To Hell
with
Johnny Manic

ANDREW DIAMOND

This is a work of fiction. Names, characters, and events are the products
of the author's imagination. Any resemblance to actual persons or events
is purely coincidental.

Cover design by Lindsay Heider Diamond. Road photo by David Everett
Strickler via Unsplash.com. Woman's eyes are from photo 185258319 by
RetroAtelier, via Getty Images.

ISBN: 0-9963507-7-2
ISBN-13: 978-0-9963507-7-8

1

The merciless Vegas sun poured in past curtains I'd left open to spite myself, washing all the color from the room and poking its lurid fingers into the eyes of my champagne hangover.

This was the day everything was going to change. This was the day everything *had* to change.

Just like yesterday, and the day before, and the day before that...

I was down to the last two hundred and fifty thousand dollars of Manis's money, and the way I was going, I could have lost it all in a single night. Maybe even in a couple hours. Or I might have hit a good streak and gone up half a million and stretched out my stay in that pampered hell for another month.

However it played out, I knew the end was near. I'd be broke, and I'd have to go out and earn a living again.

To be honest, the thought didn't scare me. In fact, it was a relief.

I'd live in a modest apartment with an alarm clock that told me when to wake up. I'd go to work at the same hour as everyone else and go home when they went home. Pick up food at the grocery store, cook for myself, clean the kitchen, watch TV, go to bed. My life would go in circles, like the hands of the clock—constrained, predictable circles that kept trouble on the outside.

Another thing was bothering me. I mean, besides the money I'd wasted and the mess I'd made of the past few months. The legal guardian of John Manis's father had been emailing me—emailing Manis—with dire reports about the state of the old man's health. His cognition was shot. His moods were getting worse. "John, it's sad. If you walked in, he wouldn't recognize you. Some days, he doesn't even know he has a son."

The facility he was in couldn't handle a case like his. The nurses and orderlies snapped at him and that made him even more agitated.

Lord, I understood that feeling. Every place I'd been in since I returned to the States felt like the wrong place, and I was always agitated. But unlike old Mr. Manis, I had some distraction. I could gamble it off. I could drink it off. I had a new group of best friends every night. I'd treat them to a fifteen-hundred-dollar dinner and make sure they were all charmed by the smooth, attentive, flattering, and charismatic John Manis.

Everybody loved John Manis, and no one gave a damn about Tom Gantry. That bugged me too. Tom Gantry was lonely as hell, the invisible heart of a seemingly charmed life, all by himself in a world no one could see or understand. Just like Manis's old man.

I called the legal guardian right there from the bed, before I got dressed, before I could get distracted or lose my resolve.

"John? Wow! We finally get to talk."

That was a relief. He didn't know Manis's voice.

He told me the old man's body was still strong. "That's the saddest part. Usually when the mind is this far gone, they only have a few months to live. He could have another year or two."

He repeated the info he'd sent in the emails. The memory care facility that specialized in cases like his cost ten thousand a month on top of what Medicare paid.

"I'll wire you the money. Two hundred and forty thousand," I said, trying to blink away the sting of the insolent sun. Why hadn't Manis done this himself a year ago? Why hadn't he visited the old man, for Christ's sake? If I had a father, I sure as hell wouldn't let him languish like that.

"You don't have to wire it," the guardian said. "You can set up a monthly draft."

"No. I'll send it today."

I had to, or else I'd blow it all that night. Two hundred forty thousand would carry old man Manis for a full two years, if he lasted that long.

That left me with ten thousand. I wouldn't have to pay for the room because the casino would comp it after all I'd lost. Their way of saying thank you, come again.

The only problem with leaving was I had nowhere to go. I could be on the road in thirty minutes, but which road? Going where? The old panic was starting to rise, and it came up slowly this time, from the depths, like a freight train gathering steam.

That meant it was going to be a bad one.

Do something, Tom!

Do what?

Something. Anything. Get out!

This was the urgency, the compulsion that had earned me my nickname at the gambling tables. The calm, well-dressed guy who arrived with a smile was John Manis. Everybody's friend. The frantic one throwing the dice and dramatically promising the crowd he'd win this time was Johnny Manic.

The real John Manis, who by now was long gone, was the guy who'd written all those addictive games that kept people glued to their phones, stacking colored jewels, running through mazes, and abusing barnyard animals. He'd sold out at age twenty-seven to a big gaming company and then posted an online manifesto denouncing the evils of the technology that had made him rich. In his dramatic middle-finger farewell to the twenty-first century, he deleted his social media accounts and told the world he was going off the grid forever.

That last part wasn't true. When I met him, he owned a cell phone and a laptop for trading stocks on E*TRADE.

But his story struck a chord among the tech workers who slaved endless hours in hopes of striking it rich. For two days, his manifesto sat on the front pages of Reddit and Hacker News while code jockeys in cubicles across the country gossiped about the lucky genius who had struck gold and then walked out on his own life.

That was two and a half years ago, and I still occasionally ran into computer programmers who said, "Wait, you're John Manis? *The* John Manis who wrote Emerald Crunch and Birdapult and Frog Slap? I thought you were, like, just a legend."

Manis would have liked hearing that. His myth was more important to him than his money. He used to say he was the greatest programmer nobody ever met.

And he would have liked to see the panic that was rising in me as I tore through the pile of clothes on the floor.

"It's not easy being me, is it, Tom?"

"Shut up, John."

It wasn't just the smugness of his tone that bothered me. It was the clarity of his voice, like he was right there in the room.

"You can't just put on my clothes and my mannerisms and expect to pull it off. This isn't a game of dress-up."

"Shut up!"

What irked me most about him, and what I admired most, was his impossible self-assurance, his unshakable confidence. The man was always at ease.

I dressed without showering, without shaving, without even brushing my teeth.

Pick the grey suit, I told myself. You'll look more composed.

I checked the mirror to see how composed I looked. The strain and excess of the past few months had puffed out in great dark circles beneath my frantic, flashing eyes. But the suit looked great.

Now get out of here, I told myself. Before you lose your nerve.

I don't remember being in the elevator, but I do remember the bustling lobby. I do remember singling out the blond-haired kid with the jeans and the black skateboard t-shirt. Jason. It was like he had a spotlight on him, like the universe was pointing him out to me, saying, That's the one you need to talk to.

I had had dinner with him two nights before, and what was it he said? His girlfriend got into grad school in Boston. He was moving east. He had a one-man business back in California, driving up and down Napa Valley helping old folks set up computers and Wi-Fi networks, cleaning viruses off their hard drives, making sure their printers could spit out photos of the grandkids. He had hoped to sell the business before he moved, but the deal fell through.

Why not sell it to me, I thought. I understood the basic tech stuff well enough. And it would give me a destination. At least I'd know which way to point the car when I drove out of town.

"Hey!" I was right in front of him now. His eyes lit up when he saw me. "You still looking to sell that computer business?"

He put on a mock frown and shook his head. "It's not happening," he said.

"No, I mean, will you sell it right now? To me?"

He looked confused, and I understood why. John Manis was a high roller, winning and losing more on one throw of the dice than his business earned in a month.

"Dude. You don't have to pity me. We have enough to make it to Boston."

"No, I'm serious." I tried to look earnest, but his expression told me I might have looked a little crazy.

"Yeah, well, it's not, like, an investment." He put on a sheepish smile. "It's just a getting-by kind of business. You wouldn't want it."

"I want it," I said, trying not to look as desperate as I felt.

"Look," I added in a quieter voice. "I know what you think of me, but I have to get out of here. I need a job. Something stable to bring me back down to earth."

He hesitated for a moment, like he thought I might be putting him on. When it dawned on him that I was serious, he looked concerned, almost disappointed.

"But," he faltered. "You're John Manis. You wrote those games. You *have* money."

"Had," I said. "I blew it." And I couldn't help adding under my breath, "Just like I blow everything."

He heard that, and his look of disillusionment threatened to melt into pity. Hadn't I spent a whole evening filling his head with stories of my travels? Wasn't I the one who treated him and his girlfriend and whoever those other two people were to their first four bottles of Dom Perignon?

"I'll give you five thousand for it," I blurted. That was half of what I had left. "That'll help you and your girlfriend get set up in Boston."

The way he smiled, I knew I could have had the business for a thousand.

I was going to pay him right then and there, but he said, "I don't want to take your money. You don't even know if you'll like that part of California—"

"I'll like it," I said.

"—or if you'll like the work. It might bore you."

He gave me his card—The Computer Kid—and told me to check out the town in Napa. He'd meet me there in three days to give me a tour and introduce me to some of his regulars.

"But call me before then if you want to back out," he said.

"Yeah, sure."

We shook on it, and the kid floated off in search of his girlfriend.

I went back upstairs and packed. The laptop, six suits, a few extra pairs of slacks and shirts. All top-of-the-line designer labels that reeked of John Manis and his ingratiating charm, his infinite self-assurance and colossal arrogance. I told myself when I got to California, I'd sell the suits on consignment, buy a few pairs of jeans and some t-shirts, and ease back into Tom Gantry.

But I'd still have to be Manis in name. I had his license, his passport, and his spotless record with the law. Manis was employable. Tom Gantry, the fugitive embezzler who'd violated parole in Illinois, was not.

After wiring two hundred forty thousand dollars back to Maryland, I drove the north road out of Vegas in an aqua-green 1963 Corvette convertible, through the sun-bleached desert that skirts the eastern edge of Death Valley. I crossed into

California near Lake Tahoe just after sunset, winding through corridors of dark Sierra pine in the crystalline twilight of a cool mountain evening.

The scent of tree sap and pine needles swelled my heart with hope. The arid wasteland was behind me. Before me was a new country, lush and green.

I'd push through to Napa in one straight shot, and in the morning I'd awake far from the empty desert and the garish oasis of excess that brought out the worst in Johnny Manic.

2

I spent the night in a motel in Napa, too keyed up to sleep. I turned on the TV and the radio and packed and unpacked my suitcases a few dozen times until the breakfast buffet opened at 6:30. I ate breakfast twice, then fell asleep.

Around 9:30, I drove north up Route 29 to the town where I was supposed to meet The Computer Kid.

By 11:00, I was ready to sign a lease on a furnished one-bedroom in a four-unit building near the south end of Main Street.

"But don't you want to see it first?" asked the landlady.

"Oh, yeah."

The place was a big step down from my suite in Vegas, and she could see the disappointment on my face. Maybe I should have prepared myself for what twelve hundred dollars a month could buy.

"You want to think about it?" she said.

"Yeah. Give me a day or two to mull it over."

She looked at my suit, which cost more than two months' rent, and when we walked outside, she glanced more than once at the gleaming, perfectly restored '63 Corvette, but she didn't say anything about it.

I left the car in front of the building and walked up Main Street, past the post office and the bank, the library, the yoga studio, and the meditation center. The immaculate sidewalks, the BMWs and Mercedes and Porsches, the guys whizzing by on racing bikes and the fit young mothers with jogging strollers lifted my spirits. This was a healthy place.

The leaves of the trees on that day in early May shimmered like they had just been washed, and the overbearing sun forced its bright abundance on eyes that couldn't absorb any more of it. I reached for the Ray-Bans in my pocket, but they weren't there. I'd left them in the car.

The difference between today and yesterday, I told myself as I crossed the street toward the organic grocery, is that yesterday I would have panicked. Bright sun, no glasses, I would have broken into a sweat and marched full speed into the nearest building. Today, I'll take my time. I'll walk nice and easy into the grocery and ride out the swell of fear. I checked my hands as I entered through the sliding glass doors. They weren't even shaking anymore. Not noticeably, anyway.

The fruits and vegetables in the produce aisle were stacked in pristine pyramids, with the staged, exaggerated perfection of a museum exhibit. Overhead lights reflected from the polished skins of impossibly bright red apples, bursting cherries, and giant eggplant. The green of the broccoli and Bibb lettuce, of the giant watermelons and fragrant basil was overwhelmingly vivid. After months in the deserts of Nevada, the lushness of the scene was extravagant, disorienting, and surreal.

And standing in the middle of it all was a tall woman in black yoga pants and sports bra. I didn't realize I was looking at her until I noticed her looking back at me.

She was a few years younger than me, in her midtwenties I guessed. The shiny straight black hair that ran to the small of her back was cut in bangs above dark eyes that looked curiously back at me and told me she was caught as much off guard by me as I was by her. Her skin was fair and moist with perspiration, as if she'd just finished exercising. Her lips were deep red and she had natural color in her cheeks, rose on white. Whether the blush was from a sudden unexpected fluster of emotion or recently completed exercise, I couldn't tell. Her strong athletic build, the straight lines of her hair, and the sharply contrasting colors of her face—black, white, red— made a bold and vivid impression.

The enormous diamond on her ring finger had obviously come from someone with a lot of money. She touched it with her thumb, unconsciously perhaps, and when I looked back up to her face, I saw a flash of insecurity in her eyes, as if she had just inadvertently revealed her thoughts.

I don't know if anyone else would have caught that flash, but with all that was going on in my life at the time, I was well attuned to feelings of uncertainty and doubt.

The whole encounter couldn't have lasted more than a few seconds, but it seemed to play out in slow motion, the way crash survivors describe the dilation of time in the instant before a wreck.

A dozen thoughts raced through my mind. You know what you look like, I told myself. You saw yourself in the motel mirror this morning. In the rearview of the car. And the way the landlady looked at you—you know you don't look well. Any woman who's attracted to *that* can't be good for you.

Another part of me asked, Who says she's attracted? I mean, who says it's *that* kind of attraction? She sees Tom Gantry. Not the flash and charm of Manis. Just honest-to-god Tom Gantry, and she can't quite turn away because maybe she's as lonely as you are and she recognizes a kindred spirit, someone she can connect with and understand.

Just smile and say hello. Give her the satisfaction of being acknowledged. That's all anybody really wants in this world. Say hello and be on your way. It doesn't have to be any more complicated than that.

And then the panic welled up, and I told myself, She's married. And besides, you've already met a woman like her and she's already met a man like you. If it was meant to work out, it would have. But it didn't, and it never will. So skip it and move on.

I swear she was reading my thoughts. The look of intrigue and fascination that had lit her face faded into disappointment as I mentally rejected her.

I turned to leave and she said, "Wait!"

But I kept going and didn't look back.

<h1 style="text-align:center">3</h1>

I walked down Main without stopping or even noticing where I was, feeling the same agitation I had felt at the casino when the crowds were watching and I had a big pile of money on the line.

In the casino, I'd respond to the panic by throwing down even more money and flashing a confident smile to the crowd. The reaction of the onlookers, the murmuring "Ooh!" or the outbursts of "Now we're on!" gave voice to the rush of energy that was driving me. I could relieve the pressure by distributing it among the crowd.

What could I do now though? What rash wager could I place to distract myself from this shapeless welling panic? The racing heart, the electricity in the veins, the overabundance of energy threatened to swell into outright mania if I didn't do something.

I didn't realize how far I had walked until I heard the skidding of tires. The sudden apparition of the black grille and white hood of a Range Rover two feet in front of me snapped me back into the present.

I had passed the sidewalk's end, passed the south edge of town, and was on the shoulder of the road.

No. I was in the lane of oncoming traffic.

The driver, a young, round-faced woman with short blonde hair rolled down her window.

"Are you all right?"

She held her hand over her heart, the fear of near-catastrophe etched into her eyes.

I ran my fingers through my hair and felt the sweat.

"Yeah. I just..." I looked back up the road toward town. "I guess I wasn't paying attention."

As I walked toward her door, she turned to check on the child sleeping in the rear booster seat.

I was standing beside her window when she turned back.

"I'm sorry," she said. "You were on the shoulder and then you wandered right into the lane—"

Her words stopped abruptly when her eyes met mine. She seemed to recoil as if suddenly confronted by something ghastly.

"I... I'm sorry, sir, but..." She hesitated. "Are you OK?"

"Yeah, I'm just a little lost."

Did I look that bad? I must have. The dark-haired woman in the grocery store triggered something in me and I hadn't walked it off yet.

"Hey, I'm sorry, lady. Sorry I scared you. I'll pay more attention to where I..."

She was leaning away from me. For a second, she wouldn't look me in the eye, and then when she did, I felt like her eyes stabbed right into me. Like she knew exactly who I was. Like her eyes said "Murderer!" and she couldn't quite cover up the thought in time.

"Go ahead and roll up your window," I said. "I know you want to."

She did.

As I stepped back from the car, I said, "I don't blame you, lady. And thanks for not killing me."

But she was already off. And she had the decency to roll away slowly instead of flooring it and peeling out.

When I turned and started back toward town, I told myself, This isn't a good start, walking into the grocery and seeing someone who sets you off like that. Walking into traffic and scaring the wits out of some poor young mom.

And then my calm voice said, Give yourself a break, Johnny. It hasn't even been twenty-four hours since you left Vegas. You know it takes longer than that to come down from a jag

like the one you were on. You have to work at it. You need a
plan.

4

Twenty minutes later, I pulled away from the curb, made a U-turn, and headed south toward San Francisco. I made it three blocks and then, for no reason at all, I turned east at the stop sign, onto a winding road that led to the top of a stony mountain patched with fields of yellow grass and clumps of dark green pine. The narrow road switched back twice as it climbed, so the town below me was sometimes off to my left and sometimes to my right.

At the top was an overlook with a gravel parking area large enough for three or four cars, a picnic bench, and a view of the valley below. I parked and walked past the bench to the low stone wall at the edge of the overlook. Beneath was fifty feet of steep brush-covered slope leading down to a thick cluster of laurel, oak, and pine.

I could see the whole of the town, a twelve-block stretch of shops and apartments. The courthouse and theater stood out because they were taller than the other buildings. At either end of town, the lush watered gardens of the big estates lined the two-lane road. To the south, vineyards climbed the rolling hills like cornrows in a young girl's hair. To the north, the valley narrowed to a deeper green, and dark pines covered the mountains.

I stood quietly for a long time absorbing the view and thinking back over the mess I'd made of my life so far. Four years of community college and then a job in the accounts department of a giant corporation. Finding a glitch in the computer system, routing some money into a bank account. My bank account. Arrested in under twelve hours.

"Why would you steal three hundred thousand dollars?" my supervisor asked. "Do you think it was a cry for help?"

"No. It was a cry for three hundred thousand dollars. You'd understand that if you'd ever been poor."

"Did you think you'd get away with it?"

"Obviously I thought I'd get away with it, or I wouldn't have done it."

I wasn't sleeping much in those days. I had too much energy. And I was sure I was invincible, sure I was smarter than everyone.

That goes away when you start sleeping again. And I slept soundly in prison, because I was contained. Because every hour of my day was planned out. When to wake up, when to eat, when to work, when the lights went out, everything. There was no way I could screw up in that place. I begged them not to let me out.

But they did, and I spent one hundred and fourteen sleepless nights in a halfway house. And it wasn't the good kind of sleepless—the kind that happens because the world is too bright. It was the other kind. The swirling into a bottomless black hole of loneliness kind.

Then I met a woman who talked to me, who listened to me, who let me put my arms around her. A kindred spirit. I followed her to St. Louis, which was a violation of parole, and I learned once again that the problem with the kindred spirit of a troubled person is that she's also usually troubled. I couldn't keep her from falling into her own black hole.

When I called my parole officer and told him where I was, he said, "You know that's a parole violation?"

"I know," I said. I was excited. I still had fourteen months left on my sentence. They'd lock me up again, and my world would be orderly, with schedules and rules and guards and boundaries everywhere.

"They're not going to put you back in that minimum-security country club prison," he said. "Not after you've fled."

I pictured a prison like the ones in the movies, with clanging steel bars and gang rapes in the showers. I would never go to a place like that.

"Tom? Tom, are you there?"

I hung up and headed south, down the river to New Orleans, then Texas, then even farther south, into the Gulf.

Then one day in Costa Rica, I met a guy who looked just like me. John Manis chased me down on Paseo Colón and asked if I wanted to play a joke on someone.

And then six months later, the sailboat and the end of Manis. The flight to Panama. The cruise ship back to the States, the green velvet tables of the on-board casino, piles of chips that grew and shrank and grew again, drowning my conscience in adrenaline. Landfall in Miami, and then the slow westward drift through the casinos of New Orleans and Las Vegas.

What have you done to fix yourself, Tom? Nothing. You just kept running west, and now you've gone as far as you can go. Unless you want to run into the sea.

I thought of the humble apartment on Main Street. It could be depressing if things went wrong. It could be one of those black holes I sometimes fall into.

And I thought of the extravagant suites on the Strip.

You could always go back, I told myself. Your credit is good at the casinos. They'll float you a hundred thousand. Maybe more. A couple good nights and...

Stop it, Tom. You're lucky you met that kid in Vegas. You're lucky you still have one more chance. You have to take it. You have to make an honest life. If it doesn't work, at least you tried.

But what if doesn't work? What if I'm stuck here all alone, and I start spiraling again?

Then the voice of John Manis broke through. It was something he said on the boat the night he died. "You worry too much."

I saw an image of him reclining on deck, beer in hand, with his easygoing smile.

"Seriously, Tom. What's the point of second-guessing yourself?"

"What?"

I was so startled by the clarity of his voice, I said that aloud. Then, embarrassed at the thought of someone overhearing me talking to myself, I turned to see whether anyone was in earshot.

I must have been lost in thought for some time, because I hadn't remembered taking a seat there on the stone wall, nor did I remember hearing the car park in the gravel behind me. But when I stood and turned, there it was. A little blue Mazda.

Its owner sat at the picnic table behind me, wearing faded jeans and a dark blue polo shirt. He looked to be in his midthirties, about six feet tall, lean and trim. He was handsome in an objective sense, with balanced, well-proportioned features, dark hair and eyes, and a sharp jawline covered with a couple days of stubbly growth.

But beyond the physical features, there was nothing likable about him. His face bore the lines of an habitual scowl, as if he'd spent years stewing over some personal grievance. He was stuffing sunflower seeds into his mouth and spitting out the shells. They fluttered to the ground like wounded moths.

He too was lost in thought, just as I had been a moment before. But unlike my meandering reminiscences, his eyes showed a more calculating look, as if he were thinking to some purpose. Thinking about beating someone up, perhaps. Or plotting revenge for whatever had etched that angry scowl into his face.

When he saw me looking at him, he stopped his chewing and spitting, his jaw clenched in a firm line, and his eyes hardened into a hostile, almost murderous look.

"What the fuck are you looking at?" he said.

I don't normally react strongly to first encounters with strangers, but this was an unusual day. First the woman in the grocery store, and now him. My feelings for this man were as powerful as my feelings for her, only they ran in the opposite direction. I hated him.

I'm not one to be rude, especially to someone I just met, but he had set the tone with that greeting, and he didn't look like the kind who was receptive to politeness anyway. So I said what I felt. "Go fuck yourself."

He watched with the hard eyes of a felon as I walked past him to my car.

Nine weeks later, when I pulled his wallet from his pants and read his license as he lay dying with a bullet in his chest, I learned his name was Roland.

But on that day in early May, as I backed the Vette out of the gravel parking lot, I had to choose which way to turn. To one side was the last hundred yards of road up the mountain. From there, it descended to the east toward Lake Berryessa and the valley, toward Nevada and the desert, the casinos and ruin.

The other option was a graceful descent into one of the loveliest towns I'd ever seen, where a striking, dark-haired woman had moved my heart in ways I didn't fully understand.

Down I went into the lush green valley, and on the way into town, I pulled The Computer Kid's card from my pocket and gave him a call.

"We're on," I said.

"Dude!" he said excitedly. "Wait'll I tell my friends I dragged John Manis back into the tech world!"

There it was—the flashy wager, played with a flourish. My chips were on the table and the audience was suitably impressed.

Before the day was out, I signed the lease for the apartment on Main Street. The wiser part of me knew I should have left. But knowing what's right and doing what's right are two different things, especially when you're at war with instincts you can't articulate and don't understand.

I understand it all now. I can articulate it very clearly. Tom Gantry wanted to kill John Manis once and for all. Or John Manis wanted to kill Tom Gantry. I was so mixed up about who I was, it didn't matter who killed whom. The important thing was that in the grocery store that morning, Johnny Manic and the raven-haired Marilyn Dupree had found each other.

The fuse was lit.

5

The apartment was furnished, but barely. A bed and nightstand, a couch, a coffee table, and a small round table with two chairs in the kitchen. Simplicity was good. The less I had, the less I needed to manage.

Jason, The Computer Kid, called that first night to say he'd be stopping in San Francisco to visit his girlfriend's parents and would be a few days late. That was good too, because I needed time to come down, and I had a plan to make it happen.

First thing, buy an alarm clock. I drove all the way down to Target at Bel Aire Plaza and picked up the clock, an analog watch, and an old-fashioned leather-bound appointment book with a page for each day of the year.

The calendar and watch were ways of imposing order on a dimension of life that was too fluid, too undefined. Without them, time had no boundaries other than birth and death, and the unstructured space in between was where everything went wrong.

People talk about freedom like it's the best thing you could ever have, but they don't understand half their misery comes from having too much of it. I finally understood that when I got to prison and my world had some structure. When I got out, my parole officer told me I had to learn to impose that structure on myself.

My phone already had a clock and calendar, but the digital stuff wouldn't cut it. My calendar had to be tangible. My watch had to tick audibly. Otherwise, they weren't real enough. They'd get swallowed up in the swirl of the days, and I would lose the battle they were supposed to help me win.

Once I had the calendar, I made a daily schedule broken down into half-hour blocks. A block for breakfast, one for showering, shaving, and dressing. Four for exercise. I could cut that down to two later, but in the early days I knew I'd need at least two solid hours to burn off the worst of the excess energy. Then blocks for lunch, reading, walking, shopping, cooking.

The evenings would be the worst, because my body and mind were still on Vegas time. At nightfall my energy would rise, and if I didn't do something to combat it, I knew I'd screw up.

This was all accounted for in the plan. In the evenings, I'd apply the tricks I'd learned in New Orleans that took me down into the nice peaceful lull that preceded my Vegas explosion. Eat a heavy dinner: steak and potatoes with sour cream, none of which I actually liked, but it slowed the blood. Wash it down with a few glasses of heavy red wine, like a cabernet.

Then take allergy meds. Three or four Benadryl brought on a smothering lethargy that was like a heavy wet blanket over the forest fire of my mind. I never liked the fog or slowness of antihistamines, but I only had to stay on them for a few days. Just long enough to break the frantic rhythm of an overwrought mind stuck in a loop of responding to stimulation that was no longer present.

After dinner, wine, and pills, I'd stay in the apartment alone and watch old TV shows on the laptop. *Dragnet* and *The Andy Griffith* show had a slow pace and a soothing simplicity, and the good guys always won. The characters were consistent and predictable. Their problems were resolved in thirty minutes. The camera focused on one or two people at a time, and my mind, no longer racing under the muting influence of the Benadryl, focused with it.

At eleven or twelve, I'd awaken on the couch, heavy with sleep. Turn off the TV. Go into the bedroom. When my head hit the pillow, I told myself I'd made it through another day. And each morning when I awoke, I found the volume and brightness of the world had been turned down another notch.

After five days, all I needed was one Benadryl and one glass of wine. I could eat a lighter meal, and I could depend on Joe Friday and Sheriff Taylor to keep order in the world.

By day six, my resting pulse was a steady sixty beats per minute. My mind moved at the same easy speed as the shoppers going in and out of the local boutiques. The shocking candy-store vividness of the organic produce aisle had faded into earth-bound normalcy. The threatening man spitting sunflower seeds at the overlook—who by the way had not appeared again—was nothing more than a sour guy having a bad day. I could even summon the image of the white Range Rover skidding into view without the memory making my heart beat out of my chest.

The only thing that still triggered me was Marilyn. Twice I saw her in the grocery store, and twice I turned and left. She noticed both times. Maybe I looked at her a little too long, but who was she to complain about that? I caught her looking at me the same way in the pharmacy, next to the post office, outside the bank.

The deli and the sushi restaurant and the coffee shop had big windows facing the street, so I could see if she was inside before I went in. A couple of times, I had to rearrange my lunch schedule to avoid her.

Get used to it, I told myself. It's a small town, and everything in it is right here on Main Street. Right outside your apartment door.

There was something reassuring in the gossip of the women at the coffee shop. The fact that they didn't like Marilyn told me the aura of danger I saw around her was not an illusion of my overwrought senses. I was seeing clearly.

But there was something unnerving about me having to tear my eyes away from someone I knew was bad for me, and about the obvious interest she showed in a guy who was just returning to sanity. I'd made a mistake like her before: the woman I followed down to St. Louis when I broke parole.

Both women had the lure of the roulette wheel: terrible odds of a spectacular payoff. Or spectacular odds of a terrible payoff, if you want to be negative about it. Most people would know to stay away. But I knew what kind of resolve I had around roulette wheels.

By the time The Computer Kid rolled into town, I'd picked up a few more tidbits about Marilyn. She lived in the big white house north of town. Her husband had made his fortune in software. He owned a tech company, the town's French restaurant, a third of the organic grocery, and a few other odds and ends.

He was a philanderer. Their marriage was a mess.

6

"Dude, check it out."

With an eager smile, Jason handed me a box of newly printed business cards. We were standing out by the Vette, on a sunny morning in front of my apartment.

"They have your name and phone number instead of mine."

I thanked him as I glanced at the cards. *The Computer Kid.* And underneath, *John Manis*, and my cell number.

"Make sure you leave one with every customer," he said. "Or else they'll be calling me in Boston and you'll be missing out on work. I updated the website too. Half your work comes in through there, so you need to check it a few times a day."

He showed me the site on his phone, how to log in and check for new work requests.

"How long are you in town?" I asked.

"Ten days. I'll take you on the rounds. Let's take your car. That thing is sweet!"

The first job we did was at a coffee shop down in Napa. Freeloaders from neighboring stores were overloading their Wi-Fi. The owner wanted an easy way to change the password every day. We adjusted the settings so the guest password would change automatically every twenty-four hours. All the owner had to do was look up the new password on her iPad each morning when she came in.

"Can you make it so the password gets printed on the customer receipts?" she asked. "Then we won't have to write it down for them."

That question got me worried. Fiddling with Wi-Fi settings was something I understood. Getting cash registers to print custom receipts was beyond my capabilities. If that was the kind of thing I'd be expected to do in this job, I was in over my head, and I'd have a lot of learning to do.

Fortunately, Jason handled it with a simple shake of the head.

"Can't do it," he said. "The Wi-Fi and the register are separate systems. Just hang up a little chalkboard above the espresso machine where no one can see it from outside. Write the password there."

That worked.

We were in the coffee shop for about an hour. Fifteen minutes of that time was actual work, and the rest was talking.

"I can't believe she paid you a hundred and fifty bucks for that," I said as we drove away.

"She paid *you* a hundred and fifty bucks," Jason said. He handed me a check made out to John Manis. "That's the going rate for a house call. Keep in mind that you've got twenty or thirty minutes of driving each way on some of these jobs. You have to make them pay."

He told me that on a good week, I could do twelve to fifteen jobs. A bad week might be four or five. I was hoping there wouldn't be too many bad weeks. It wasn't just the money that worried me, it was the amount of free time I'd have.

As we drove back up Route 29 toward town, I started making a list in my head of activities to fill in the thirty-minute blocks of time I'd laid out in my appointment book. Hiking, reading at the library, maybe trying yoga. Learning how to cook new dishes using fresh vegetables from the organic grocery. These weren't necessarily things I wanted to do, but if I made myself do them, they'd keep me busy and out of trouble.

When I got home that day, I penciled in an hour of online research every night for the next two weeks. That would help me come up to speed on Wi-Fi routers, computer viruses, smart TVs, and some of the other products we were dealing with.

7

Over the next few days, The Kid and I did a number of jobs that had piled up while he'd been away in Vegas and San Francisco. One was at a winery, and one was at a little three-person accounting office, but all the rest were in private homes.

We'd go in and hook up a new TV to a bunch of peripherals, make sure everything was working, and give the owner a summary of how to use the remotes. Most of the time, I was figuring it out as I was doing it, and Jason was an invaluable guide.

We'd go into a house where some old guy's computer was choked with viruses, and we'd slowly clean the thing up using antivirus software that anyone could download from the internet for free.

The next job might be something as simple as helping a harried mother set parental controls on every device in the house.

I couldn't get over how much some of these people were paying us to do stuff they could have done on their own.

"They all have money," Jason said. "You see what kinds of houses they live in. Yeah, they could do it themselves, but why should they if they can pay someone else to do it? It's like, do you really want to wash your own car?"

"Well, yeah," I said. I had it penciled into my calendar twice a week to keep me busy.

"OK." Jason laughed. "But you have a really nice car."

I was surprised at how grateful our customers were for the simple work we did. We got gushing thank-yous from moms stuck at home with sleeping toddlers, from old guys who spent their mornings on the phone with investment advisors, and from work-at-home people whose infected laptops we restored to their former vigor.

As modest and mundane as the jobs were, there was something deeply satisfying in doing useful work, in seeing the appreciation of ordinary people whose days I had made just a little easier. Though it was less than Johnny Manic used to wager on a single bet, the money I got from an honest day's work was worth more to me than all the piles of cash I'd squandered in Vegas.

The nagging reservations I'd felt on first seeing my apartment began to fade. Sure, the kitchenette was too small, the stainless-steel sink was somehow stained, and the compressor in the ancient fridge groaned jarringly to life every thirty minutes before suddenly shutting down again. But there was nothing in the place to tempt or provoke me. The glitz and bustle of the casinos that had brought out the manic in Johnny were fading into memory.

Those top-chef restaurants in Vegas and Miami and New Orleans with their two-hundred-dollar bottles of wine had always put me on edge because I knew I didn't belong in them. Looking back, I realized how much I had overplayed my role when I felt out of place. I got carried away and poured on the charm and let the money flow like water to smooth over my discomfort. No one ever seemed to see through it. They got swept up in the ride and carried away right along with me.

Jason and I had some good talks in the car. He wanted to know how I'd managed to blow all my money. I gave him the basic outlines of the story. I'd left Costa Rica and boarded a cruise ship in Panama. The ship, bound for Miami, had a casino. That's where I discovered I had a gambling problem.

Of course, I left out the parts about why I was always on edge, about what I'd done to Manis, how I'd gotten his laptop, his license, his passport. How I'd cut my hair to match his passport photo. How many times I looked back and forth between the picture and the mirror. My terror of being found out.

I didn't tell him how much I secretly liked losing the money I had stolen. It was a form of punishment and soothing evidence of divine justice. It told me there was someone or something in the universe I couldn't lie to, no matter how much I ran or hid, no matter how duplicitous I was or how long I refused to confess. Someone knew and was making me pay, and a desperate part of me hoped there'd be absolution in that, when the money was all gone.

Another part of me flourished with the attention of the onlookers and the way they responded to my money and my daring. I told Jason all about that, about how I always played the showman at craps and roulette.

"It's ego," I said. "When you can draw a crowd every night and get them cheering for you, it's all ego." I didn't tell him how the noise drowned out the voice of guilt.

He wanted to know about Miami and South Beach and the nightclubs.

"Unfortunately," I said, "I spent more time in the casinos. And the ones down there aren't that glamorous. They're mostly slots, and those get boring fast."

Drifting from Miami to New Orleans, which had better casinos, to Vegas was like moving from codeine to OxyContin to heroin.

He was fascinated by all of it, and I even threw some humor into the stories of my bigger nights—enormous wins and crushing losses—the way a drunkard embellishes the escapades of which he's most deeply ashamed. After a few days, The Kid thought I was the most fascinating thirty-year-old he'd ever met, but all that stuck with me in recounting my binge was that I couldn't remember the names of any of the people I'd been with during those reckless nights.

Talking about those days and all the things I'd done wrong helped put the present in perspective. In this small, clean town where I could walk to everything I needed, a roast beef sandwich and a bottle of beer in the deli was more satisfying than all the meals I'd eaten in all those fancy restaurants, because I didn't have to try to live up to an image that wasn't me. My job, as simple and modest as it was, had one great psychological advantage over my former life of selfish frenzy. For the first time in almost a year, I could honestly say I was leaving people better off than I had found them.

That was such a balm to my conscience, it even shut John Manis up. At the end of my first week of work, I noticed the smug apparition of the man on the sailboat hadn't visited me for days. The cool, self-assured voice whose taunts had increased throughout my stay in Vegas had finally gone silent. Perhaps he had nothing left to say.

"You miss it?" Jason asked as we cruised north up Route 29 with the top down.

"Huh?"

"The old life."

"No."

"Aw, come on! You must miss it!"

"OK, actually, yeah. It's just not something I need. Junkies miss their needles, but it's not the solution to their problems."

"What do you miss most?" he asked. "The money?"

I didn't want to answer that, but he was watching me, waiting for a response.

"Winning?"

"No," I said as I pressed the accelerator with compulsive force. "I miss the drama."

"Dude, slow down!"

"Regular life, you know..." I pushed the pedal all the way to the floor. "It's like one dead level. And that scares the hell out of me. But that's how I'm going to have to live from now on, if I'm going to keep living."

He pressed his hands against the glove box. "Seriously, man, slow down!"

The kid was genuinely scared.

I slowed down.

8

On our last day together, The Kid and I left early for a long drive down Route 29 then up Route 12 through Sonoma.

"New customer," Jason told me. "He's hella impatient."

We had the top down in the Vette. I turned to see his short blond hair dancing in the wind.

"Hella?"

He laughed. "I was wondering if you'd notice that."

When we arrived at the house—an old craftsman that had fallen into disrepair—I understood what The Kid meant.

A gaunt old man, bent and spotted like an overripe banana, stood in the doorway waiting. "'Bout time you got here!"

"Eight thirty on the nose," Jason said happily as he slammed the door of the Vette.

As we approached the porch, the old man watched eagerly through thick oversized glasses that magnified his eyes to owlish enormity.

Inside, the cottage was darkened by heavy velvet curtains pierced by narrow slices of dusty golden sunlight. The living room was a time capsule of ancient flea market finds: a white satin couch with yellow stains, a settee with carved wood legs, a mahogany coffee table, a tarnished silver tea service. All of it spoke of the gentle-looking woman, recently departed, whose face appeared in framed photos beneath the porcelain lamps. The one of her alone, young and smiling in a light silk blouse, had the years of her birth and death etched into the bottom of the silver frame.

The man had bought a laptop and a keyboard, a gigantic monitor, and a new desk to put them on. All of it sat in the living room, in boxes shipped from an online retailer.

"You gonna do some programming?" Jason asked with a playful grin.

"No," said the old man flatly. And that was the end of that conversation.

The kid and I cleared out a space in the den for the desk, which we had to assemble. Jason whispered, "You don't usually have to put furniture together, but you never know. The cranky ones like..." He nodded toward the man who stood in the other room with his back to us. "They never tell you everything when they call. Just make sure to bill them for all your time."

After we set up the desk, the man watched closely as we unboxed the giant monitor. It was practically a Jumbotron. It took four hands to set it on its stand, and when we did, it covered almost the whole surface of the desk.

"I can't use a tablet," the man said. He tapped his thick glasses. "Don't have the eyes for it anymore."

I got the new laptop out of the box and plugged in the monitor and keyboard.

"What happened to your old computer?" Jason asked as I clicked through the setup questions.

"It got too slow."

"It was probably just a virus," he said. "I could have fixed that."

The old man gave a dismissive wave as if to say it wasn't important. I asked him if he wanted a password on the new computer, and he said no.

"Email?"

"No."

"You must have email," I said. "Don't you want me to set it up?"

"Just get me on the internet."

"You have Wi-Fi?"

"'Course I do."

After I connected the Wi-Fi, I stood and ushered the old man into the chair. "Take it for a spin."

He bent his head over the keyboard and pecked at the keys with his crooked index finger. In a minute, he loaded up a porn video of an over-muscled guy being serviced by two naked women on a blanketless bed. He cranked up the sound until their moaning filled the room, then he grabbed the edges of the monitor and pressed his giant owl eyes into the blonde woman's crotch.

"Jesus!" muttered The Kid, and we both turned away at once.

"Go wait in the car," he said. "I'll get the check."

When we pulled out of the driveway a few minutes later he said, "Sorry, dude. I had no idea. But I can't promise you there won't be more like him. You never know what you're walking into when you make house calls."

When he handed me the check I made a mental note of the name and vowed not to go back there again.

As we headed back toward Route 12, he said, "Let's stop and get some lunch. 'Cause we got a long drive ahead."

The second and final job of the day was way up past Cloverdale, more than an hour to the north.

"The Lemonade Lady," Jason said. "She's your meal ticket."

"What do you mean?"

"She'll call you to plug in the radio or change the channel on the TV. She just wants company. You gotta sit and chat with her for an hour. That's the unwritten contract."

The Lemonade Lady lived in a white ranch-style house that didn't look like much from the street. She opened the door one second after we rang the bell, as if she'd been waiting on the other side all morning.

She looked to be in her seventies, with dark hair and eyes, lively and alert in a purple muumuu with a matching headband.

"Jason!" she cooed. She gave him a quick hug, and then when she turned to look at me, her eyes lit up. "Oh my," she said, putting her hand to her heart. "You've brought a friend!"

"This is John," said Jason. "He'll be taking over starting tomorrow."

"Oh!" She couldn't have been more delighted if Jason had just delivered her a new grandson. "Well come in! Come in! I've made some lemonade."

And then Jason silently mouthed the words as she said them aloud. "Fresh squeezed."

We toured the back garden with her, glasses in hand, and she showed off her olive tree, her avocado tree, her prize roses, and a dozen other kinds of flowers whose names I don't remember.

Then the three of us sat at a table on the back patio and she made eyes at my suit and gabbed about her granddaughter who was twenty-four and "unattached." She managed to slip that little tidbit into the conversation three times, with the emphasis always falling on the word "unattached."

After thirty minutes, I was eyeing the lemonade pitcher like an hour glass. Once we emptied it, I figured, she'd let us go.

I drank four glasses, which simply delighted her, and then my heart sank when she stood and said, "Let me get the other pitcher from the kitchen."

When she walked into the house, I asked Jason, "What are we here to fix?"

Jason smiled and said, "Dude, we *are* the fix. She likes having a young person to talk to. She misses her grandkids."

"Seriously?" I asked. "She pays for that?"

"Don't let the modest house fool you. She's loaded. And there are worse things to spend money on. A lot of people up here drop five hundred bucks on a bottle of wine and they think that's a great time. To each his own, right?"

"So we're not actually fixing anything?"

"Oh, don't worry," he said. "She'll come up with something."

It took her ninety minutes to come up with something, which turned out to be her printer. She had just received a package with new ink cartridges and needed someone to install them.

"They're delicate, you know. And with today's electronics, there's always the risk of electrocution."

Jason and I, brave young lads, performed the heroic swapping out of cyan, magenta, yellow, and black, sparing the old lady a violent high-voltage death.

As I put the empty ink cartridges into a mailer for recycling, Jason said under his breath, "I'm telling you, dude, she's good for at least one call a week. And boy does she love you!"

"It's just the suit," I said.

"Then you better take good care of that suit."

Funny he said that, because I had blocked out most of the coming Saturday to drive to San Francisco and dump the suits at a high-end consignment shop. Every time I looked in the mirror, the suits reminded me of Vegas. Even worse, they reminded me of Manis.

Part of my plan in coming here had been to get back to being myself. I was more a jeans kind of guy. But if the suits were working for me, why get rid of them?

When I dropped The Kid off at his parents' house that afternoon, we shook hands.

"Dude, you're gonna ace this," he said. "And don't worry if you don't understand every new product on the market. You can always look up what you don't know."

I wished him good luck in Boston.

9

The next three weeks went smoothly. Some days I had three or four jobs. With all the driving I had to do, those could be twelve-hour days. Some days I had only one job, so I had to come up with ways to do to fill the empty thirty-minute blocks on the calendar.

I had my suits dry-cleaned and bought matching hangers to hang them on. That made the closet more organized. I bought a cheap old dresser so my socks and underwear wouldn't lie around in plain sight.

I rented a steam cleaner and got some of the stains out of the carpet, and I bought a used vacuum cleaner to keep the floors tidy. I bought matching stainless steel flatware to replace the mismatched knives and forks that the last tenant had left. That made the silverware drawer look more orderly when I slid it open. I bought matching plates, matching sheets and pillowcases for the bed, and I shined my shoes.

When there was nothing left to clean in the apartment, I'd go out and clean the car. A thorough job, inside and out, would take five to six thirty-minute blocks. If that didn't fill the afternoon, I'd look up a healthy recipe online. Walking to the grocery store, buying the ingredients, and walking back took one thirty-minute block. Prepping and cooking took one to two blocks, depending on what I made. Eating and cleanup occupied another block.

On some nights, my hour of online research stretched into three or four hours. I learned more about antivirus software. I learned how to work around glitches in the Android operating system that ran most smart TVs. I learned how to recalibrate inkjet printers, how to sync photos between phones, PCs, and

Macs. I learned which Wi-Fi routers had the best range, and which had the best reviews among gamers for handling heavy game and video traffic.

When my evening research time cut into my TV time, I'd open up the appointment book, erase "TV" from the thirty-minute blocks and write in "Wi-Fi research," "virus research," "product research," or whatever I'd actually been doing. That gave me a true record of my time, so that on Sundays, when I went to the coffee shop early and reviewed the week, I could see I had something to feel good about.

My customers liked me. I saw it in the way they welcomed me, and I felt it in the way they listened to my stories, to my opinions and advice. I was developing a solid confidence, rooted in a true sense of self-worth, not the bluff and bravado of the guy in the fancy suit making a big show of throwing the dice.

I hadn't had a single panic attack since my first day in town. I was back in shape from doing one to two hours of daily exercise. The apartment was starting to feel like home. I was picking up new clients through word of mouth, and because I penciled in blocks of time for it each day, I was even learning to cook.

The only thing that was bothering me was I couldn't sleep. It wasn't the kind of insomnia I'd had in Vegas. It was the other kind. The kind where you're staring at the ceiling and it's two o'clock and then three o'clock and then four o'clock and you're asking yourself why the life that feels just fine in the light of day feels so empty in the dark of night.

I'd had a thousand tiny victories in the six weeks since I'd rolled into town, and no one to share them with. No one to talk to about all the little things that added up to everything. No one to share the meals I had just learned how to cook.

The loneliness scared me, because it pointed to the downside of the ride I'd been on for months in Miami and New Orleans and Las Vegas. It pointed toward the bottomless black hole that would suck me in. And the black hole had no antidote. The heavy meals and wine and Benadryl that could break the high side of the cycle wouldn't work on the down side. They'd only make things worse.

One evening, when I had no fingernails left to chew off and couldn't muster the energy to shop or cook, I picked up the leather-bound calendar book and erased everything from 7:30 on.

I told myself I'd walk down to the restaurant at the south end of town, the one with the bar, where there'd be people and noise to lift the weight of loneliness. I told myself I could take a night off, strike up a conversation with someone new, get out of my own head for a while, away from the thoughts that would darken a solitary evening.

On the street outside, I told myself it was the middle of June. I'd been here six weeks and hadn't made a real friend. It was time for my world to expand.

As I approached the restaurant, I told myself I didn't have to clench my fists so tightly when I walked.

10

The Bohemian Sage was a typical California architectural identity crisis. The façade was a twenty-foot-high outward-leaning grid of glass and steel, like a modern airport terminal, while the interior looked like a stripped-down nineteenth-century warehouse, with exposed brick and thick, rough-hewn beams supporting a high, bare ceiling.

The name didn't fit either. There was nothing bohemian about the place, and I didn't smell a whiff of sage anywhere. It was all hip-modernist inside, dark wood and brushed stainless steel—the kind of place where lawyers on TV shows go after work to unwind and flirt with colleagues.

Twenty or so white-clothed tables stood in the front section of the restaurant, all occupied. The diners' chatter rose to the high ceiling and then echoed back in a shapeless murmur that gave the place a warm, lively feel.

In back, a dark wood bar edged with steel stretched almost the width of the building. An aisle dividing the tables ran from the host's podium in front to the bar in the rear. I scanned the crowd as I walked through, and lo and behold, there was Marilyn Dupree at a table for four. Her husband sat across from her. I didn't recognize the other couple.

Marilyn said a few words to the woman beside her. Her voice, smooth and cool, stuck with me. I hesitated for a second.

You don't need to be here, I thought. You could go up the street and get sushi.

But I didn't want sushi. And I couldn't avoid her forever.

So what if she sets you off, I told myself. A little spark of light in the darkness isn't going to kill you.

I took a stool on the left side of the bar and ordered a gin and tonic.

As the bartender poured it, I caught snippets of the conversation behind me.

"Again?" That was Marilyn, not happy about whatever "again" was referring to. A voice I guessed belonged to her husband replied with a short, dismissive comment. I only caught the tone, not the words.

"Why don't you move back there if you like it so much?" That was Marilyn, frustrated.

I didn't catch her husband's response.

"Oh, Bastian, come on!"

She was chiding him about something.

My low-backed swivel stool was bolted to the floor. I turned a hundred and eighty degrees and looked toward their table. She looked at the same time and it turned into one of those awkward meetings of the eyes where neither person can look away.

Her husband, Bastian Chakra, sat across from her with his back to me, and in a second he turned to see what had caught his wife's eye. He smiled and raised his glass, and I waved hello. That was my first interaction with the wealthiest man in this wealthy little town, the guy everyone except me seemed to know.

He was forty-one years old—fifteen years older and half an inch shorter than his wife—bald on top, with golden-brown hair on the sides, a sandy-brown mustache, and zero body fat. I knew that because on Saturday mornings, he put on his spandex cycling outfit and rode with a group of other balding fat-free millionaires on a carbon fiber racing bike through the center of town.

From watching him at the coffee shop, at the grocery store, and at a couple of lunch spots around town, I learned his diet consisted of egg whites, kale smoothies, and fat-free lattes. I had heard he liked to drink, and I learned that night he drank only one thing: vodka and soda with a twist of lemon, because it had no sugar and he could put down eight or ten of them without getting love handles.

During one of our long drives, The Kid told me Bastian had made his money in software, first with a company he'd helped to found when he was twenty-one, and later through a lucky investment in a second company that took off. People said—and Bastian himself joked—that he wasn't all that bright. He just had the good fortune to be in the right place at the right time, twice. That was fifty million dollars' worth of good timing.

He and Marilyn had been married three years and had moved here from San Francisco a year and a half ago. I knew some of that from coffee shop gossip, and some from the social pages of the local weekly that people left on the tables at the front of the grocery store.

After waving hello, Bastian turned back to his dinner guests, who were finishing their desserts. Marilyn's eyes remained fixed on me.

I turned back to the bar and drank the rest of my gin and tonic.

"Looks like you have an admirer over there," the bartender said as he poured a glass of wine. I couldn't tell if he was smiling or smirking, so I ignored his comment.

"You ready for another?" he asked.

"Sure."

He dumped the ice from my glass, then added new cubes from a silver scoop and poured in a generous shot of gin.

"You're new here," he said.

"I've been here a few weeks," I said as he topped off the glass with tonic.

"I've seen your car. That is one sweet ride!"

He slid the glass across the bar and then walked off.

As I took the first sip, I heard people getting up from the table behind me. One couple said goodbye, and then a man said, "I'm gonna stop at the bar for a drink."

"You don't need any more," Marilyn said.

"I want to talk to this guy," Bastian said. Somehow, I knew he meant me.

A few seconds later, he appeared to my left, and as soon as he put his glass on the bar, the bartender stepped up and filled it with vodka and soda and a fresh lemon wedge. He didn't even have to ask.

Bastian wore a light-grey suit, tailored to show his trim waist. His light-blue shirt was open two buttons too far, to show the golden new-age pendant nestled in the mat of curly hair between his fat-free pectoral muscles. The pendant looked like a peace sign with the three lines in the middle replaced by phalluses.

When he saw me looking at it, he lifted it from his mat of chest hair and said, "Pretty cool, huh? It's an ancient Indian symbol of male fertility and penile enlightenment."

"East Indian or American Indian?" I asked.

He looked confused, as if the question had never occurred to him. "I don't know." He dropped the pendant back into its hairy nest and took a sip of his drink.

Marilyn later told me the pendant had been designed by the daughter of Bastian's spiritual advisor during her third stint in rehab.

I noticed a few other things about Bastian in that first meeting. He wore a platinum bracelet on his left wrist and a Patek Phillipe watch on his right. The platinum wedding band on his left hand, inlaid with sparkling diamonds, looked small and plain compared to the giant jewel-encrusted monstrosity on his right.

"You like that?" he asked with a smile. "It's a Super Bowl ring. I bought it from a down-and-out New York Giants cornerback for eighty grand." He extended his hand and said, "Bastian Chakra, and you're John Manis."

I stood and shook his hand.

Marilyn walked up to the bar and stood to Bastian's left. She looked at me over his shoulder, directly in the eye as if to ask, Now are you going to introduce yourself?

My answer to that was no. Her look was too direct. Too forward. There was something presumptuous in it, like she thought I owed her something.

I didn't like the fact that she'd planted herself in a place where I couldn't look at the person I was talking to—her husband—without seeing her too. I forced my eyes away from her. I leaned my elbows on the bar and stirred the ice in my gin and tonic with the thin black straw, not looking at either of them.

My heart was thumping hard and fast. The sight of her face and the sound of her voice had an effect on me I couldn't explain—like the roulette wheel I had pried myself away from had come to hunt me down. Through the din of the crowd, I thought I heard the voice of John Manis, who had been silent for weeks. "It's called a crush, my friend. Everyone gets them."

I turned to see if he was standing behind me.

"I hear you write code," Bastian said.

"I used to," I replied, turning my gaze back toward my glass. I could feel her eyes on me, and my pulse was rising. I started breathing deep and slow to keep calm. I wanted desperately to leave, and even more desperately to talk to her, but not in front of her husband. I had to work hard to keep quiet and not look at her.

"Well I have an offer you might like," he said. And then he launched into his pitch. His new company was building software for law enforcement.

"Oh, come on, Bas," Marilyn interrupted. "You're building it for third world dictators."

"Shut up," Bastian said with a backhanded wave over his shoulder. It was a quick, dismissive comment, spoken not with venom or hostility but simple impatience, as if he were speaking to another man's dog. And it stung my heart to see him treat her like that.

I looked up at her instinctively. I couldn't help it. Part of me wanted to see how she had taken it, and part of me wanted to let her know I would never talk that way to anyone.

She was looking away at that moment, toward the far end of the bar, with her hand raised to get the bartender's attention. If Bastian's remark had any effect on her, I couldn't see it.

Bastian blathered on about his company, bouncing his leg on the footrail of the bar and speaking rapidly like someone who'd had too much coffee. "Our system hooks into surveillance cameras. It does facial recognition and connects what it sees to a database of criminal profiles so the cops can track the bad guys."

He didn't look at me when he spoke, and the timing of his hand gestures didn't match what he was saying. I had the feeling he was repeating a sales pitch he'd given a thousand times before.

"Bad guys?" Marilyn said. "Seriously, Bas, you sound like a kid." Then she said to the bartender, "I'd like a whiskey sour."

"Bad guys," Bastian insisted. "That's what you call them."

Marilyn turned her eyes to me and said, "What would you like to drink?"

I still had half a gin and tonic, so I said, "Oh, I'm good."

"Are you?" she asked. There was a hint of sarcasm in her tone, and a hint of flirtation, though I wasn't sure if it was intended to provoke me or her husband.

"He said he's good," Bastian snapped.

Marilyn shrugged and turned her attention to the whiskey sour the bartender was mixing.

Bastian turned back to me and said, "The company's doing great. We just have to work out some problems with the facial recognition engine. Check this out."

He reached into his jacket and before I knew it, he had his phone out and was taking a photo of me.

"Whoa!" I said. "Whoa! You don't just go taking people's pictures without asking."

Marilyn turned and looked at me sharply, her eyes narrowing at the corners, as if the video recorder had just gone on in her brain.

"See this," Bastian said. I could hear the effects of the alcohol more clearly in his voice now. "Look at this photo. The light above your head casts shadows under your brow, your nose, and lips. And watch."

He tapped the "Identify" button. A little blue wheel spun for a couple of seconds before giving way to an old black-and-white photo.

"Ha! Look at that," he said. "That's a Navy fighter pilot from the second world war! What kind of facial recognition is that?" He squinted at the image. "I mean, it does look like you. But seriously, it says 'US Navy, 1944' right in the photo."

"He doesn't like having his picture taken," Marilyn said. "Can't you tell he's shy?" This time, her mocking tone was aimed at me.

"Yeah, fuck off," Bastian said, as if he were speaking to a person of no consequence. She reacted with indifference, as if she were beyond caring what he thought.

Bastian went on talking about his software without looking at either one of us. He was watching the bartender and rattling the ice in his empty glass. "If we close two of the four contracts in negotiations, that's a hundred million right there. But we need another top-notch programmer to get the software back on track..."

As he jabbered on, Marilyn and I studied each other's faces with the unguarded curiosity of children. The voices in the room faded into the background. What I saw in her eyes and what I think she saw in mine was that this whole scene was only about her and me. We were communicating on a frequency no one else was tuned in to.

My heart was beating so hard and fast, I could feel the artery in my neck throbbing. I saw the same artery pulsing in her neck. The luster in her eyes as she looked at me showed the same feeling of enchantment that was racing through my own heart. She broke into a smile, and a whole other dimension of her character appeared. It was a sudden flash of joy, of pure happiness, and it made me smile.

We continued to look at each other while Bastian yammered on like a television in the background. "...revolutionize law enforcement... disrupt the status quo... this is your chance to get in on the ground floor."

"So what do you say?" he asked. "You interested in leading a software team?"

I wouldn't have taken a job with him even if I did know how to program. He looked like a nineteen-seventies swinger and talked like a car salesman.

"No thanks," I said. "I appreciate the offer, but I don't write code anymore."

"So what are you going to do?" Bastian asked. "Plug in printers for old ladies? I hear that's what you're up to. Driving around in a Corvette, diddling with rich people's iPads."

"That's more my speed right now."

The bartender stopped and refilled Bastian's drink.

Bastian took a sip and shook his head. "Makes no sense," he said. "No sense at all, a programmer of your caliber doing mindless crap work." Then he added excitedly, "I can up the offer. Stock options too."

"No," I said.

Bastian let out a sigh and said under his breath, "Well, shit..."

He put his drink on the bar and picked up his phone. He touched the button and the photo of the World War II pilot appeared again.

"So we're stuck with this," he sighed. He swiped left and a new photo appeared. "Ha! Look at that," he said derisively. "The second match is just as bad. Some convict from Illinois."

It was the mug shot from my arrest. Bastian's drunken tone told me he had dismissed it as an obvious mismatch, but my heart was pounding right up into my throat, because—what about Marilyn? Did Marilyn see that?

I didn't know. I wasn't sure if she even *could* see it from where she was sitting.

I looked at her just as she was turning her face away, so I couldn't read her expression.

"What's the next match?" I blurted, my voice an octave higher than it had been a moment before. I stood up from the stool and leaned over the phone so Bastian would turn it toward me and away from her. My palms were in an icy sweat.

"The next match?" Bastian said drunkenly. He swiped the screen and a photo of John Manis appeared. I knew that photo. It was from an article in a tech journal reporting the sale of his game company, and it looked enough like me that I could have put it on my license and no one would bat an eye.

"Next is John Manis," Bastian said. "But it doesn't do us any good when that's the third match. It should be the first."

I backed away from him and took my seat again, pressing my hands into my thighs to hide their shaking. I wanted to see if Marilyn was watching, but I didn't want to turn and look right at her.

She had to be watching, I thought. What else would she be doing?

The panic I had felt in the casinos when the stakes were high was now rising to full intensity. Only here, I couldn't play it off. I couldn't turn to the crowd with a cool smile and a witty remark as I threw another ten thousand dollars onto the table.

I glanced at Marilyn for a second to see if she noticed my agitation, then I quickly looked away. I had already seen those dark, lustrous eyes enough times to know they took in everything. She had to have caught it all. She had to have seen my furtive glance and rising panic.

I quickly grabbed my glass and drank down the rest of my gin and tonic.

"You want another?" Bastian asked, staring into his phone.

"No," I blurted. Too loud. That was too forceful, I told myself. You shouted. Then I swallowed hard and said in a more reasonable tone, to try to prove that I was calm, "I don't want anything."

"Oh, you want something," Marilyn said coolly. Her sharp, observant eyes narrowed at the corners. "It's been written all over you since the day we met."

"You two know each other?" Bastian asked absently, still looking at his phone.

Marilyn ignored him. Then she said something that just floored me. It was coincidence, to be sure. A remark any witty, observant person might have made, given my name, the way I had blurted out my words, and the level of agitation I was showing. But it shook me nonetheless.

As the bartender passed by, she said, "How about another drink for Johnny Manic?"

Without looking up from his phone, Bastian slurred, "His name is Manis. John Manis."

Marilyn replied cool and easy, "I don't think so."

11

The next thing I knew, I was holding a guy by the lapels of his rumpled brown suit. I had run smack into him in the doorway as I hurried out. I wouldn't have grabbed him, except if I didn't, we might both have gone over backwards.

"Sorry," I blurted as I let go of his lapels.

When I tried to smooth them out, he brushed my hands away and gave me a sour, irritated look.

"I wasn't looking where I was going—"

"No, you weren't," he barked.

"—and I didn't see you, and crap, I can't remember if I paid my tab."

I looked back toward the bar where Marilyn and Bastian sat with their backs to me. They were talking to the bartender.

I thought I said goodbye before I left them, but I wasn't sure. I thought I left cash on the bar to pay my tab, but I might not have.

The bartender looked up just then, looked at the man I'd run into, and he pointed at me and shook his head.

"What's that mean?" I asked frantically. "Why's he pointing at me and shaking his head?"

The bartender waved a receipt.

"You didn't pay your tab," the man said. "You trying to skip out?"

Bastian grabbed the receipt from the bartender. He turned and looked at me, then pointed to himself and gave me a thumbs-up. I nodded thanks.

When I turned back toward the door, the man I'd run into was staring at me, but it wasn't the angry stare you'd expect from someone you'd just collided with. He seemed to be assessing me methodically, almost clinically. He looked closely at my eyes, which must have looked frantic if they showed anything of what I felt. Then he looked at my brow. I was suddenly aware that it was sweating. Then his gaze went down to my shaking hands, which I slid into my pockets. Then back up to my eyes, where too much was going on at once.

"You OK, pal?"

Now I remembered who this guy was. I'd seen him in the grocery store picking up coffee and a sandwich. He ate corned beef, and the sandwich guy and the store manager and all the cashiers called him Lou.

Every time I'd seen him before, he'd been in uniform. He'd pull up in his patrol car once in the morning and then again around lunchtime, every day like clockwork. Coffee and a banana for breakfast. Coffee and a sandwich for lunch.

He looked to be in his forties, trim, with thinning hair and a serious, almost dour expression. His suit was a size too big, like he had bought it off the rack and hadn't bothered to have it taken in.

Normally, I'd be put off by a guy staring at me the way he was. But a guy who'd just been run into the way I'd run into him had every right to be angry, and this guy wasn't angry. He was completely in control of his emotions, and I admired that. It actually put me at ease.

"I asked if you're OK," he repeated.

"Huh? Yeah. I just got a little rattled, you know?"

He was still quietly examining me, and I felt the need, almost the compulsion to explain myself.

"That woman," I nodded toward the bar.

"Marilyn?"

"You know, I just... Wait, you know her? I guess everyone knows everyone. Small town, right?" I forced a smile that got no reaction from him.

"I got rattled. I just got, I don't know." I looked around, as if there might be someone there to help me out. But who did I expect to find? John Manis? I licked the dryness from my lips.

"Sometimes there's just too much going on at once. You ever get that feeling?" His immovable expression told me he didn't. "You ever get, like, a panic attack? Do cops get panic attacks? Is it like a test you have to pass to get onto the force? I mean, you seem pretty calm. You seem like—"

I poked him a couple times in the chest, just to see if he'd react.

"Stop that," he said, swatting my hand away. "How much have you had to drink?"

"I don't know." I ran my fingers through my hair. "I had one when I came in." I shifted my weight from one foot to the other and then back again. "And then I had another." I ran my fingers through my hair again and let out a long loud breath.

"Stop fidgeting," said Lou.

"Sorry. That guy," I nodded toward the bar, "started jabbering at me and I don't do coding anymore, and his damn wife wouldn't stop staring at me."

"You driving?"

"No, I'm walking. *You're* staring at me too. You know that? You stare. It's not polite. I'm right up there." I pointed up the street toward my apartment.

He stepped out my way without taking his eyes off me.

"Go home," he said.

On the walk back to my apartment, I thought of Marilyn and Manis and my little apartment, and now that The Kid was gone, I had no one to talk to and I drove around all day by myself and then at night I ate alone, and in the mornings I woke alone, and in my date book I tried to write my biography looking forward instead of backward, filling in the hours of my life the way they were supposed to play out, and all the entries for little piddly things that didn't matter, and Marilyn Dupree was beautiful, absolutely beautiful, and she saw something in me and I saw something in her, and whether or not it was something good, something was better than nothing in this place I suddenly realized I was in, in this life that I just woke into, that all of a sudden seemed emptier than the Nevada desert.

What the hell happened back there, I asked as I listened to the echoing clop-clop-clop of my heels on the empty sidewalk.

I don't know.

But it really bugged me that my suit was nicer than Lou's because he stood on the right side of things and I didn't. He made it his life's work to try to do right by everyone, which is not only an impossible task but a thankless one as well. No wonder he looked so sour.

And I had a 1963 Corvette and a closet full of two-thousand-dollar suits and I had never done a damn thing for anyone.

What happened back there?

I told you, I don't know.

Stop running your fingers through your hair. Through your sweat-soaked hair. You're going to pull it all out.

Then I was at the door of the apartment building. Then I was inside. The air was hot and smothering. Into the kitchen, open the windows and the wine and go through the checklist.

Are you in danger this minute?

No.

OK. Long exhale, and we come down a notch.

Pacing in the living room.

Will you be in danger ten minutes from now?

No.

Good. Another long breath, out through the nose, and we're down another notch.

Drink down the whole glass in two gulps.

Is it safe to sleep here?

Yes.

Exhale. Let your shoulders drop.

Will you be in danger tomorrow, or the next day, or the day after that, in this tiny little town where everyone knows everyone, where you can't turn around without running into that woman or that cop?

Panic!

Back into the kitchen. More wine, red like blood.

Marilyn Dupree was beautiful and that cop's probing eyes were like the goddamn Inquisition poking a shovel right into Manis's grave and I'm stuck here living paycheck to paycheck and when my mind isn't on fire a black hole is going to swallow me, and the gin and the tonic and this whole bottle of wine and six Benadryl won't put me to sleep tonight, and I can't go through this again. I can't, I can't, I can't!

At the kitchen window, the calm, easy voice of John Manis counseled me. "You're losing your grip, Tom. Of course you'll go crazy if you try to think of everything at once. Pick one thought from the chaos and try to hold on to it. Just one. That's where we start."

I closed my eyes and in the whole spiraling mess of the collapsing universe there was only one thing that didn't look hideous and terrifying and wrong.

Marilyn.

Marilyn Dupree with the dark eyes and the fair skin and the lips as red as love.

12

The next day, when I needed gas and Marilyn was filling the tank of her black Mercedes, I kept on driving, all the way to the next town, and got gas there.

I didn't know I was still wound up from the previous night's encounter until I got to my first job.

"Slow down," the man said as I explained how to configure the antivirus software I had just installed for him. "And you don't have to pace when you talk. This isn't a university lecture."

The day after that, I didn't have sushi for lunch because I could see Marilyn through the restaurant window.

I got through two jobs without shaking or pacing, and every time I checked the speedometer on the Vette, I was no more than ten miles an hour over the limit. I only needed two glasses of wine and one Benadryl that night.

On the third day, my nerves were back to normal, my mind was clear, and my pulse was an even sixty.

But I wasn't paying attention. As I came around the end of the bread aisle in the grocery, I ran smack into her. She was wearing a black cotton summer dress and a pair of black flats.

"John," she said. "What does it mean when your computer says there are bad sectors on the hard drive?"

That was it. No hello or anything. Just a technical question. I had imagined many scenarios in which we'd finally get a chance to talk alone, but none of the conversations started like this.

"It means your hard drive is going bad," I said. "You need to back up all your files and replace the drive."

I stood and waited for the next question, which I knew would be something like, "Is that something you could help me with?"

I could see the mind behind her dark eyes working on the wording, gathering the nerve to ask. I could see the question forming on her lips. But it didn't come out as I expected.

"Come to my house," she said. "Bastian's away."

Then she wheeled her cart to the checkout, calmly and slowly, as if nothing had just happened. I followed and stood at the register behind her with only a loaf of bread. The way she turned and smiled at me while the cashier rang up her order, and the way I smiled at her, our feelings must have been obvious to anyone watching. The cashier looked at Marilyn and then at me, then quickly turned her attention back to the scanner, as if embarrassed at having intruded on someone else's affair.

In the parking lot outside, Marilyn got in her car and I got in mine. I followed her six miles north, and then we turned onto a long stone driveway that led through a stand of trees to a large white Italian villa with a terracotta roof. There was a marble fountain in front and a pool in back, and six million dollars of house in between.

Marilyn didn't look at me as she took the bag of groceries from her car. The front door of the house opened as she made her way up the steps, and a short, dark-haired woman in a maid's uniform said, "Buenos días, señora."

The housekeeper took the bag from Marilyn, and Marilyn said, "Buenos días, Esme."

Esme nodded hello to me, then retreated into the house. Marilyn turned and smiled. "I'll give you a tour," she said.

I followed her through the kitchen and a sitting room that looked out onto the backyard pool, through a living room and dining room full of expensive mismatched furniture, and back to the main entrance.

"Nice house," I said.

"Isn't it?"

I followed her up the broad curving stairway, into the hallway of the second floor. I could feel the nervous energy in her quick steps. I had the same jittery energy in mine, the same rising sense of power, pulsing and fluid, that ran through me when I approached the tables in Vegas. She hesitated at the entrance to the master bedroom, squeezed my hand as if for reassurance, and said, "Not here."

She turned as if to continue down the hall toward one of the other rooms, then she stopped and said, "Yes, here."

We walked in together. To the left was a tall cherrywood dresser. Beyond that was a walk-in closet larger than most bedrooms. To the right was the sprawling master bath. We continued straight ahead, toward the French doors that opened out to a balcony. On the right side of the room stood a desk and divan. On the left was a king-size bed neatly made in pale green.

She was in front of me, walking toward the desk, and I looked at her in a way I had been trying for weeks not to look at her. The sway of her loose summer dress only hinted at the contours of my desire. The pressure inside me kept rising, but it didn't have the usual edge of fear, because I knew there'd be an outlet for it soon.

I looked back toward the bed. The nightstand to the left of it held a stack of business books. Not the kind about how to manage your money, but the kind about how enlightened corporate leaders think, how to corner the market on innovation. The kind of stuff tech CEOs read while they eat their fat-free yogurt.

The nightstand on the right held a scented candle, a lamp, a jar of lip balm, and a stack of books. *The Great Gatsby*, *Moonstone*, and a couple of crime novels by Jim Thompson and Charles Williams.

Marilyn walked to the desk and stood by the laptop and printer with her back to me in that dress I just wanted to pull off of her. For a moment, I thought she was going to say, "This is the computer. See what you can do about that hard drive."

Instead, she twisted the wedding ring from her finger and laid it on the desk.

"There's no point in pretending, is there?" She turned to face me, and I walked toward her.

We had weeks of foreplay behind us in those skirting encounters around town. The spark of a single kiss ignited it all at once. From there it was just a few steps to the bed. And let me tell you—a frustrated, unhappily married woman has more pent-up passion than any single woman anywhere, and she can push it all out through her hips with shocking and magical intensity.

* * *

In the calm that followed, I was staring up at the Art Deco lines of the tray ceiling, which didn't go with the Victorian crown molding, which didn't go with the classical marble entrance or the razor-straight lines of the modernist pool out back.

"Who designed this place?"

Marilyn was watching with crossed eyes as her fingers stretched a lock of long black hair up toward the ceiling. "Bastian worked with six different architects. He kept firing them."

"Why don't you have a garage?"

She let the lock of hair drop back onto the pillow. "Bastian thinks it's morally wrong for cars to live in houses when so many people are homeless. Now he wants a helicopter so he won't contribute to traffic between here and San Francisco."

"He's very thoughtful," I said. "Why didn't you take his name?"

"Marilyn Chakra? Are you kidding? Sounds like a new-age porn star."

"The way you move that body of yours, you could be a porn star."

"No, it's the new-age stuff I hate." She turned her head toward me. "You know, Bastian Chakra isn't even his real name? His name was Timmy Smith, but his spiritual advisor told him he should change it, to channel cosmic energy and tap into his karmic potential."

"Did it work?"

Marilyn shrugged. "I can't tell. But something changed. I mean, now he likes boys and wants a helicopter."

"What do you mean he likes boys?"

She frowned. "What do you think I mean?"

"Like schoolboys?"

"No, but young. Twenty or twenty-two. Vigorous and willing." She rolled onto her back and looked at the ceiling. "But only as a diversion from women. He's had so many women, he needs a change now and then to keep from getting bored."

I had wondered why the housekeeper didn't react when we went upstairs. Maybe this was just how they lived.

"So can you fix my hard drive?" Marilyn asked.

"Are you serious?"

"Yes. I'm serious."

"Is that all you wanted me for? My technical expertise?"

"That's it," she said, smiling. "How was I to know you'd attack me? You seemed so shy out in public. Almost like you were scared of me." She traced a line down the middle of my chest with her index finger. "I don't have any cash. Will you take what I just gave you as pay? Or does that make you feel like a prostitute?"

"No, I'll take it," I said.

She propped herself up on both elbows and said with a mixture of earnestness and teasing, "You can come back for more if the job takes longer than expected."

13

After lingering a while in bed, I went to the desk and opened Marilyn's laptop. A message about "bad sectors" popped up. "Try running disk repair," it said.

Marilyn walked up behind me and put her hands on my shoulders. I pointed to the monitor. "That's all you have to do," I said. "Back up your drive and run disk repair."

"If I had done that," she said, pulling her long black hair back from her face, "you wouldn't be here."

"Do you have an external drive I can back this up to?"

She opened the top drawer of the desk and pointed at the three hard drives inside. "Pick one."

I chose the drive on top and as I plugged it into the laptop, she reached over my shoulder and snatched some papers from the printer in a gesture that seemed sudden and impulsive.

"What's that?" I asked.

"Insurance."

She took an envelope from the desk and crossed the room to the dresser, where she stood and wrote.

An icon appeared on the computer screen showing the external disk I had just plugged in. It said "BAC Backup."

What was BAC? I thought for a second. Bastian Chakra. His middle name must start with A.

I clicked the icon to see what was on the drive. Documents, spreadsheets, PowerPoint presentations, and folders labeled "Business" and "Personal."

I turned to look at Marilyn, still standing at the dresser, still writing. That's a lot of writing to put on an insurance document, I thought. Maybe she's adding notes for her agent to change the policy.

"You mind if I shower?" she asked without looking up.

"Go ahead," I said.

She put the pen down, folded the papers, and laid them on the dresser. Then she picked up a small round mirror and looked into it as she applied a coat of dark red lipstick.

"Who puts lipstick on before they shower?" I asked.

"I'm not sure about this color," she said. "What do you think?" She blew me a kiss.

"I like your natural color better."

"Me too."

She picked up the folded papers and pressed her lips against them, imprinting a dark red kiss. Then she slid the papers into an envelope and sealed it.

"Are you having an affair with the insurance agent too?" I asked.

She gave me a hot, angry look and said, "Don't be rude. You knew I was married when you walked in here. If you wanted something exclusive, you should have looked somewhere else. And no. The insurance agent is dull and unattractive."

She wiped the rest of the lipstick from her mouth with the back of her hand.

"Sorry," I said. "It was a joke."

"It wasn't funny," she said. And she went into the bathroom.

Looking back at the computer, I clicked on Bastian's Business folder. Then I clicked on Loans and saw a long list of documents. Why did he have so many? The dates on the files were all recent, all within the past few months.

I opened one of the documents. A loan for one million dollars against a movie theater he owned in Oakland granted eight weeks ago.

I opened another. A loan against a car wash for one hundred and fifty thousand dollars, taken six weeks ago.

Another document. A six-hundred-thousand-dollar line of credit for one of his software companies.

You have to stop this, I told myself. This is how you got in trouble the first time, embezzling from the corporation. And then you were back at it the minute you got your hands on Manis's laptop. You tore through everything until you found his passwords, his online accounts, all his money.

What got me going in Manis's case was a series of emails I had found between Manis and his money managers. He criticized them relentlessly for being too conservative, and eventually wrested control of his investments from them, against their advice. They finally washed their hands of him and pushed all his holdings into E*TRADE so he could manage them himself. That's how I got at them.

Whatever Bastian was up to was none of my business. But he was definitely up to something...

I closed out all the documents and unplugged the drive. It didn't have enough free space for me to back up Marilyn's laptop anyway. I dropped it back in the drawer and chose another drive. This one was empty, so I started the backup. The computer said it would take twenty-six minutes to complete.

I heard the shower go on in the bathroom.

Twenty-five minutes of backup left.

She'll be in there a while, I told myself as I tapped my fingers on the desk and watched the colored circle spin.

Twenty-four minutes left, and I didn't hear any splashing in that shower. She hadn't gotten in yet.

I looked back at the bed and wondered if Marilyn would ask the maid to change the sheets before her husband returned. I walked to the dresser and picked up the envelope she had just sealed. It had no stamp or address. I put it back.

I wondered what was in that giant walk-in closet.

Then the regular patter of water on the shower floor broke into uneven splashing. She was in.

I walked back to the bed and put on my pants and shirt. Then I went into the closet and flicked on the light.

Bastian's stuff was on the right. Hers was on the left. She had thirty or forty dresses neatly arranged on hangers: mostly cotton, and mostly black or red. Beyond those hung thirty fancy gowns, like prom dresses only nicer, and I bet she never wore any of them twice. She had a few dozen blouses and skirts on hangers, piles of yoga pants and jeans, dozens of pairs of shoes and boots lined up on the floor and stacked in cubbies that climbed the rear wall.

On the right side of the closet, Bastian had a bunch of jackets, neatly pressed shirts, a dozen belts, and only a handful of ties. He liked to wear his collar open, like me.

There was a stack of cherrywood drawers on his side. The top one was full of cuff links pressed into a black velvet tray. Who wears cuff links? And without a tie? The next drawer was full of watches. Sixteen fancy Swiss timepieces that probably cost a few thousand dollars each. I remembered him at the bar the other night, with his Patek Phillipe watch, his platinum bracelet, and his gaudy rings. He liked adornment.

She had a similar stack of drawers on her side, but I told myself I wasn't going to open them, because I had already pried far enough. They're full of diamonds, I guessed. I bet that's what they're full of.

She was still splashing in the shower. She wouldn't be out anytime soon.

I opened the top drawer. Yup. Diamonds. And sapphires. And rubies and emeralds. Earrings, pendants and studs. The next drawer down was full of necklaces, and below that, bracelets on black velvet, all in perfect order. I wondered if she put the stuff away herself or if she had the maid do it.

Then the shower went quiet. I slid the drawer closed and returned to the desk. Eighteen minutes left until the backup was done.

What was in that Personal folder on Bastian's hard drive? Anything like the treasures in his closet? And what was Bastian doing in his personal life that would lead him to neglect a wife like Marilyn? To be so dismissive toward her, as he'd been at the bar the other night?

I opened the drawer and looked again at his backup drive. It was slim and black with a USB plug on a short wire, identical to the other two drives—the one now plugged into the computer, and the one beneath it in the drawer.

Marilyn walked from the bathroom to the closet, a white towel wrapped around her body, and another twisted in a turban around her hair.

I thought about slipping Bastian's hard drive into my pocket as I watched the colored circle spin onscreen. But I resisted the temptation. Sixteen minutes left.

Marilyn came out of the closet wearing a green cotton dress. She unwound the towel from her head and began to brush out her long black hair.

"Are you hungry?" she asked.

"Very."

"We have leftover Thai food in the kitchen."

"That sounds great."

As I stood from the desk, she laid the brush on the dresser and ran her fingers through her hair one last time.

At the door, we kissed. She smiled. And then she whispered in my ear, "You left the light on."

"What light?"

"In the closet."

<h1 style="text-align:center">14</h1>

I saw Marilyn again the following day, but not the way I'd expected. She had texted in the morning to say Bastian would be home all day. "But we'll meet up again soon. Looking forward to it!"

Around 11:30 that morning I walked into the deli on Main Street, and who did I see? Bastian Chakra and Marilyn Dupree standing at a tall table near the front window. Marilyn was holding a ticket for the sandwiches they had ordered. My heart raced at the sight of her. Even in faded jeans and a light-blue t-shirt, she was lovely. I wanted to put my arm around her, pull her toward me, and kiss her lips. But Bastian was standing beside her.

"Hey you two!" I spoke too loudly and gave a cartoonishly exaggerated wave. The woman behind the deli counter and a few customers looked at me.

"Well if it isn't Johnny Manic," Marilyn said with an amused smile. "I bet he can resolve it for us." She looked me up and down in a provocative way.

Bastian was wearing blue-gray wool slacks and a fresh white dress shirt unbuttoned to show his mat of chest hair and his golden pendant. He was bouncing one foot on the floor, as if he'd had too much coffee, and he said, "Look, John, I was serious about the job offer. We're always on the hunt for top talent. A guy like you could take us to the next level."

"I'm not interested," I said. "What did you want me to resolve, Marilyn?"

When I caught her eye and felt that spark in my heart, I was sure I gave us away. But if she noticed the spark, she didn't seem to care. And I'm pretty sure Bastian didn't pick up on it at all. He didn't seem to be tuned in to anything happening in her world.

"Bastian says you can't leave the country without a passport," Marilyn said. "And I say you can."

"You can," I said.

"See, Bastian?"

She had a calm, even tone, but Bastian dismissed her abruptly. "You can't leave the country without a passport."

"Sure you can," I said.

"Yeah? How?" Bastian asked.

I leaned on the table between them and spelled it out. "You go down to southern Texas and you find a yacht or a fishing boat going south. Give the captain some money to drop you off on a beach in Mexico. Pick any small town. They don't have cops sitting on every beach looking for people getting off of private boats."

"Does it have to be Texas?" Marilyn asked.

"It could be Southern California," I said.

"You see, Bastian?" she said. "I was right."

"Yeah, but once you're in Mexico, you're stuck," Bastian said. "You can't cross back into the US. You can't go anywhere."

"You can go south," I said.

I didn't bother explaining the rest of it. When you get down to Guatemala, Honduras, and El Salvador, those countries where the government doesn't seem to function at all, it's mostly rural. It's woods and farms and hills and unpaved roads with the occasional cop or soldier. If you need to cross a border, you slip someone cash. Just don't try it at a major crossing. Stick to the rural outposts.

The roads down there are hard, especially when you don't have much money. You have to pick up odd jobs along the way, or you have to beg. You're hungry most of the time, you're covered with bug bites, and you start to smell because you can't always find a place to wash. People don't think about those things until it's too late.

That whole part of the world is hot as hell and filled with snakes and scorpions. By the time I got to Costa Rica, I had had enough. All I wanted was to get back to the States.

As the woman at the deli counter called out number forty-eight, Bastian said, "I read your manifesto."

He meant Manis's infamous denunciation of modern technology.

"I totally agree with the idea of unplugging," Bastian said. "Getting off the grid, ditching the mobile phone and the whole digital life. I do it for ten minutes every day. It lets my spirit open up."

The deli woman called forty-nine and Bastian said curtly, "That's us. Get the food."

Marilyn got up and did what he said.

"You still believe that?" Bastian asked. "That technology has overwhelmed us and made our lives poorer?"

"For the most part," I said. "But it's here to stay, so we have to make our peace with it."

"Can you make peace with writing code again? Leading a team of developers?"

I shook my head. "Sorry. That's just not where I'm at right now."

He looked at me impatiently as he tapped his gaudy Super Bowl ring on the marble tabletop. "I guess you're OK on money then? I mean, you obviously can't be making a living doing what you're doing now."

"I'm fine," I said.

Marilyn returned with the sandwiches. "Are you getting anything?"

I didn't want to stand there and eat with them. Bastian was fidgety and unfocused, like a twelve-year-old boy who'd been forced to sit still too long. I felt guilty about what I was doing with his wife, and jealous that she would leave the deli with him instead of me. On top of that, I felt a pang of frustration with myself. Marilyn's words from the day before came back loud and clear. "You knew I was married when you walked in here. If you wanted something exclusive, you should have looked somewhere else."

The old agitation was beginning to well up, only it had a different flavor this time. In Vegas, it was pure compulsion to get back to the felt-covered tables and let the adrenaline flow.

Marilyn tapped into that same adrenaline. She hit every one of my buttons without even trying. Talking to her was easy and natural, like picking up a conversation that had been running for years. She was the antidote to the emptiness and loneliness that had been creeping in over the past few weeks, the only person in this little town whose pull was strong enough to keep me from falling into the gaping black hole that threatened to swallow me on those long sleepless nights. She fit with me and I fit with her, and I wanted her. Only I couldn't get to her. Not with her husband sitting right there.

If I thought about it too much, I'd start to freak out. I looked around at the other patrons and asked myself, Do you really want to ruin their lunch with one of your episodes? Just leave. That's the obvious solution, right?

But the thought of her leaving with Bastian while I went back to an empty apartment brought me down hard, straight down into the dark and bottomless flip side of my agitated highs. I could feel it coming, and I didn't want anyone to see me like that. I had to get out of there.

"I asked if you wanted anything," Marilyn said.

"No. I'm not hungry."

"Then why'd you walk in?" Bastian asked.

"I don't know," I said. "I don't know why I do half the things I do. Every place I walk into lately turns out to be the wrong place."

I meant that as a jab at Marilyn, but if she caught it, it rolled off her the same way Bastian's insults did.

"You want our pickles?" she asked.

"No thanks."

"Try one," she said.

A mischievous, teasing smile lit her face as she lifted the pickle spear from her plate and pushed it into my mouth.

I turned my face away. Bastian gave her a hard slap on the thigh and said, "Stop that!"

"Why do you put up with her?" I asked.

"She gives me what I want," he said. "And if I can't get it from her, she doesn't mind if I get it from someone else."

"Who says I don't mind?" Marilyn asked. She picked up her napkin and wiped my cheek and chin before I could pull away. "Tell him what you do when you're traveling, Bas."

"What do I do when I'm traveling?" Bastian asked indifferently as he bit into his sandwich.

"Young women. Nineteen-year-old boys. Whatever comes your way, right?"

"All right," I said. "I don't want to get into your business."

"Where are you going?" Marilyn asked as I turned to leave.

"Away." My heart was sinking fast.

"I'll call you tomorrow," she said.

I didn't turn to see how Bastian reacted to that, but her words pushed the up button on the elevator that had been dragging my heart down into hell. She'll call me tomorrow!

Five seconds after all was lost, I left the deli with my head in the clouds, and even Manis couldn't reach me with his taunts. All he could do was roll his eyes and say, "This again."

15

At the grocery, I bought the same turkey sandwich I would have gotten at the deli. I took it to one of the tables up front, but I was too keyed up to eat.

I wondered if Bastian and Marilyn fought in private, and what those fights might look like. After spending an afternoon in her bed, I knew Marilyn wasn't the kind to hold anything back. Beneath her cool surface was a cauldron of emotion that she had no trouble expressing.

Bastian, on the other hand, seemed indifferent and tuned out. Why were they even together? What could be more infuriating to a passionate woman than a man who refuses to engage with her emotions?

I'd been drumming my fingers on the table as I thought about that, and at some point I must have started rapping my knuckles too loudly. The couple at the next table gave me a pointed look.

"Sorry," I said.

I had no jobs that afternoon and I needed something to do. I could wash the car again. Or vacuum. Or go for another goddamn hike.

The couple gave me the look again, and I looked at my hand knocking on the table. My knuckles hurt.

"Sorry," I said again. I left without touching the sandwich.

I walked back to my apartment and checked Manis's email. His dad was doing much better in the new home. The doctors had changed his meds, he got along well with the nurses, and he wasn't so agitated.

Good for him.

I wondered where Marilyn and Bastian were now. They must have left the deli. What sorts of things did they do together? Maybe he took her shopping. Maybe he was out buying her things I could never afford.

I opened the fridge. A cup of yogurt and an open box of baking soda. The fridge was so empty, the shelves didn't even have stains from things that used to be there.

Then I went back to the living room and checked to see if any work requests had come in through The Computer Kid website. There was one from late the night before.

Hey Jason. Tried calling but no answer. Got a new TV to surprise Edgar, but can't connect it to Wi-Fi no matter what I try. At my wit's end! Can you check it? He'll be home in two days and I want it working when he arrives. (Birthday, you know!) Hi to Marnie! When do you guys leave for Boston? -Jennifer

She didn't leave her last name or number, so I called Jason and asked if he knew a Jennifer who lived with an Edgar. He gave me her address and phone number. No one answered when I called, so I drove out to the house because there was no way I could spend another minute alone in that damn apartment where the only sound was the groan of the refrigerator.

Ten minutes later, I was approaching a mission-style house at the foot of the hills just outside town. I spent the entire drive thinking about Marilyn and Bastian. Maybe they were back at the house now. In the bedroom. Maybe he commanded her to take off her clothes the same way he commanded her to shut up, to get the sandwiches from the deli, to stop flirting with me. Did she obey? The thought made my blood boil.

Something sent my anxiety up a notch as I pulled into the drive but I couldn't put my finger on what it was. That's always a bad feeling, when you're trying to worry about one thing, and then you start worrying about something else and you don't even know what it is.

"Get a hold of yourself," Manis said as I climbed the steps to the porch.

"Shut up, John."

I rang the bell and heard two voices inside. A young child far back in the house said something I didn't catch. A woman approaching the door called back to him or her. "Try to find your shoes, OK? Mommy will be right back."

Then it hit me. It was the car in the driveway that had put me on edge. The white Range Rover with the black grille. That was the one that had almost run me over my first day in town. The memory of it came back so clearly, it made my heart jump. And I was sure Bastian and Marilyn were getting it on.

Then Jennifer opened the door. The round-faced woman with the short blonde hair.

"Jennifer?"

I tried to sound polite, but my thoughts were such a mess the name came out twisted with agitation and anger. I smiled politely. Her eyes fixed on mine with a look of surprise and fear, and she recoiled momentarily before she recovered herself.

"Oh." She put her hand to her heart, just as she had done the day she almost hit me. "I'm sorry. Can I help you?"

"I'm here to fix the TV."

She blinked, uncomprehending.

A voice from the back of the house called, "Mama?"

"To help you connect the new TV to the Wi-Fi," I said.

Her eyes went wide. "Oh my god! How did you know I have a new TV?"

The alarm in her voice sent my pulse and blood pressure up. I could feel the sweat forming on my brow.

"You submitted a request through the website," I said. My hands were starting to shake. "About your TV."

Then I saw her put it all together. "Oh!" she said. "Oh, God. I was expecting Jason. I'm sorry."

She looked me over silently for a few seconds the way Lou had done the other night at the restaurant. Like she was going through a mental checklist. Eyes, posture, eyes, hands, eyes, mouth, eyes.

I said, "He moved, you know. To Boston." My mouth was getting dry.

"Right," she nodded. "Right, um..." She looked back into the house, toward where the child's voice had come from.

This woman didn't trust me. She was polite and sweet-natured and had an aura of warmth, but she was scared of me.

She wasn't going to say it, so I did. "You're not comfortable with me coming in."

She hesitated, started to shake her head as if she wanted to say something kind and reassuring, but her discomfort was too strong. She just couldn't get the words out.

The child called again. "Mama?"

"That's alright," I said. "I get it."

Whatever she saw in me that made her uneasy sparked the same compulsion to explain myself that I'd felt the other night with Lou. I had a reason for being keyed up. I thought, You would be too, lady, if you had a brain like mine and a heart that can do two hundred beats a minute round the clock and you had to leave Marilyn Dupree in a deli with a guy you know treats her like shit, and then you go back to an empty apartment where you have nothing to do but think about the things you don't have and the person you can't be with.

I didn't say any of that, but the thoughts ran through my mind and I felt every one of them, and the way her eyes went wide, I think she could feel the energy coming off me.

I clamped my mouth shut and focused every ounce of energy on *not* ranting, not dumping this all on her, like I'd done to Lou the other night. I think she was waiting for me to say something, anything, but I wasn't going to let myself ramble incoherently on this poor woman's doorstep.

"Well look who's in control of himself today," Manis taunted. "Way to take the reins! You've managed to avoid making an ass of yourself."

"Shut up!" I whispered angrily.

Jennifer, who seemed to have been frozen with fear while I stood silently staring at her, cocked her head at that remark, like a dog when it hears a strange voice. I gave her a little nod and said as politely as I could, "You have a nice day, ma'am."

She shut the door as I turned and left.

I started the car with a little too much gas, accidentally gunning the engine. I looked up a second later to see her watching me from the window beside the door.

I tried to back slowly onto the street, but that didn't work. I left tire marks on her driveway as I peeled out of there.

It was still early afternoon. I had many hours to fill before dark, and then I'd have to deal with night, having nowhere to go and nothing to do.

I drove up to Calistoga and back. I drove to the overlook above town. I moved all the dishes in the cabinet left of the stove to the cabinet on the right, and then I moved them all back again, because they obviously didn't belong on the right. They didn't belong on either side, so I stacked them on the counter.

I found an absurdly complex chicken recipe on the internet that kept me busy for over two hours. I screwed it up and forced myself to eat my mistake.

At 7:30, it was still light out, and I had nothing to do.

I opened Manis's laptop and started poking around Netflix, looking for movies Marilyn might like, and wishing she were here with me.

What *would* she like, I wondered.

Probably noir. Probably an old crime movie like *The Killing*.

"Who cares what she likes?" Manis asked.

I looked around but didn't see him.

"How did you get in here?"

"You and your infatuations," Manis said. "There's only one thing men and women want from each other. It's perfectly enjoyable by itself. Why complicate it with emotions?"

"You don't like her, do you, John? You don't like her because you know I can't hear you when she's beside me."

I typed the title into the search bar. *The Killing*.

"You're never happy unless something is bothering you," Manis said. "Think how miserable you'd be without your problems."

"Shut up, John."

Netflix didn't have *The Killing*. As I tried to think of another title, Jason called.

"Hey dude!" His voice always reminded me of sunlight.

"Hey man. How's Boston?"

"Awesome! The apartment rocks. The music scene rocks. Love being in a real city. How's town treating you?"

"OK," I said. "But I'm getting a little bored."

"Hey, uh... I heard you had a little incident with Jennifer today."

"Where'd you hear that?"

"She called me."

"Oh," I said. "Did she find someone to fix her TV?"

"Naw, dude. Her husband will do it when he gets home. He's good with that stuff."

There was a brief, awkward pause. Then he got to the point.

"Hey, um... You know Jennifer can be a little high-strung."

"Yeah? She didn't really strike me that way, but OK."

"Well, you know, like finicky. Sensitive."

"What are you trying to say?"

"You might just want to avoid her," he said.

I thought about that for a moment.

"OK."

"But don't take it personally or anything. She gets bent out of shape sometimes. Her husband's been away for two weeks, she's all alone with a three-year-old, and she's a nurse at a psych hospital. You'd be on edge too if you spent your whole day around toddlers and crazies."

16

The next morning, The Lemonade Lady called to say she had accidentally drowned her iPad in the pool. I wasn't sure if she wanted me to fix it or preside over its funeral.

"Do you think you can resuscitate it?" she asked.

"I can come take a look," I said, knowing it was hopeless and assuming she knew that too. "If I can't fix it, we can get a new one and transfer your files and settings."

"Oh dear," she said excitedly. "That could take hours!"

I'd been up there twice since The Kid left, and both visits tested the limits of my patience and my bladder. Last time I was there fixing a loose cable, she had dyed her hair and put on makeup. I could just see her measuring out the lemonade and searching for a suitable dress for today's visit. An occasion like this might even call for a hat.

We made an appointment for three p.m.

Then I got a text from Marilyn. "Bastian's gone. Come over."

I called her back. "What are you doing?"

"Come over for a swim."

I put on a pair of swim trunks under my pants, grabbed the car keys and forgot all about The Lemonade Lady.

I was so excited at the thought of seeing Marilyn in a bathing suit, I wasn't paying attention to how fast I was driving. About a mile short of her house, I heard a siren behind me and looked up to see flashing lights in the rearview. I checked my speed before I slowed. Fourteen miles an hour over the limit.

I let off the gas and drifted onto the shoulder. The cop followed about sixty feet behind. A minute later, Lou was standing beside my door.

"You in a hurry?" he asked. I could see his face more clearly in the daylight than in the dark of the restaurant. The deeply etched lines that ran from the edges of his nostrils to the corners of his mouth showed he hardly ever smiled. His brown hair was thinning on top, and his thin cheeks were just beginning to sag. He removed his sunglasses to reveal dark, serious eyes that projected an air of no-nonsense efficiency.

"Sorry, Lou. I wasn't paying attention to how fast I was going."

"License and registration."

I found the registration in the glove box and handed that to him along with my license. He went back to his car, and for the next few minutes nothing happened, except for me picturing Marilyn in a bathing suit.

Finally, he returned with his sunglasses on and a ticket in hand. "You're fourteen miles over the limit. You realize fifteen is reckless driving in California?"

"I didn't know that, Lou. I'll be more mindful."

"Is this your current address?" he asked as he handed me the ticket and returned my license.

"No, I live on Main, remember? You asked me the other night if I was driving, and—"

"I remember," he cut me off. "That license was issued four years ago in Maryland. If you're planning on sticking around, get a California license."

He handed me the registration and said, "You'll need to register the car in state as well and get California tags. Where'd you get this thing?"

"Vegas," I said.

He nodded. "Well, it's a nice ride." Then he took his sunglasses off. "Let me ask you something, Mr. Manis." His dark eyes were piercing and intense. I looked away from them to the nameplate beneath his badge. It said Eisenfall.

"What is it, Lou?"

"You're doing house calls now? Fixing computers in people's homes?"

"You've heard of me?"

"You disappeared a few years ago," he said.

"I burned out," I said. "And decided to take some time off."

"Yeah. I read your manifesto. Seems like it's the whole town's summer reading. Where were you between the time you wrote that and now?"

"Jamaica," I said. "France, Spain, Italy, Honduras, and Costa Rica." I could prove all of that, because I had John Manis's passport with dated entry and exit stamps from each of those countries.

"How'd you wind up here?"

"I just kind of drifted in," I said.

He nodded. "From Vegas? Where you bought this car?"

"Yeah."

He nodded again, still friendly, but there was an uncomfortable probing tone to his questions. "And now you're helping people with computers."

"We already established that," I said. "There's no running away from technology, Lou. I mean, I tried. And then I came back and I guess this is my way of making peace with it."

Something in his face told me he didn't like that answer.

"You disappeared with several million dollars, didn't you? That's what the articles say."

"Yeah." I was starting to get uncomfortable.

"And now you're living in a—I'm sorry, what kind of apartment?"

"A one-bedroom on Main."

"A one-bedroom on Main, making house calls. And these people you're visiting, are they wealthy?"

"Everyone around here is," I said. I didn't like where this was going.

"And they're older?"

I had a feeling he already knew the answer.

"Yeah," I said. "Most of them are older. Young people don't need tech help, because they get it. They grew up with it."

"Uh-huh. So this is a kind of humanitarian mission you're on? Because a guy with a few million bucks doesn't need to do house calls for fifty dollars a day."

"It's a hundred and fifty," I said defensively. "Per call." My right hand gripped the knob of the shifter. When Lou glanced down at it, I did too. My knuckles were white, so I relaxed my grip.

"How much did you lose in Vegas?" Lou asked, looking a little less friendly than he had a minute ago.

"Oh, I lost some," I said, pressing my feet into the floor and trying to lean back in a seat that didn't lean back. "But not enough to worry me." That sounded like a lie, even to me.

I felt trapped in that little car as he looked me over.

"You have too much coffee this morning?" he asked.

"Why, is that a crime? I didn't have any coffee."

Why would he ask that? Was I that fidgety? Was I shaking? I wanted to look at my hands, but then he'd look at them too, and they might be shaking, and then he might ask me more questions. Or even worse, he might look at them just long enough to make a point that he noticed, and then not say anything at all.

Lou nodded. "Sorry to grill you," he said. "I like to keep tabs on what's going on."

"Yeah, well, that's your job, right? I mean, what good is a cop if he's not keeping an eye on things?"

"Have a good day," he said. And he turned and walked back toward his car.

"I respect that, Lou. I really do," I yelled after him. "And I'm not always..." I was going to say "having a breakdown like I was the other night when I ran into you," but there was no point. He wasn't listening.

I sat there for a minute wondering what had triggered him to grill me like that. So I was the new guy in town, so what? And so what if I had an unusual story? Maybe he's just suspicious by nature, or maybe too many years of police work got his brain stuck in a rut of treating everyone as suspects even when there was no crime.

Well, I told myself, other than a fling with a married woman, I'm not doing anything wrong. I'm earning an honest living, and I'm helping people. That cop can dig all he wants, but unless he goes down to Costa Rica and digs up John Manis, he won't find anything on me.

I pulled slowly off the shoulder back onto the main road with Lou Eisenfall following a hundred feet behind. In the mile between there and Marilyn's house, I drove exactly the speed limit.

What if he starts checking up on Manis's past, I wondered. What could he find?

I had done plenty of searches myself, so I knew it would be hard for him to dig up anything. Manis's mother was dead. His father was so far gone with Alzheimer's, he hardly remembered he had a son. If Manis had close friends back in Maryland, he never spoke of them. The only photos of him still in circulation were the ones from a couple of online news articles, and they were low-resolution snapshots that looked enough like me not to raise suspicion.

The online version of his hometown newspaper had a two-paragraph article about the climbing accident that had severed the tip of his left pinky and the surgeon's successful effort to reattach it, but there was no photo.

I turned my thoughts back to Marilyn. As I pulled into her driveway, I could feel the strands of her long black hair running through my fingers and smell the scent of her skin.

Halfway up the drive, I checked the rearview. Lou Eisenfall had parked his cruiser at the entrance to the property.

17

Esme, the housekeeper, answered the door and told me in Spanish that la señora was at the pool in back. She walked me through the kitchen, to the rear of the living room and left me at the French doors. I crossed the patio and found Marilyn in a black bikini by the poolside, her long body stretched on a white canvas chaise lounge beneath a matching umbrella.

"What took you so long?" she asked.

"I got pulled over."

She picked up a piña colada from the table beside her and took a sip.

"By a cop?"

"Lou Eisenfall. He's a real hard-ass."

Marilyn shrugged. "He's a cop. Where's your bathing suit?"

"Under my pants."

"Take them off," she said. "You make me nervous standing there in slacks."

I took off my shirt and pants and sat in the chair beside her. Between us was the small table that held her drink, her sunglasses, and a novel.

"Where's Bastian?" I asked.

"Shopping for helicopters."

"I didn't like that little stunt you pulled in the deli yesterday."

"What stunt?" she asked as she took another sip of her drink.

"At the table. With the pickle. It's like you were trying to flaunt the fact that there's something between us. Like you wanted to rub it into your husband's face."

"I did," she said simply.

83

"Is that how he treats you?" I asked.

"He treats me like I treat the maid," she said angrily. "Calls me into the room when he wants something and the rest of the time I'm invisible. I'm not important enough for him to rub things in my face. That takes effort, and no one puts effort into things they don't care about. Would you like a drink?"

"Not now," I said.

She stirred the straw in her piña colada and drifted into thought as she gazed at the glassy surface of the pool. After a long minute, she said absently, "You want to know a secret?"

"Tell me," I said.

"My name isn't Marilyn."

"Really?"

"Well, it is now. But it didn't used to be."

"What was it before?"

"Mary Lou," she said. "Mary Lou Dupree. Doesn't have much of a ring, now does it?"

"It sounds kind of country," I said.

"It is country," she said. "My father worked at a gas station, and my mother used to take his money and hide it in cans in the pantry when he was drunk, just so we'd have enough to get through the winter."

"That sounds almost tragic."

"It almost was," she said. "But I wasn't going to let my life be a tragedy. I wasn't ever going to be hiding cash in cans. You know what my mother got for all her anxiety and planning?"

"What?"

"Ulcers. And cancer. And it didn't work anyway."

"What didn't work?"

Her straw made a slurping sound as she finished the last of her drink. "Sure you don't want one?"

"No thanks."

She called Esme and asked for another piña colada.

"What didn't work?" I asked again.

"My mother's plans. Hiding money from my dad and the bill collectors who were always hounding us. You know what she used to say to me? She used to say, 'Be sure to eat in school, because there might not be any dinner when you get home.' What kind of thing is that to say to a child?"

The anger in her tone told me the words still hurt.

"While all the other kids were learning, I was worrying about my world falling apart. And it did. I came home one day and found all our stuff on the lawn. We'd been evicted."

Esme came through the French doors and set a new piña colada on the table and took the empty one.

That was the first eviction, she told me. "After that, you live your life like the next disaster is just around the corner. Where did you grow up?"

"Maryland," I said.

I gave her John Manis's story as I knew it. She listened attentively and asked lots of questions, but her tone was nothing like Lou Eisenfall's. She came at John Manis with the curiosity of a new girlfriend eager to know what makes her man tick. I even told her about some of my gambling misadventures. She was as intrigued as Jason was by those tales. I didn't tell her how much I had really lost. I didn't want her to know I was broke.

It bothered me to see how the story of Manis fascinated her. I wanted to tell my own story, because I knew, after the childhood she had just described to me, that she would understand. The only person I'd ever told my story to was my parole officer. He asked what made me think I'd get away with routing three hundred thousand dollars out of the corporate accounts system into my own bank.

"You thought you were a real genius, didn't you?"

I said, "Yeah, actually I did. My teachers used to say, 'Tom, you're so smart. If only you'd apply yourself.' I *was* applying myself. I don't know why they didn't get that. I was applying myself just showing up to class. The other kids didn't have to drag their mom out of bed in the morning and force her to take her meds, shove her onto the bus, and hope she'd make it through the day without another breakdown. The other kids didn't live in a cramped apartment where clothes were piled on top of dishes on top of magazines on top of cartons of Chinese food that still had food in them."

I wanted Marilyn to know I understood her. Her need for security and my need for order were symptoms of a common past. That's what provided the spark of mutual recognition that first day in the grocery store. I mean, I couldn't have articulated at the time exactly what we might have had in common, but I felt it in the first look we exchanged. I get you, and you get me. That was what scared me, and that's what made it so hard to turn away.

But there at the poolside that day, I blew it. I played it safe and told her all about Manis, about who I was supposed to be instead of who I was.

We talked for almost an hour, and she told a story very much like the story of me becoming Manis, only she had started her makeover at an earlier age. She said she realized by the end of high school that to distance herself from the life she wanted to leave behind, she'd have to polish every surface. She worked hard to undo her Carolina accent. She exercised every day and taught herself to look people in the eye when she spoke. "That makes a huge difference in how people perceive you."

"I know," I said. I learned that when I became John Manis.

She described the same feedback loop that I had discovered when I took on my new identity.

"Act confident," she said, "and people believe you. They like you, and then you become more confident."

After she finished her second piña colada, she stood and said, "Let's swim."

"You go ahead," I said.

She walked toward the edge of the pool, her fair skin contrasting sharply with the black bikini, her hips swaying gently with each step. She dove without breaking stride, her smooth body lengthened in a graceful arc above the placid surface it was about to shatter. The pool seemed to swallow her without a sound.

She glided silently along the bottom and came up on the other side facing me, her silky black hair flattened against her head and shoulders. She put her back to the wall and spread her arms along the edge and kicked her legs beneath the water, like she was pedaling a bicycle in slow motion. She fixed her steady gaze on me, her slow-blinking eyes framed by thick black lashes. The soft smile and the way she offered up everything I wanted beneath the distorted lens of shimmering blue water made my heart race.

"You coming in?" she asked.

I was too mesmerized to respond. She didn't wait for an answer anyway.

For the next few minutes, she swam laps beneath the water, her grace and strength on full display. She'd go under and swim half the length of the pool in two or three powerful strokes, then come up and take a breath. I could feel the firmness of her muscles as she pressed forward, the energy and vitality of the body she'd surrendered to me just the other day. She never slowed.

When she got out, she was breathing deeply and her cheeks were flushed. She stood in front of me to dry off, her chest rising and falling with each breath.

"God, John! The way you look at me! Do you have any idea how sexy that is?"

She smiled, bright and beautiful like the sun as she wiped the last drops from her cheek and neck. Then she let the towel fall to the ground and whispered playfully, "Let's go inside."

18

In bed an hour later, as she lay nuzzled against my chest, I said, "Why did you tell me that? About Mary Lou?"

"We're not always born who we want to be. Sometimes we have to make it happen."

"I understand that," I said.

"Mmm." She yawned. "I thought you would."

She slid her hand over my chest and rested it on my shoulder. "Are you hungry?" she asked.

"Starving."

"Let's go out somewhere. In town."

She kissed me and got up and went to the bathroom. I was about to stand up and dress when Esme walked in and asked in Spanish where la señora was.

I pointed to the bathroom.

A pang of jealousy stabbed my heart. Why didn't Esme care that I was in la señora's bed? What went on in this house when I wasn't around?

Esme tapped at the bathroom door.

"Just a minute," Marilyn said.

"Señora?"

"Esme?"

"Un hombre está abajo. Quiere hablar consigo." A man downstairs wants to talk with you.

Marilyn came out of the bathroom wearing a silk robe. "That's the plumber."

She walked into the closet and threw on a pair of leggings and a t-shirt.

Before she left the room, she said, "Ten minutes, OK? Then we'll go."

"No rush."

I noticed the hard drive I had hooked up to her computer the other day was still plugged in, like she hadn't touched the laptop since I'd left.

I sat at the desk in my underwear, removed the drive, and put it back in the drawer on top of Bastian's drive. Then I sat quietly staring into the drawer.

Bastian was up to something and the evidence of it was on that drive. Why had he taken out so many loans? Why all at once and all so recent?

I turned and looked out through the open bedroom door. Wherever Marilyn and Esme and the plumber were, I couldn't hear them.

I felt a stirring of the old agitation tingling in my fingertips. Not the scary kind, but the good kind. The kind I felt when I found the glitch in the corporate accounting system, when I found Manis's E*TRADE account, and when I drove into Vegas that first day with a seemingly inexhaustible supply of cash.

I took Bastian's hard drive from the drawer and plugged it in. I scanned quickly through the Business folder, looking again at the loans he'd opened.

Then I saw he'd backed up several email accounts onto the drive. I knew there was more than I could look into before Marilyn returned. So I unplugged the drive and walked back to the bed, picked up my pants, and slid the drive into the pocket.

"Once a thief, always a thief," said Manis.

I didn't look around to see where he was. I didn't want to give him the satisfaction. I put on my pants and asked in a voice as casual as his, "How did you get in here?"

"Relax, Tom. She's not in the room."

"Go away."

"What *are* you up to this time? Even I don't get it."

"Get out of here," I snapped.

"Who are you talking to?" Marilyn asked.

I turned to see her standing at the door, giving me a funny look.

"Huh? Oh, I was just thinking out loud."

"*That's* how you talk to yourself?"

I shrugged. "Sometimes I don't like what my mind has to say." I picked up my shirt and put my arm through the sleeve. "Are you happy with every thought that goes through your head?"

She put out her hand, palm forward, like a traffic cop. "OK, whatever. You want sushi?"

"Sushi sounds good."

"Let me change."

She disappeared into the closet.

A minute later, as I was tying my shoes, she came out in a white backless summer dress.

"How's this look?" She did a slow three-sixty, watching me over her shoulder.

A beautiful smile lit her face. "You don't even have to say it, John. I can see it in your eyes."

When we left the bedroom, I noticed the letter she had sealed the other day was still on the dresser by the door. She had printed her name and return address in the upper left corner in a neat, looping hand. But the envelope had no stamp or address.

19

At the sushi restaurant on Main Street, nestled between a wine bar and a chocolate shop, Marilyn ordered enough to feed four people.

"You're too ambitious," I said.

"No, I'm starving."

"No one can eat that much," I said.

"Watch me."

I liked that she had a big appetite.

Lou Eisenfall must have liked it too. He sat in his cruiser across the street for twenty minutes, watching us on and off, when he wasn't diddling with the laptop mounted between the front seats.

He hadn't been at the end of the driveway when Marilyn and I left her house. He hadn't followed us into town, either. He just happened to be there when we arrived.

Marilyn had a forward manner, in a literal, physical sense. She leaned across the table when she spoke. She put her hand on my knee when she emphasized a point. She picked up food with her fingers and put it in my mouth. The body language of lovers was unmistakable. You could see it all through the restaurant's big plate glass window. Which is why Lou Eisenfall's presence out there unnerved me. He was already more interested in me than I wanted him to be. I didn't need to make a public display of what I was doing with another man's wife.

"Is he bothering you?" Marilyn asked.

"That cop? Yeah."

"Why? Are we doing something illegal?"

"He really grilled me this morning," I said. "When he pulled me over."

"He's like that," Marilyn said. "Are you worried about him seeing us together?"

"A little, yeah."

She nodded and then looked down at the table, thoughtful and withdrawn. She put the piece of tuna roll that she had just dipped in soy sauce back on her plate and wiped her hands.

When she looked up again, I saw a slow-burning anger in her eyes.

"Well I don't give a shit what Lou Eisenfall thinks," she said defiantly. "When Bastian was with another woman at the French restaurant—which we own—" she added bitterly, "when he was drunk and kissing her in front of the other diners, Lou drove them both back to the inn at the winery where she was staying. You know why? Because he didn't want Bastian to make a scene, or to crash his car while he was drunk.

"When Bastian sideswiped a car in town because he was getting a blowjob while he was driving, Lou Eisenfall wrote him a ticket for failure to control his vehicle, and then Lou drove the woman out of town."

The color was rising in her face, and the vein on the side of her neck that had throbbed in unison with mine at the bar on the night we met was pulsing quick and hard.

"My husband," she said, "does whatever the hell he pleases, wherever he pleases, with whomever he pleases. When I walk into a store or a bar in this town, everyone knows who I am and what my husband does. When they look at me they don't have to say a goddamn word, because I know exactly what they're thinking. When I walk into my own restaurant..."

She choked up for a second and put her hand to her face before forcing herself to continue.

"...my own fucking restaurant, they say, 'Good evening, Ms. Dupree.' But all I hear is 'Good evening, doormat.'"

Her voice was rising now, and the other patrons were looking at us. Lou was looking at us.

"I sit there eating a meal most people can't even afford, and I pretend people aren't looking at me, that they aren't judging me for selling myself out. For being the stupid wife of a vapid man who can't keep his goddamn dick in his pants."

Her voice began to break. "So what if Lou Eisenfall sees us? So what if anyone sees us? What's the point of this charade?"

I put my hand on hers. "Calm down."

"I will not calm down! I need to say this."

"You don't have to say it in here." I looked around at the other tables, at the customers who turned away, pretending they hadn't been looking at us.

Marilyn looked down at the table, then said in a quieter tone, "Fuck Lou Eisenfall. He's supposed to stand for justice, but all he wants to do is avoid a scene and preserve the peace. He should be arresting Bastian for having sex while driving. Instead, he's helping him smooth it over."

She lifted her napkin from her lap and dropped it on the table. "I'm sorry, Johnny. I'm not hungry anymore. Will you take me home?"

"Yeah," I said. "Yeah, sure."

She called the waitress over and asked for the check.

"I'll get that," I said.

"No, I will. I haven't been a very good date," she said softly, as if she were ashamed of herself. "I can't let you pay for this."

<h1 style="text-align:center">20</h1>

When we walked out a few minutes later, she put on sunglasses to hide her swollen eyes. Lou's cruiser was gone, but on the walk to my car, I saw another thing I didn't like. A little blue Mazda parked across the street, half a block up. Roland glared at me through the open driver's window. His angry eyes followed me from the restaurant until we passed his car.

I thought back to the first time I'd seen him up there at the overlook, and it occurred to me that maybe my perception wasn't distorted that day. There really was something wrong with the guy.

Marilyn and I walked arm in arm. I turned to look at her, to see if she had noticed his nasty glare. But she had her head down.

We didn't speak on the drive back to her house.

"You want me to come in?" I asked when we came to a stop in the driveway.

She shook her head.

"What are you going to do?"

"Dunno," she whispered.

"All right. Well, let me know if you want to hang out. Or if you just want to talk."

My phone chimed.

"Oh, crap. The Lemonade Lady."

"Is she a customer?"

"Yeah. She lives way up in Sonoma County." I pointed north.

"Well, go tend to your client," she said. "I'm afraid I won't be much fun today."

She opened the door to get out, then stopped and turned.

"You know, it's been a long time since anyone has looked at me the way you looked at me at the pool this morning. When you've been treated like shit long enough, you start to think that's all you're worth. Then *you* come along, a stranger out of nowhere, and every time you look at me I see your whole face light up, and that's just..." She stopped for a moment and thought. "It's like spring after a long winter. Everything that's been dead for as long I can remember suddenly returns to life."

We kissed, then I headed up north for some lemonade.

<h1 style="text-align:center">21</h1>

The Lemonade Lady's iPad was still in the bottom of the pool when I arrived. It looked like a staged murder scene. She spent an hour reminiscing about it over lemonade and cakes. All the photos she had taken, all the news articles she had read, all those YouTube videos of kittens and tornados.

"They're gone," she said. "Just gone!"

I assured her the internet had survived the loss of her iPad, and the kitten videos would look even better on the new model.

She said she had already ordered it, and it would arrive in a few days. Could I come back and help her set it up?

"Of course."

"Oh, and by the way," she added, "I have two friends who need your help, but don't let that Sylvia get you alone in her wine cellar. She'll try to put her hands on you!"

For the next few days, I kept busy, driving to and from house calls, hooking up game consoles and listening to Sylvia compliment my nice firm muscles down in the wine cellar as I tried to get her to explain what exactly she wanted me to fix.

Bastian was working from home those days, so I didn't see Marilyn.

I spent my evenings poring through the contents of Bastian's hard drive. He had taken out ten million dollars in loans, leveraging every piece of property he owned, both business and personal. But I couldn't figure out what he was doing with it.

He hadn't put the money into any bank account. I knew that because his bank statements were on the hard drive. He wasn't paying off creditors, though he certainly had plenty of those, including the IRS, to whom he owed hundreds of thousands of dollars.

I found an email exchange between Bastian and his company's board of directors. They asked him to put a few million into the company to keep it afloat and he refused. Why wouldn't he be willing to rescue his own company, after he had just taken out ten million in loans?

Then I started digging into his personal emails. That's when the loans began to make sense. There was one account in which all the messages were between Bastian and a woman named Olivia. A burner account just for her, with nine months' worth of messages. Some of them included photos. Olivia was good-looking, but she was no Marilyn. She had dark hair and dark olive skin, and from what I gathered, she was from a wealthy Colombian family.

Bastian had been hooking up with her at a cabin near Shasta Lake, and in San Francisco and LA and Vegas. She liked the jewelry he had bought her, and the clothes, and the hotels he put her up in. He liked everything about her. His love letters were formatted like business presentations and included bullet points.

What I love about you...

- Sweet
- Charming
- Understand me
- Smell good
- Excellent Karma
- Decisive
- No BS
- Dress well
- Eat right

Her emails were bossy and demanding. She told him what to wear. She instructed him to stop hanging out with one of his business partners because the man told stupid jokes and laughed too loudly. Bastian's white convertible Mercedes was her idea. She didn't like the Porsche he had owned when they met because it was too loud. He had to get rid of it, she wrote, but he must not accept a penny less than sixty-five thousand dollars on the trade-in. She told him what to eat and scolded him in all caps when HE LOOKED AT OTHER WOMEN. I knew her type from my time in Miami: rich, spoiled, controlling.

She seemed to be exactly what Bastian needed. Marilyn let him do whatever he pleased, but deep down, Bastian was a kid who wanted his mommy to tell him he couldn't have that helicopter.

In their last email exchange, Olivia wanted to know how "the plan" was coming along. He replied that he had a few more things to arrange with the bank, and then they were on.

Over two nights, I read the full nine months of correspondence to figure out "the plan."

Bastian was going to abandon his life for her. His company would run out of money and go under. His house here and his house in San Francisco would be foreclosed because he hadn't paid the mortgage in months. He would skip out on his debts to the IRS. He was borrowing all he could, with no intention of ever paying it back. He and Olivia would run off together.

And what? Leave Marilyn to clean up the mess? It must have been some mess if he wasn't going to try to salvage anything.

In her emails to Bastian, Olivia referred to Marilyn as "the witch."

I tried to imagine how Bastian could extricate himself from his life the right way. Divorce Marilyn. That could take a year, and she might take half his money. Sell the house here, the San Francisco house, the software company, and the other holdings. That might take a couple of years. Then pay the IRS.

Maybe Bastian didn't have the patience to spend years cleaning up his life. Maybe he wouldn't have much money left in the end. Maybe it made more financial sense to cut and run.

I went back through his business emails and read the dire messages from his lawyers and accountants. The problem with the IRS was bigger than back taxes. It sounded like fraud or something criminal.

Whatever the case, he had just borrowed ten million dollars and stashed it somewhere. But where?

Olivia wanted to know too.

"Don't worry," he wrote. "It'll be there when we need it."

"I'm tired of the lake house, tired of waiting," she wrote in her most recent message. "When are we going to do this?"

"Soon," Bastian replied. "Very soon."

Those messages were eight days old.

As I read through the last of them, Marilyn kept texting me.

"Lonely."

"Angry."

"Tired."

"I wish he would leave. I just want to see you."

Little yellow emoji blowing a kiss.

At 9:47 on our fourth night apart, she texted "Meet me at The Sage in 30."

22

We returned to the restaurant where we had first met and took two seats at the bar. I put my hand on her shoulder as a friendly greeting, and she turned and kissed me on the mouth. I pulled my head back in surprise.

"What?" she asked. "Is something wrong?"

"Just..." I looked around to see if anyone had noticed. "I don't think we should do that in public."

She put her hand over her mouth, as if to cover her faux pas. "Sorry." Her breath smelled of sour whiskey.

"What would you like?" the bartender asked.

As soon as the words were out of his mouth, she said, "Whiskey sour."

"What about you?" the bartender asked.

"How about a pale ale?"

I turned back to Marilyn. "Where did you tell Bastian you were going?"

"I told him I was going out. That's all. How have you been?"

"Busy. At least by my standards. Seven jobs in four days."

I could tell something was weighing on her. As the bartender slid her drink in front of her, she put her thumbnail into her mouth and was about to bite it. Then she pulled it out, looked at her manicure, and decided to pick up her glass instead.

"What's bothering you?" I asked.

She was quiet for a long moment, then she said, "I didn't like the conversation at the house today. Bastian met with his board of directors by the pool. I eavesdropped from the upstairs window."

"Yeah?"

She twisted her glass in circles on the bar, looking worried. "It was tense. Almost hostile. Esme was supposed to bring them coffee and sandwiches. I went down to the kitchen and told her to prepare the trays and let me carry them out, so I could listen."

She gave me a dire look. "Bastian's company is going to run out of money soon." Again, she put her thumbnail into her mouth. This time, I pulled it out for her.

"I don't know why he doesn't tell me these things. Maybe because he knows how I worry, but... What?"

"Nothing."

"You looked like you were going to say something."

I was going to say something about the things I'd seen on his hard drive, but I figured it would be better to let her finish.

"No," I said. "Go on."

She drank half her whiskey in two gulps.

"The thing that really worries me," she said, "is what one of the directors said. He said, 'You'll never raise another penny from investors if you're not willing to put in any of your own money. You have to put some skin in the game, Bas.' And Bastian shook his head. 'No way. Not another dime.'"

She looked at me nervously and said, "Do you know how much money he's sunk into that company? And now he's going to let it go under!"

I was starting to get uncomfortable, seeing how nervous she was and knowing I had more bad news for her. I was trying to think of a way to tell her about all the money he'd been borrowing, but I didn't know how to do that without telling her I took the hard drive. Maybe it was time to confess to that.

Marilyn's phone chimed as she drank the last of her whiskey sour.

"It's Bas," she said. "He wants me home."

"For what?"

"God only knows. Maybe he'll talk to me now. He wouldn't before."

She texted him back, though I don't know what she said. Then she waved the bartender over and asked for the check.

"I'll get that," I said.

"No you won't. I just unloaded on you again, and I won't make you pay for that."

The bartender laid the check in front of her. She put down her credit card and as he took it, she said, "Wait, one more whiskey sour. Would you like another beer?"

"No thanks." I wasn't even halfway through the first one.

"Sorry if I'm preoccupied," she said, "but I worry about money even when we're rolling in it. I know it's just one company and Bastian owns other things, but the thought of losing any of it makes me think of losing it all, and I never want to be poor again. Never!"

The bartender set another whiskey sour in front of her, along with the check. "That feeling of the world slipping out from beneath your feet..." She picked up the glass and took a sip. "Once you've felt it, you always fear it."

She put her hand on my knee and smiled. "How far do you live from here?"

"About four blocks."

She leaned in and whispered, "Let's go to your place. We can be quick. And let's not talk about marriage or money or anything else that's horrible."

23

Two days later, I was back at Marilyn's. She was smiling when she answered the door in a blue silk robe embroidered with a golden dragon.

"Johnny!" She gave me a kiss.

"Your cheeks are flushed."

"I know," she said, touching them. "I had a piña colada. Is that an awful thing to do at..." She turned and checked the grandfather clock. "One eighteen in the afternoon?"

"Not at all. Were you at the pool?"

"I was on my way," she said. "But..." She looked over her shoulder in a coy, playful gesture, to see if Esme were nearby. Then she opened her robe to show her bare body. "I couldn't decide on a bathing suit. Want to come up and help me pick one out?"

You can guess where that led. All I needed was one look at her and I couldn't think about anything else.

From the bright, mischievous manner she had shown at the front door, and her quick, light steps up the stairs, I expected her to be in a playful mood.

But as soon as she closed the bedroom door, I could see something wasn't right. Her eyes had a hint of that frantic look I used to see in the mirror in Vegas. It was just a hint, but I recognized it, and it made me uneasy.

"Come on," she said. "Don't look like that. We don't have much time."

"Don't look like what?"

"Like you're thinking. Come here." She pulled me in for a kiss.

In bed, she was wild, in a scary kind of way.

103

"Are you OK?" I asked when we were done.

"Yeah." She was still breathing hard, playing with her hair as was her habit after sex.

"You didn't get off," I said.

"I don't always. But I still enjoy it."

"What's bothering you?"

"Nothing," she said defensively. "Why does something have to be bothering me?"

"Something is off," I said. "When you answered the front door, you were smiling. But when we got up here—"

She interrupted angrily. "Don't judge me, OK?" She sat up and gave me a hard, sharp look. "I am what I am. If you don't like me, then find someone else."

"Whoa, wait a minute. Who's judging you? I didn't say anything about not liking you—"

"Then why are we talking about this?" She stood and picked up the silk robe from the floor and went into the bathroom.

"Why are we talking about what?" I asked. "I don't even know what we're talking about."

She shut the bathroom door.

As I listened to the water splashing in the sink, I wondered what the hell had gotten into her.

While she was in there, I took Bastian's hard drive from my pocket and slipped it back into the drawer, beneath hers.

Marilyn came out of the bathroom wiping her face and walked straight to the closet without looking at me.

I put my pants on and followed her in. She had already put on a pair of underwear and was hastily fastening a bra.

"Why are you getting dressed? I thought you were going to the pool."

"I'm going to San Francisco," she said coldly.

"But I just got here."

"Why does everything have to be about you?" She yanked a black cotton dress from a hanger and pulled it over her head.

"Why did you invite me over if you were about to leave?"

"Don't pretend you didn't have your own reasons for coming here," she said.

"What the hell is wrong with you?"

"What the hell is wrong with you?" she shot back.

She pulled her hair into a ponytail and wrapped it with an elastic band as she stepped past me. Then she opened a cherrywood drawer filled with earrings and chose a pair of brilliant diamond studs. She fastened them to her ears and held up a mirror and turned her head from side to side.

"Those look nice," I said.

She glared at me, put the mirror down, and took the studs out.

Then she chose a second pair, half the size of the first. She put those in, checked the mirror, and approved.

She pushed past me again and picked up a pair of Mary Janes from the floor. "I'll see you tomorrow," she said as she pulled the shoes on.

She went out the door and down the stairs while I stood there wondering what in the world had got into her.

On the dresser were two letters. The one from the IRS, which was addressed to her husband, had been torn open. I pulled the pages from inside as I heard the front door slam below. The letter said Bastian owed over six hundred thousand in back taxes and penalties. I slid the pages back into the envelope without reading any more.

Is that what set her off, I wondered. Combined with what she overheard the other day about Bastian's company running out of money, that would give her plenty to worry about. Maybe she's scared that Bastian is hiding deeper secrets. I suppose you can sense those things when you're married to someone.

The second letter was sealed and still unaddressed. Holding it up to the light revealed nothing, but when I pressed the back of the envelope flat against the contents, I could see the outline of Marilyn's lips printed in dark red.

I looked at the return address she had written in the upper left corner. Marilyn Dupree had beautiful handwriting.

24

I drove into town, got coffee and a sandwich and sat at a table by the front window of the coffee shop, trying to sort out my thoughts while four young moms with writhing toddlers chatted at the next table.

Why would Marilyn be going to San Francisco? To talk to a lawyer? A divorce lawyer? Well good for her, if that's what it was. But why wear diamonds with a simple black dress and no makeup...to meet a lawyer? That didn't make sense.

And then my mind began to wander. Say she divorced Bastian. What would she do? Find someone even richer? She certainly wouldn't settle for me. She could barely disguise her disappointment at seeing my apartment the other night. Security and comfort were first and foremost with her, and those were things I could never provide.

I pictured her with a new man, in a new house even bigger and more tasteless than Bastian's. She'd be happily in love while I was still driving up and down the valley plugging in wires and drinking lemonade with lonely old ladies, making just enough to pay my bills.

The thought of her with someone new made me sick with jealousy. I left the second half of my sandwich untouched, left the chatting moms and screaming toddlers and drove up the mountain road for some fresh air. I passed a little blue Mazda coming the other way as I ascended, but I only vaguely registered the fact.

As I rounded the last bend, I noticed another car parked at the overlook. When I got closer, I saw it was Marilyn's black Mercedes.

106

The first thing that went through my mind was, She doesn't want to see you anymore today, so keep driving.

And then I thought, Screw that. If she doesn't want to see me, she can go somewhere else. She's supposed to be in San Francisco anyway. I cut the wheel hard into the gravel parking area and pulled in so fast I had to slam on the brakes to avoid hitting the picnic table.

"Jesus, Johnny! What the hell is wrong with you?"

She'd been standing with her arms folded across her chest, looking out over the town, but the sound of my car skidding across the gravel made her turn abruptly. She had the angry look of someone who had just been rudely startled, but there was something else beneath the anger. An air of anxiety, unsettled and heavy.

"Hey Marilyn. You look good."

"Oh, shut up."

She walked over to the car as I was getting out. "Have you been following me?"

"No." I shut the car door.

Her eyes narrowed. "Have you?" she demanded.

"No. Why would I follow you?"

"Because you're weird. And you're here. Where have you been?"

"I had lunch in town. What do you care?"

Her hair was still pulled back in a ponytail, as it had been in the closet when she'd tried on the two pairs of diamond studs. Only now, the studs were gone. When she saw that I noticed, she gave a little start, her right hand shot to her ear, and she blushed.

"Where'd your diamonds go?"

"What diamonds?"

"The ones you put on before you left the house."

Her face reddened all the way up to her forehead and her dark eyes flashed with anger. "Mind your own business, John." She turned toward her car.

As she opened the door, I said, "You could have lied, you know."

She turned and looked at me with a sullen, pouting face.

"You could have said, 'I took them off. They're in the car.'"

For a second there, she looked like she was going to cry. Then her face went blank, as if she had cut off her emotions all at once. She got into the Mercedes and drove away without a word.

I walked to the picnic bench and looked out over the valley, which was as beautiful and green as the day I'd first seen it. I could now make out where Marilyn's house was, six miles north of my apartment, a white speck with a red roof surrounded by green.

I don't know how long I stood there, or even what I was thinking. But I do remember turning and seeing black-and-white sunflower shells scattered on the dusty ground beside the picnic table. I knelt and picked one up. It was still wet with saliva.

That was Roland's blue car that had passed me on the road. And Marilyn had lost her diamonds. Her second-best pair of diamond studs that she had chosen deliberately instead of her best.

25

I didn't see Marilyn at all the next day. The day after that, I stopped by her house around five p.m. and found her in the kitchen. I told her I had run into Lou in the grocery store that morning.

"What does Lou have to say?" she asked.

"He says I should stay away from you."

"Oh, God," she scoffed. "He's so annoying."

"How does he know Bastian?"

"Lou talks to everyone," Marilyn said. "And Bastian talks to anyone. Lou's been in this house a dozen times, and not just to haul Bastian home when he's drunk. He's come by once or twice just to chat."

"Well, he doesn't like us airing our affair," I said. "I think we should keep a lower profile."

"And I think we should fuck in the town square while Bastian watches."

From the other room, I heard the sound of ice cubes dropping into a glass, and then the cap of a bottle being unscrewed.

Marilyn said loudly, "Pour me one, will you?"

"What do you want?" Bastian replied.

"Bastian's here?" I whispered.

"Bourbon," Marilyn yelled. "With ice." Then, to me, she added, "He's not here. He's drunk."

"Why didn't I see his car out front?"

"Because Esme is washing it over there." She pointed to the side of the house.

Bastian walked in with a drink in each hand. Vodka and soda with a wedge of lemon for him, bourbon for her.

"Hey! Johnny!" he said with a cheerful smile. "How's Marilyn treating you?" His voice was loud and his face was red from drink. He looked like he'd been at the bottle for at least a couple of hours.

"I'm treating him well," Marilyn said. "How many drinks have you had, Bas?"

"I don't know. Who's counting?" He handed her the bourbon and asked if I'd like anything.

"No thanks," I said. "I was just on my way out."

"No you weren't," Marilyn said. "Bas, we have a dinner for twelve tonight, remember? How are you going to make it if you're in this state already and it's only five fifteen?"

"Pffft!" He waved the question off. "As long as I don't stop, I'll be fine. It's when you stop drinking—" he took a sip of his vodka and soda—"the sleep catches up with you. You drink, Johnny?"

"Not so much," I said.

"Well what do you do for fun then?" He didn't wait for an answer as his addled mind skipped on to the next thought. "Where are we in that series?"

"What series?" Marilyn asked.

"That Netflix series," Bastian said as he wandered absently from the room. "The funny one."

Marilyn shook her head. "We haven't watched Netflix in months. You must have me confused with one of your girlfriends."

I heard the TV go on in the other room.

"Ok," I said to Marilyn. "I'm out. I'll see you later."

"Where are you going?" she asked angrily.

"The Lemonade Lady," I said. "Her new iPad arrived—"

"Tell her you'll see her tomorrow."

"I can't. She wants me to—"

"Come upstairs," Marilyn said. "I want to talk."

26

When we got upstairs, she closed the bedroom door to shut out the sound of the television. Bastian had the thing on full blast, tuned to some awful sitcom with a laugh track.

Marilyn set her drink on the dresser beside the unstamped envelope that bore her return address. She put her head in her hands and let out a long, weary breath. "Oh my god, he's driving me crazy."

"Why did you marry him?"

"We didn't start like this," she said. "We started with a honeymoon, like every couple that gets duped into chaining themselves together."

She took a sip of her drink and added, "You know we both like sex. A lot."

"I can tell."

"And neither of us makes any pretense about enjoying other people."

"Wait," I said. "Were there others? Before me?"

"What difference does it make?" she asked.

"Well, it makes a difference to me," I said. "If I'm sleeping with a woman, I like to think I'm special. At least in her world."

"You're sleeping with a married woman, remember? And you are special. But I'm not the first person you've slept with either, so get over it."

Her bluntness stung.

"You know what happens in a relationship like ours?" she asked. "I mean an open marriage, like Bas and I have. Eventually, the man gets bored of the woman, especially a man as unfocused as Bastian. I married him because we had the same ideas about relationships and sex, and I thought this was the best bet, all things considered. And yeah, it was also because he had money. I'll admit that. And now I have the life I deserve. Because I'm horrible, Johnny. I'm weak, and I'm insecure, and I'm horrible, and he treats me like shit because I deserve it."

"You don't deserve it," I said.

"I do," she insisted. "You know, I signed an agreement before we married that said if I initiate a divorce, I'd get a one-time payment. It would basically be enough to live on for a year, and nothing more. I signed that, because I was sure I'd be able to hang with anything for the money and the freedom this life offered. But there were no restrictions on him in the prenup. If he initiated a divorce, the standard laws applied. I could take all his money. Or half of it. Or whatever the courts would give to a stupid, slutty little gold digger."

"Don't talk about yourself like that."

She drank the last of the whiskey and looked forlornly into the empty glass.

"I didn't think he would ever leave me," she said. "And it turns out, he didn't have to. All he had to do was make me miserable enough to want out. And now he's done it. Now he has another woman, and if I want to file for divorce, he can skip out with his one-time payment and be done with me forever."

I wondered if by "another woman" she meant Olivia, the Colombian woman he'd been planning to run off with.

"What?" she asked, looking closely at my face. "You're thinking something."

"Well," I said, "he's been screwing around with other women for a long time."

She shook her head. "This is different. He's in love."

"How do you know?"

"Because I'm his wife. I know." Again, she watched me closely. "Johnny, why do you look so guilty?"

"I don't," I lied. "I just feel bad." I felt bad that I already knew what she was telling me. "I mean, you're in a horrible position."

"But maybe I'm not," she said. "Maybe he loves her enough to leave me. Maybe he'll initiate the divorce after all, and I'll get something out of it."

No, I thought. He won't. I had to tell her.

"Marilyn—"

"I want another drink," she said as she crunched an ice cube.

"Marilyn—"

My phone chimed. The Lemonade Lady.

"What's bothering you?" Marilyn asked.

"God, I don't even know where to start with this."

The muffled laugh track from Bastian's idiotic show seeped in beneath the bedroom door to mock my troubled thoughts.

"Well I'll tell *you* something," she said. "The other day, Bastian left his phone in the kitchen. I found a text from a woman named Olivia. I scrolled back and read a few messages before Bastian returned and I had to put the phone down. They were planning to meet. Tonight, at a cabin Bastian rented up at Shasta Lake. A cabin he took me to before we were married."

She put her glass to her lips and sipped the runoff from the ice. "I need another drink," she said. "Do you mind going back downstairs with me?"

"Wait," I said. "Before we go down—"

"You can tell me on the stairs." She picked up the unaddressed letter from the dresser and opened the door. Fake laughter crept up from below, accompanied by Bastian's drunken "Haw haw haw!"

"He tried to back out of tonight's dinner," Marilyn said. "So he could drive up there and see her. I told him no way. You planned this dinner. You invited all those people. I didn't let him know I was onto his plan, but I told him I'd be damned if I was going to entertain a dozen of his friends all by myself. That was two hours ago. That's when he started drinking. Come on."

She went through the door and we walked side by side down the stairs.

"What did you want to tell me?"

"It's too loud here," I said.

"What?"

"It's too loud with that stupid TV. I'm not going to shout it."

I followed her into the dining room. She slid the sealed envelope between two liquor bottles, then dropped some ice into her glass and poured another bourbon.

"You want one?"

"No. I have to drive up north to see—"

"The Lemonade Lady, I know."

The laugh track from the television blared from the other room. Bastian slapped his knee and laughed his idiotic laugh. "Haw haw haw!"

"Bas, turn that down!" Marilyn yelled.

"What?" Bastian turned the TV down. "What did you say?"

"Thank you," Marilyn said.

He kept the sound down, and I could see him through the archway from where I was standing. If I told her now about all the things I'd found on his hard drive, he'd hear me.

"You were going to say something?" she said. I was beginning to hear the alcohol in her voice.

This wasn't the time, so I changed the subject.

"Why did you leave San Francisco?" I asked. "There's so much more to do there. It seems you'd be happier—"

I stopped midsentence because of her reaction. She blushed from her neck to her forehead and had that same caught-red-handed look I had seen on the overlook two days before.

"Well that was the problem right there," she said. "There was too much to do in the city, for both of us. And believe me, I wouldn't have left that life for this one without good reason."

I gave her a look that showed I was waiting for more, but she shook her head and said, "I'm not going into that. It won't do you any good to know."

She lifted the envelope from the liquor tray and made a motion as if she were going to throw it into the trash, but she stopped when she saw there was no garbage can. She walked to the other side of the liquor table and made the same abortive motion, then stood there looking confused.

"I swear there used to be a garbage can here."

"What's in the envelope?" I asked, remembering that she had told me on day one it was an insurance policy.

"Nothing," she said absently. And then with a look of resignation, she slid the envelope back between the liquor bottles and said, "Johnny, you should go."

My phone chimed with another text from The Lemonade Lady. "Where are you?"

"Yeah," I said. "I'm late."

"No. I mean away. From me. Forever."

I shook my head. "No way. I could never do that."

"Johnny." Her eyes flashed with a mixture of sorrow and anger and fierce determination. "I mean it. You have no idea how horrible I am."

27

It was a little past 5:30 when I left Marilyn's house. The first half of the drive up to Sonoma County was on smooth, freshly-paved blacktop. Then, about fifteen miles up, the paving crew had abandoned their equipment for the evening on the shoulder—a milling machine, a paver, a dump truck, and a steamroller—and at that point, the road became rough again.

The Corvette's steering wheel shook more than usual, which made me think the front wheels were out of alignment. But I didn't give it too much thought, because my mind was occupied with Marilyn and her problems. I felt bad for her and wanted to help her out. But there wasn't a whole lot I could do beyond offering moral support and reminding her not to pick on herself when her life wasn't going right.

"Ah, the drama," said Manis. "The lady in distress, and her knight in shining armor!"

"Shut up, John."

When I arrived at The Lemonade Lady's house at 6:20, I noticed my front left tire was low. That's why the steering wheel was shaking. I made a mental note to check it again before I left.

A green Ford Explorer was parked in the driveway beside the old lady's BMW. As I walked up the drive, I could hear her voice coming from the backyard.

"But wait till you see him, dear. He's not just a fixit guy."

Good Lord, I thought. Who is she pimping me to now?

I rang the bell at the front door, even though I knew the old lady was out back. I didn't want to be paraded in front of her guests like a show pony. I wanted her to come to the door, give me the iPad, and let me work.

"Oh, Johnny!" she gushed. She wore a pink and purple muumuu and stood there with her arms extended, like I was supposed to walk into them for a warm embrace.

"You look nice," I said.

She smiled. "Johnny, you have to meet my granddaughter."

"I'd be delighted," I said.

"Come, come!" She pulled me by the hand. "She's out back. I've told her all about you!" And then she added in a sly whisper, "And she's unattached."

"Unhinged is more my type."

"Oh, Johnny." She giggled. "You're such a wit!"

The granddaughter, who was about to go to law school, was twenty-four years old with a heart-shaped face framed by long golden-blonde hair. In the first minute of conversation, she showed herself to be level-headed, practical, and smart. And she liked me. A lot.

"It's just the suit," Manis said. "No one likes *you*, because you're insane."

I ignored that.

The old lady prodded me to tell my life story. Game programmer, sold out for millions, wandered the world, then got bored and gave up the life of the globetrotting millionaire so I could fix grandma's iPad.

I told it better than that, but I have to admit, when I listened to myself recount the tale, I understood why Lou Eisenfall was suspicious.

Young Ms. Lemonade was captivated by the story and by the whole Manis persona, which made me feel like an impostor and a fraud.

I could hear Manis laughing at me.

"Don't you wish you'd met her first?" he asked. "Instead of that hot mess you've been screwing?"

I slammed my hand onto the table so hard I startled my companions.

"Sorry," I said. "I have a thing about flies."

I made a show of checking my hand for a squashed insect. Fortunately, my little outburst didn't ruin the flow of the evening. The conversation picked up where it had left off. I held my wrist beneath the table and checked my pulse while the granddaughter talked of law school. Ninety beats per minute was not a problem. I could come down from that in a few minutes.

Grandma had prepared some food for the occasion, and we talked for about two hours.

Finally, around 8:30, I told them I had to get going. Not that I had anywhere to go. I just didn't want to be there anymore.

"Oh, what a shame," grandma said. "We didn't even get to the iPad. But you can come back in a few days, can't you?"

"Of course."

I said my goodbyes and walked back to the car. The front left tire was almost flat. I debated for a moment whether I should call a tow truck, then I decided against it. If the old lady thought I might be stuck, she'd fix up a bed and insist I stay the night.

I drove a mile back toward the main road, keeping my speed to about ten miles an hour. Then I pulled over and found the jack and the spare. I've changed tires before, and it's taken about twenty minutes. This one took over an hour. The handle didn't fit the scissor jack, so I had a hard time raising the car. Then it got dark. I lost one of the lug nuts and spent ten minutes looking for it before I realized I had put it in my pocket.

Once the spare was on, I put the flat into the carrier beneath the trunk and headed out onto the main road. A mile south, I stopped at a gas station to relieve myself of a gallon of lemonade, and to wash the filth from my hands.

If you're wondering why I'm boring you with these details, think back to a turning point in your own life. A day when everything changed for better or worse. Think of the long series of seemingly insignificant events that laid the groundwork for you to be in the right place at the right time. Or the wrong place at the wrong time.

By the time I got back on the road it was after ten, and I was dead tired.

28

About halfway back to town, on a long, straight stretch of road where the old rough pavement met the smooth new blacktop, two sets of headlights approached. I was going south. They were coming north.

The first car was drifting in and out of its lane. The second car was some distance behind and catching up fast. As it came up on the first car's tail, it crossed the yellow line, directly into my lane, and if I didn't move, we would have hit head-on and we'd both be dead.

I pulled the wheel to the right. The Vette shot out of the lane onto the shoulder and almost into a ditch before I nudged the wheel back to the left.

I had one tire on the road and one in the dirt when a white streak shot by about ten feet to my left—that was the first car. It was illuminated by the headlights of the second car, the one that was in my lane. That one passed only two or three feet from my door with a whoosh, leaving a red smear across the starlit night.

I ran off the shoulder into the dirt and drove parallel to the road for a couple hundred yards before slowing to a stop. Then I heard a loud crash on the road behind me.

In the rearview, I could see one dim set of taillights stopped on the opposite shoulder, about a third of a mile back, where the paving equipment was parked.

I turned my head and saw a second bright set of brake lights a little farther down. The driver came to a full stop, then his reverse lights came on and he backed up.

I sat there on the shoulder for a minute, trying to catch my breath. They say your life flashes before your eyes when you're about to die, but all I saw was a white streak and a red streak.

After my heart stopped racing and I could breathe normally, I turned and looked again. The taillights were glowing dimly on the car that had crashed. The other car was just in front of it, in the main driving lane beside the paving equipment. Against the red of the second car's taillights, I thought I saw a person moving beside the wreck.

I swung my car around slowly and drove toward the crash. My hands were still shaky on the wheel, and I was going about ten miles an hour. The low beams of the Corvette didn't reach very far, so I could only see the dim shadow of the figure up ahead. Judging by the size, it was a man. It looked like he was trying to yank the driver from the mangled car.

I put the high beams on and saw that it was indeed a man. He was pulling violently on the occupant of the wrecked car. On the driver of the white convertible Mercedes.

Jesus, I thought, that's Bastian's car! Why are you pulling on him like that?

I was still a good distance away when the man turned his back to me. He was yanking the driver the wrong way. If you want to get a driver out of a car, you pull on his left side, the side by the door. But he was pulling the driver's right arm across his body.

"You bastard! What the hell?" I hit the gas, he gave the body one last yank, then ran up the road, jumped in his car, and took off. I should have noted his license number, but the bloody arm hanging from the driver's door of the white Mercedes caught my eye, and I had a sudden flashback of Bastian laughing drunkenly in his home earlier that evening.

I slowed alongside the mangled convertible and saw Bastian's balding head hanging forward at an unnatural angle. He had hit the rear of the steamroller, probably at sixty miles an hour.

I pulled up a few yards past the wreck and left the Vette idling in the lane. The front of the Mercedes was crumpled, the white hood pitched upward like a volcano. The windshield had shattered, and the deflated airbag was covered in blood. Bastian's right arm had been pulled across his body by the man who'd just driven away. His right wrist rested on his left knee, and his watch, that sixty-thousand-dollar Patek Phillipe he liked to show off, was gone. His rings were gone too, the platinum wedding band and the Super Bowl ring that was studded with diamonds.

His left arm hung unnaturally low over the outside of the door. He had probably been resting it on the door when he crashed. The impact must have pulled the limb from its socket.

I knew from the tilt of his neck he was dead. And he reeked of alcohol.

I stepped back and looked at the car. On the rear quarter panel was a three-foot-long red scuff mark. The car that had passed must have tried to come back into the lane too early. It had bumped him, but not hard enough to leave a dent. Not hard enough to knock him into the steamroller. Maybe Bastian just overreacted and lost control of his car.

I looked down the road where the cars had come from, but it was too dark to see any tire marks. Even in daylight, they'd be hard to spot on that fresh black pavement.

I looked up the road where the red car had fled and saw only darkness.

Then I heard sirens coming from the south. Bastian's car must have had one of those systems that automatically calls 911 after a crash.

I thought to myself, This doesn't look good. I'm standing next to the car of the man whose wife I'm screwing. He's dead, and he's missing a hundred thousand dollars' worth of jewelry. The only sensible thing to do in this situation is leave.

I walked back to my car, pulled on my seatbelt, and was about to hit the gas when the headlights set something gleaming on the road up ahead. I got out and picked it up, then jumped back in the car and hauled ass back up north, away from the sirens.

Ten miles up, I pulled off onto a side road and looked at the item in my hand. It was Bastian's platinum bracelet. The impact must have torn it from his wrist and sent it flying up the road. Why the hell didn't he take his arm off the door when he got sideswiped? Wouldn't you want to steer with two hands at that point? A sober person would. But he hadn't been sober for hours.

The bracelet had a thick platinum chain that went around the bottom of his wrist, and a platinum plate on top, encrusted with tiny blue-white diamonds that spelled out his initials: BAC, which, by the way, also stands for Blood Alcohol Content.

Bastian was supposed to be at dinner with Marilyn and a dozen other people that night. What was he doing up on that stretch of road?

My first thought was that I should return the bracelet to Marilyn. My second thought was how would I explain how I had gotten the thing in the first place? Would I just blithely toss it on the bed and say, "Oh, I saw your husband last night. He dropped this."

There would be an investigation and Lou Eisenfall would have his nose in it. Lou who was already suspicious of me. Lou who knew I was having an affair with Marilyn.

I should have chucked the bracelet that night. I should have wiped it clean of fingerprints and tossed it into a sewer.

But the shock of almost getting killed, the shock of seeing Bastian dead and robbed had rattled me. I hadn't felt that kind of trauma since the night John Manis and I went sailing in Costa Rica. And what had I done then? I buried the body and hid the evidence, so my lonely conscience bore the entire weight of a crime the world could have mourned. And where had that gotten me? Into a life of imposture, duplicity, and deceit. Into the bed of a married woman, and a maze of guilt and denial out of which I couldn't find my way.

I heard the waves beating against the boat. I saw John Manis sitting at ease on deck, popping the cap off a bottle of beer.

"You're already in it up to your neck," he said. "And you're not rich anymore. Why don't you hock the bracelet?" He was smiling and jovial, pleased with himself as usual.

"No."

"Oh come on, Tom!" he scolded with a light, mocking tone. "You didn't turn down *my* money. Don't start developing morals now. You can't afford them."

Before I slid the bracelet into my pocket, I turned it over and looked at the inscription on the back: an unfamiliar twelve-letter word that didn't look like any language I had ever seen.

29

The next day, the crash was the talk of the town. The story started with Bastian and Marilyn in a group of twelve at the French restaurant. Bastian arrived drunk and got drunker. He and Marilyn fought. The maître d' couldn't talk any sense into Bastian, so he called Lou Eisenfall to try to smooth things over.

While Lou consoled Marilyn, who was crying, Bastian slipped out and drove away. Lou drove Marilyn home. The rumor was that Bastian left to see another woman, who was waiting at a house by a lake. When I finally got to talk with Marilyn, she confirmed that.

"That's what we were fighting about," she said. "In front of everyone."

Bastian's blood alcohol when he died was point two four. Three times the legal limit. The talk in town centered on the circumstances of the crash and the fact that he'd been robbed of all his jewelry while he was either dead or dying.

The police were looking for the car that had left the red scuff mark on the rear quarter panel of Bastian's Mercedes. They were having trouble identifying tire marks on the fresh new asphalt, but they could see that Bastian's car had crossed the white shoulder line after it had been bumped, then had veered left and crossed the center line. Bastian then overcorrected, steering too hard to the right, and slammed into the parked steamroller.

People were divided about whether the crash was the result of the red car's impact or of Bastian's drunken overreaction to being bumped. They were also split over whether he had been robbed by the driver of the red car or some opportunistic passerby. The answers to those two questions, people said, would determine whether the incident was a murder or a hit-and-run accident.

The police had put out a plea for witnesses, but I wasn't about to come forward. The first thing they'd ask is why I left the scene. And if Lou Eisenfall was on the case, he'd start digging into my past. I was never sure how well my new identity would stand up to scrutiny. All it would take was someone running my fingerprints.

I waited until the following afternoon to call Marilyn. When she answered, she sounded numb, like she had cried herself out, or had taken a tranquilizer, or both.

"I'm sorry," I said. "What a terrible thing. How are you holding up?"

"I'm not," she said. "And I keep getting questions from cops and lawyers."

"I'd come by, but—"

"Don't. Just... Maybe in a few days. Not now."

"Yeah, all right. I hope you get some rest. I don't know what else to say."

"There's nothing to say."

For the next few days, I kept to myself. I didn't have any work, and except for one trip up to the overlook, I didn't leave town. I checked in with Marilyn twice a day via text, and each day she thanked me and told me to stay away.

With nothing else to do, I eavesdropped on the gossip in the coffee shop and the deli. I read the local news sites, which were full of the story, though the Chronical and SFGate down in San Francisco didn't give it much more than a blurb that could be summarized as "Napa entrepreneur dies in suspicious crash."

Four days after the crash, I started getting restless. I had no work scheduled, and no idea when I might get any. The blank spaces in my date book made me nervous. I thought about calling The Lemonade Lady about her iPad, and I thought about Bastian's platinum-and-diamond bracelet, which was worth a lot more than one of my house calls.

I could hock it, but I'd have to do it somewhere far away. I had enough cash in the bank to carry me through the end of the month, but after that…

That bracelet is worth thousands, I told myself in a voice that was starting to sound more and more like John Manis's. Why let it go to waste? Isn't that just compounding the tragedy of Bastian's senseless death?

I went back and forth on the idea for a couple of hours before I managed to talk myself into it.

You might get a few thousand for it, I told myself. That would give you some cushion. Otherwise, Johnny, you're living paycheck to paycheck. Take the bracelet to San Francisco. You'll find a buyer there.

A trip to the city sounded nice after all those days cooped up in my apartment.

Before I left, I reread all the stories about the crash on all the San Francisco news outlets. I checked the video coverage as well. They mentioned the stolen Patek Phillipe watch and the Super Bowl ring, but not the wedding ring or the bracelet.

I put on a button-down shirt, wool slacks, and a pair of black Oxfords. You don't go selling platinum and diamonds in jeans and a t-shirt.

As I pulled away from the curb with the bracelet in my pocket, I asked myself if San Francisco was far enough. Should I go farther south, just to be safe? No. The bigger the city, I thought, the less you stick out. No one notices you in San Francisco.

But where would I sell it? How much could I get for it? Enough to cover rent, utilities, and car insurance?

These were the questions running through my head as I headed south past the edge of town with the convertible top down. They were practical questions about the future. I wasn't thinking at all about the present until I saw the blue flashing lights of Lou Eisenfall's cruiser in my rearview.

As I eased the Vette slowly to the shoulder, my left hand went instinctively to my hip pocket, to cover up the thing I didn't want Lou Eisenfall to find.

30

"What is it, Lou? I wasn't speeding."

"License and registration," he said. The guy had no expression on his face. It spooked me, because I couldn't read him, and I didn't know what he was going to do.

I pulled my wallet from my back pocket and handed him my license. Then I got the registration from the glove box.

He took the documents and went back to his car without a word, leaving me alone to think.

I checked the rearview every thirty seconds, but he didn't seem to be doing anything other than looking into the screen of the laptop mounted between his cruiser's front seats.

Stop looking in the rearview, I told myself. You're checking every thirty seconds, and that looks suspicious. Keep it to a minute, at least. Or better yet, don't look at all. But will that look like I'm trying not to look?

I felt the bracelet in my pocket and wondered, what if he arrests me? They always search people when they arrest them. Always. I could see him asking, How'd you come by this, Johnny? I could see the dark suspicion in his eyes and hear the accusatory tone as clearly as if Manis himself were speaking.

But what could Lou arrest me for? I hadn't done anything.

Well, he had pulled me over and I hadn't done anything. What was to stop him from taking it a step further?

Then I thought about the dealer I had bought the Corvette from in Vegas. At two in the morning. Who sells cars at two a.m.? Well, it was Vegas. But was the dealer legit? He had a lot full of exotic cars, and a showroom that looked like the Vegas of the 1970s, flashy and seedy at the same time. Had he sold me a stolen car? Is that what Lou was figuring out? That I was driving a stolen car?

No, I thought. He pulled me over before. If the car was stolen, he would have noticed it then. Besides, I had the title back in the apartment. It looked legit. But then I thought, I have no idea what a Nevada title is supposed to look like.

What the hell is Lou doing back there?

I wanted to look in the rearview, but I told myself not to. I looked in the sideview instead at just the wrong moment, and our eyes locked. It looked like Lou was about to get out of the car, but then he hesitated. Why?

Because you looked at him, stupid. Anytime your eyes meet someone else's unexpectedly, it throws them off. Just for a second. Even Lou.

Finally, he opened the door and walked back to the side of my car.

"Everything all right?" I asked. My mouth was dry as the desert, and I knew my words came out sounding nervous.

Lou handed me a ticket and said, "Your brake light is out." He must have noticed I was sweating. It was a cold sweat. "You OK?" he asked.

"Yeah," I said. "Fine." I took the ticket with my right hand and slid my left over my hip pocket.

He noticed. I tried to distract him with another question. "Hey, uh..." I held the ticket in front of my face but couldn't read it. "Is this something I could get pulled over for again?"

"If you get pulled over today, just show them the ticket. If I see you driving tomorrow with that broken light, I'll write you up again."

"Thanks, Lou." I don't know why I said that. "How's Marilyn?" I don't know why I said that either. My nerves were on edge and I wasn't thinking straight.

"About as distraught as a woman should be under the circumstances. I'm surprised you haven't been by to comfort her."

The way he said "comfort" made me angry, but I held my tongue.

"Anything else, Lou? Am I free to go?"

"You're free to go," he said.

When I pulled away, I wondered how Lou knew I hadn't been by to see Marilyn. Was it because I had asked him how she was doing? Or had he been keeping an eye on me?

31

I was so paranoid about getting pulled over again I stopped on the way to the city and had lunch while a mechanic replaced the bulb in my taillight.

As I rolled into San Francisco, all I could think about was getting rid of that damn bracelet. I drove straight to Mission Street, figuring I could sell it there, no questions asked.

The first pawnshop I went into was filled with guitars and video game consoles and crappy jewelry. I left without even showing them the bracelet. I went to a couple other places before I found one that had decent stuff. The guy offered me eight hundred dollars. I said no way.

A pawnbroker will give you ten percent of an item's value, so the guy was basically telling me the bracelet was worth eight thousand, which meant it was probably worth fifteen.

That gave me a better idea: find a high-end jewelry shop where they appreciated this kind of thing and they'd give me a fair price.

I found a place near the financial district that fit the bill, with white satin beds of glistening diamonds encased in glass beneath glaring lights.

When I walked in, a young guy in a suit asked if he could help me.

"Yeah, I want to sell this bracelet."

He hesitated a moment, then said, "This is not a pawnshop, sir."

"I know. That's why I'm here." I pulled the bracelet from my pocket and said, "A pawnshop can't appreciate a piece like this."

When I held it out to him, I noticed he was looking at my face, not the bracelet. I thought, You're nervous, Johnny, and it's showing. The kind of person who has enough money to own a bracelet like this wouldn't be acting like you in this situation. Don't talk like you're in a hurry.

I think those were my thoughts, but maybe it was Manis talking. It was getting harder to tell the difference. Whoever thought it, it made sense, so I went with it.

I draped the bracelet over my hand like a woman selling jewelry on the Home Shopping Network.

"This is platinum," I said. "The diamonds are all brilliant blue. Take a look under the light."

He took the bracelet and stepped into a bright beam of light shining down from the ceiling.

"Where did you get this?" he asked.

"I bought it."

"For how much?"

"Fifteen thousand."

He nodded, which told me I got the number right.

"And why are you selling it?" he asked, glancing first at my shirt and then at my pants.

In that moment, I saw myself through his eyes. My light-blue Oxford had been through three wearings without being washed or pressed and had a faint trace of mustard on the breast pocket. That came from my lunch in Vallejo. My pants, charcoal-grey dress slacks that had been part of a suit I no longer owned, hadn't been pressed either. The crease was no longer crisp, and the wool was thinning on the right pocket, where I kept my keys.

"I don't like it," I said. "It's too gaudy."

He frowned. "I actually think it's quite elegant. What does BAC stand for?"

"Blood Alcohol Content."

"Excuse me?"

"It's hotter than hell in here. Why do you keep the lights so bright?" I felt like I was in one of those old crime films where they have the spotlight on the guilty guy during the interrogation.

"Sir?"

"Are you interested or not?" I asked impatiently.

"Well," he said, looking again at the bracelet. "We occasionally sell a piece like this on consignment."

"OK."

"You'll have to sign a form."

"Yeah, sure."

"And show me some ID."

"Wait," I said. "Consignment? How long does that take?"

"A piece like this? It could go in a week. Or it could take a year."

"A year? I can't wait a damn year." I took the bracelet and turned to go.

"Hey wait," said the guy.

I turned. "What?"

He stared at me for a long couple of seconds as if to memorize my face. "What's your name?"

"Lou."

Then I went to another jewelry shop and they told me the same thing. Nice piece. Consignment. It might sell in three months, or six months, or never. The monogram was a problem. No one's going to buy a bracelet with someone else's initials.

So I went back to the pawnshop where the first guy had made his offer and hocked the thing for eight hundred bucks. I was pissed off because the guy tried to haggle me down. He knew I'd shopped it around since I first came by, and the fact that I was back meant I hadn't found a better offer. So he tried to squeeze me, but I stuck to eight hundred, and I got it.

I was keyed up when I drove out of the city. It was the same feeling I'd had when I left Vegas: I couldn't get away from there fast enough. I kept finding myself right on the bumper of the car in front of me. I'd check the speedometer, ease off the gas, and a minute later I'd be tailgating again.

Slow it down, Johnny boy, I told myself. You don't want to get pulled over again. But as soon as I hit the highway, I thought, Lou Eisenfall can pull me over all he wants. He can tear my car apart, but he won't find a thing. I have eight hundred bucks in my pocket, and I want to take Marilyn out to dinner.

As I wove through traffic on Route 80, I texted her. "Dinner and drinks tonight?"

Some of the cars I was passing were honking at me. If they hadn't been driving so damn slow, I wouldn't have to weave around them.

Marilyn wrote back, "Leave me alone."

That wasn't the answer I was looking for. We hadn't seen each other in days, and we sure weren't having any fun apart. So I decided to stop by.

32

The fresh air and the long drive soothed me. When I got to Marilyn's, I was nice and calm. There were four cars parked outside the house. Marilyn's black Mercedes, a police cruiser, a BMW, and a Jaguar. Esme was beating the dust out of a rug on the front step.

"Buenos días, señor."

"Buenos días, Esme. Is Marilyn in?"

She pointed toward the rear of the house. I walked through the kitchen and found Marilyn at the table on the back patio with Lou Eisenfall and two other men in suits. A silver tray with a silver coffee pot sat at the center of the table. The men had coffee cups. Marilyn had ice water.

She looked up at me, and I read her expression instantly. She was angry, sullen, and exhausted, trying to contain the worst of her emotions in front of the guests, but I could see her patience was wearing thin.

"Did I ask you to come over?"

The two men in suits turned to look at me. They were both middle-aged, one thin and one thick, like an ex-football player.

"No," I said, "but I thought you might like some company."

"I have company," she said. "But they'll be leaving soon." That was a not-too-subtle hint that she was done with whatever discussion they'd been having.

Lou said, "Hello, Johnny."

I told him I got the taillight fixed and he said, "Good for you."

The thick man said to Marilyn, "It's probably a good thing, in the long run, that you didn't return the policy. I don't like the drinking clause. You shouldn't have initialed it. We can strike it—"

"No," said the thin man, shaking his head. "No, no, no."

Marilyn explained later what that was about. Bastian had revised his life insurance policy, raising the payout from three million dollars to ten million. The agent knew Bastian liked to drink, and if anything was likely to kill a forty-one-year-old in perfect health, it was driving drunk in a fast car. The agent had added a clause to the new policy that said if Bastian died as a result of drunk driving, there would be no payout.

Bastian had signed the policy, then brought it home to Marilyn. Marilyn had signed and initialed it too—three months ago—but she never returned it to the agent. In the meantime, Bastian's old three-million-dollar policy had lapsed, so he had no insurance at the time of his death.

The lawyer said, "Marilyn, the policy was dated three months ago and signed by both of you. The fact that you forgot to return it—"

"Who says I forgot?" Marilyn asked.

I thought of the unaddressed letter she had kept on the dresser upstairs.

"Well, obviously," the lawyer said, "it was an oversight. But as long as it's signed, it's valid."

"Sorry," said the thin man, shaking his head again. "If she didn't return it to us—"

"You *will* be sorry," the lawyer interrupted, "because I know the law and you don't. You should be ashamed of yourself. This is no way to look out for your clients."

"I have company interests to look after. Besides, Bastian was drunk when he died. There's no guarantee we'd pay a dime on that policy."

The lawyer argued that if the impact from the red car had caused the crash, then alcohol would not be to blame, and the insurer could not invoke the alcohol clause.

"If the red car caused the crash," Lou said, "then we're dealing with a homicide." Lou's eyes drilled into Marilyn, who

I could see was nearing a breakdown. She was quietly wringing her hands, and her eyes were beginning to moisten.

Lou stared at her the way poker players examine each other when they're looking for a tell, for a crack in the façade that might give a clue about what the person is really thinking. I didn't like him looking at her like that.

The lawyer said, "Give me the signed policy, Marilyn. I'll take care of it."

She hesitated, looking for a moment like a deer in the headlights as all eyes were on her.

I felt bad for her, having to deal with all this in the wake of her husband's death. They may not have had the best marriage, but still, it had to be a shock to lose someone so suddenly and violently.

I thought again of the envelope she'd slid between the liquor bottles the last time I was over.

"Do you want me to get it, Marilyn?"

"Get what?" she asked, as if in a fog.

"The insurance policy. It's right in there." I pointed toward the dining room.

Lou turned and looked at me sharply. "Why do you know where the policy is?"

"Why do you have to be such a prick, Lou? The policy's in an envelope right over there."

Marilyn shook her head slowly.

"What?" I asked. "Did you mail it?"

She shook her head again, and Lou looked back and forth between the two of us. I could see the dark prosecutor's mind at work behind his narrowed eyes, trying to weave together the threads of a conspiracy.

Marilyn Dupree was stuck in a miserable marriage. Then Johnny Manic came along and they fell in love and plotted to get rid of Bastian. They'd make it look like an accident. Marilyn had a brand new ten-million-dollar policy on her late husband's life, and Johnny knew exactly where she kept it.

I swear, I was reading his mind. Right there, in front of everyone, Lou said, "Where were you the night of the crash, Johnny?"

That sent a jolt of fear through my heart, and I think it might have shown.

"I was up north," I said. "Way up north."

"That's pretty vague," Lou said. "Where up north?"

"Past Cloverdale."

"What were you doing up there?"

"Working."

"At night?"

Marilyn said, "Jesus, Lou, do you have to interrogate him right here? Don't you think it's enough I lost my husband? Don't you think it's enough I have to think about him being robbed as he was dying? After we parted the way we did? After that awful fight in the restaurant? Have some fucking decency!"

Then she turned to the lawyer and the insurance agent. "I have no time for you and your stupid papers. Get out of my house! All of you!"

The lawyer and the agent hesitated for a moment, looking at each other. Then they both stood.

The lawyer said softly, "When you have time, Marilyn, give me the policy. Or I can send someone by to pick it up. Just let me know."

Lou continued to stare at her as the other two turned to leave. He made no effort to conceal what he was thinking.

"Don't you look at me like that," Marilyn said. "Don't you dare look at me like that."

Lou stood to leave.

"You think I killed my husband?" she asked bitterly.

"I didn't say that," Lou said.

"Your eyes did," Marilyn said. "Your eyes said exactly that."

"Lou," said the lawyer. "Leave her alone."

"I have some news for you," Lou said to the lawyer. "Since this is a possible homicide—"

"The coroner hasn't ruled on that yet," said the lawyer.

"Regardless," Lou said, "when I have a potential homicide, I dig into the circumstances leading up to the event. Bastian took out a ten-million-dollar policy on his own life three months before he died, with you as the beneficiary." He pointed to Marilyn.

"He also sucked ten million dollars out of his businesses in the past few months, did you know that?"

"What?" said Marilyn weakly.

"He borrowed everything he could against everything he owned. God only knows where that money went, but I don't like the fact that the new policy matches up almost exactly to the amount he borrowed. I don't like the fact that he's dead, or the way he died, or the fact that only one person—" he turned his gaze from Marilyn to me—"or maybe two stand to benefit from all this."

Marilyn's face went pale, and she had to steady herself with both hands against the table.

"That's enough, Lou," said the lawyer. "You have no business talking to her like that."

"You gonna sue me?" Lou asked. "You're a contract lawyer."

"No, Lou. I'm going to punch you right in the fucking face if you don't shut the fuck up."

"Get out," Marilyn said. "All of you."

33

As the other three left the house, Marilyn stood with her hands pressed against the table. She was breathing deeply, with long, slow exhalations to calm herself.

Esme came out to the patio carrying a tumbler filled with whiskey and ice. She must have heard the tone of the conversation from inside. Marilyn took the glass and said, "Gracias." Esme returned to the house without a word.

"I hate that man," she said softly. "I don't know who the hell he thinks he is. He was with me the night Bastian died. He drove me here himself, and he stayed for twenty minutes. Where the hell does he get off saying things like that?"

She took a sip of whiskey, and then another. "You want some?"

"No thanks," I said.

The color began to rise in her cheeks. I couldn't tell if that was from the liquor or if it was just her regaining her composure after that tense encounter.

"Johnny," she said. "Come inside."

We went into the kitchen, and I thought about what Lou had said about Bastian borrowing all that money. I had been planning to tell Marilyn myself, but now I didn't have to. Now she knew.

Marilyn opened the fridge and said, "Will you please have a beer? It makes me nervous if I'm drinking and you're not."

"Sure."

She opened a bottle of beer and handed it to me. Then she threw her arms around my neck and kissed my cheek. "Thank God you're here," she said. "Thank God for you."

She pulled away and picked up her whiskey from the counter and held it up for a toast, but she wasn't smiling. She still looked shaken. I tapped my bottle against her glass and we both drank.

I thought about telling her the other half of what I had found on Bastian's hard drive, about his plan to run away with his new lover. But Marilyn already knew about her, at least to some extent. She had said she knew her husband was in love. She knew the woman's name was Olivia. She knew Bastian wanted to meet her at the cabin by the lake the night he died. What was the point of telling her more, now that Bastian was dead? Why add to her troubled thoughts?

But it was already on her mind.

"Do you think he was planning on running away with her?" she asked, her dark eyes troubled with thought.

"Bastian? Run away with who?"

"Olivia," she said bitterly. "The woman he was meeting at the lake."

"I don't know."

"Why would he borrow ten million dollars? If he wanted cash, he could sell a business, or one of his buildings. He owns an office building, you know." Her eyes had a distant look, and her voice was hollow, like she was just talking out her thoughts as they arose and wasn't expecting any answers.

"Did you know he was in trouble with the IRS?" she asked absently.

"Was he?"

"He owed a lot of money," she said. "Maybe that's why he borrowed ten million dollars. But I couldn't see him owing that much. I mean, ten million in taxes? That's a lot." She drank down the rest of her whiskey, then she went to the fridge and opened a beer.

"Maybe that's why he changed the insurance policy," I said. "Maybe Lou was onto something when he talked about the numbers matching up. If Bastian did run away, he would have left you with ten million in debt—"

Those words struck her like a blow.

"—and a ten-million-dollar policy to pay it off. You'd still have the house."

It took her a few seconds to recover from the idea of being alone and in debt.

"It wasn't Bastian's idea," she said softly. "I told him to up the policy. But I think..." She trailed off, staring at the floor, lost in thought. "I do think he was going to run away with her. And just leave it all behind. Leave me and his businesses and every other responsibility behind."

She looked up at me with a light in her eyes as if it had all just become clear to her that moment. "He was always going away," she said, "and I never understood why. I mean, why would he want to leave all this?" She pointed vaguely around the room. "This house he built? And why..." Her voice faltered. "Why would he want to leave this?" She ran her hands over her chest and hips. "Am I so horrible?"

She gave me a helpless, pleading look and repeated, "Am I?"

"No," I said. "Not at all." I put my arms around her and pressed her against the island in the center of the kitchen as I kissed her.

"Stay here, will you?"

"I'm not going anywhere," I said. I kissed her again.

"Let's watch a movie. I don't want to think. I don't want to feel anything anymore."

I went to the living room and turned on the TV. She went to the dining room and got the bourbon.

34

The following day was Bastian's funeral, which we agreed I would not attend. "It wouldn't look right," Marilyn said. I wondered if Lou Eisenfall's suspicion and innuendo had gotten under her skin. She had never made an effort to hide our affair before.

I was one of the few people in town who didn't go to the funeral. The French restaurant was closed. The grocery store, of which Bastian was part owner, had only one cashier on duty, and the town seemed empty. The high clouds that had rolled in the night before had begun to thicken, threatening a long, drenching rain.

I had no work that day, so I drove up to the overlook and sat on the stone wall above the valley, which looked somber and leaden beneath the heavy grey sky, like a vista from a Pacific Northwest winter. The first time I had gone up there, I remembered, the sun was shining and the valley was one bright promise. Now it was heavy and dark.

Sometime since my previous visit, a car or truck had bumped the wall next to where I sat and knocked a few stones loose. I threw chips of broken mortar into the bushes and trees below, and watched absently as a little blue Mazda made its way up the winding road I had just climbed in the Corvette.

Someone should collect these stones, I thought, so they can repair the wall. A breeze stirred the thick, moist air. I should collect these stones. Why leave it to someone else? That's how things go left undone.

I picked up two large stones from the ground behind me, along with several smaller ones and stacked them on the wall. Most of the stones had fallen below and were still within a few feet of the wall, though some had tumbled farther down toward the bushes and trees.

I hopped over the wall and started collecting the pieces, stacking them neatly where I had been sitting a minute earlier. I heard a car pull into the gravel lot as I went down the hill after two big grey rocks. As the first raindrop landed on my nose, I thought, I should put the top up on the Vette, before it starts to pour.

As I walked back up the steep slope toward the wall, I saw Roland standing by the rock pile I had made. His jaw was moving, but he wasn't spitting sunflower seeds this time. He had an unfriendly look on his face, like he was waiting for me to get close so he could push me back down the hill.

The way his jaw was working, I couldn't tell if he was chewing something or just compulsively clenching it like an angry man trying to control his rage.

"Enjoying Marilyn?" he asked.

"Who are you?"

"Her last fuck. She's something, isn't she?"

His hard eyes searched my face like a target. I didn't like being below him on that steep incline. There was something wrong with the man. He was the kind you'd cross the street to avoid having to walk past. And he was wearing Bastian's Patek Phillipe watch.

I walked up to the wall a few feet to his right. He turned his body toward me like a fighter wary of letting an opponent get on his blind side. I set the two big rocks I'd just collected on top of the wall and pulled myself up beside them. Before I could stand, he took a step closer. I remained crouched atop the wall, my right hand a few inches from the larger of the two rocks I'd just brought up.

"I asked you a question," he said.

His hand went toward his pocket, which was bulging with what looked like a gun. His jaw kept clenching, and his eyes were moist. The fear that had been growing in me was now rising toward panic. But this wasn't the vague, unfocused kind of panic I was used to. This fear, like the fear of a cornered animal, had a single deadly focus.

What kind of asshole carries a gun in his front pocket, I wondered. And why are his eyes so moist? Is he going to cry? Christ, the guy looks crazier than I ever looked.

"Sorry," I said. "What was the question?" My body was so flooded with adrenaline, I really couldn't remember.

His hand slid into his pocket. "I asked how you like that cun—"

In one fluid motion, I grabbed the rock beside my hand and sprang forward with a sidearm throw as he pulled the gun. The rock traveled three feet before hitting him square between the eyes and knocking him backward toward the picnic bench. The gun went off as he toppled over, and the sound stopped me cold. It was so near and so loud, I was sure I'd been shot.

Roland lay on the dusty ground cursing, with his right hand covering his right eye and the bridge of his nose. "Jesus! Fuck that hurt!" His left hand waved the gun in my direction, and he let off another shot, which missed.

That snapped me out of my terror. I threw the second rock and hit him in the chest. I think it knocked the wind out of him. He moved his gun hand to the spot I had hit, and I thought, Run? Or take the pistol?

As he raised his hand for another shot, I jumped sideways off the wall. He let off a wild shot, and I threw a handful of dirt into his eyes.

He cursed again, and I went for the gun, which was in his left hand, up near his dirt-filled eye, which he seemed to be trying to rub. I pulled the gun down to try to get it away from him, and it went off just under his chin, taking off a chunk of the left side of his jaw.

He started moaning and thrashing, and I jumped out of the way, thinking the gun was going to shoot again. But he dropped it as he writhed in terror. He touched the wound with his left hand, and grasped at the dirt with his right, like it was a blanket he could pick up to comfort himself. He kicked his heels against the ground, like a man having a seizure, and I watched in terror as his cries began to gurgle. Then he started choking and spluttering.

Jesus, I thought. Jesus, what do I do? I felt his terror as vividly as if it were my own, and I wanted to end it.

I looked around, and it seemed the nearest person had to be down in town, miles away.

I looked back at him, coughing blood and kicking his legs up and down, and I couldn't bear it. I picked up his gun and shot him in the chest. Then he was quiet.

What do I do now, I wondered. I had shot him just to stop the terror in my own mind, so I could figure out how to help him. It only occurred to me afterward that I had killed him.

And then again I looked around.

No one in sight. No cars coming up the road.

This is John Manis all over again, I thought. Only this time you did it with a gun. Try saying *that* was an accident.

It was self-defense, I told myself. And then the cool, mocking voice of John Manis chimed in. "Go tell Lou it was self-defense."

"Shut up, John." I said that out loud. "Shut up!"

This isn't the sea at night, I thought. This is a public road, and we're in daylight, and anyone might drive by at any minute. We have to act quickly. What do we do? What do we do?

"The first thing," Manis said, "is to calm down. Take a few deep breaths, and don't think about anything at all. Just breathe."

I did.

"Now you have to move the body," said Manis, cool and easy. "Away from the road, where it can't be seen."

Over the wall, I thought. Down into the bushes.

I heaved Roland onto my shoulder and dropped him over the wall. From there, the slope was steep and he was easy to drag. I went down about fifty yards, well into the trees and shrubs, before I thought about the blood.

How will I get rid of the blood?

"The rain will take care of it," Manis said.

The first fat drops of what promised to be a long, heavy storm had begun to fall.

"Take his clothes off," someone said. Me or Manis, I don't know who.

I took his clothes off, along with Bastian's watch. I took his keys, his phone, and his wallet. I checked his license while I was at it. Roland Morel of San Francisco, California. He had another license too. Roland Lefevre of Portland, Oregon. And another. Roland Marchand, Denver, Colorado.

This guy's worse than me, I thought. I'm only two people. But at least he's consistent with the names.

By the time I got back up to the parking area, it was raining hard.

What about his car, I thought. And his bloody clothes? And *my* bloody clothes? And the gun? The gun was lying in the mud.

I wiped the blood from my hands onto his clothes, then I found a plastic grocery bag on the floor of the Vette, carefully wrapped his clothing and the gun, and put the bundle into the trunk. I put the top up to keep the rain off the seats, then I checked his car.

It was unlocked. I opened the rear driver-side door to find fast food bags all over the floor. The car smelled of burgers and fried chicken. There was a duffle bag on the back seat. I pulled it out and opened it. It was full of clothing. I pulled out a rumpled blue Oxford shirt, removed my shirt, which was stained with blood on the shoulder and back, and put on the Oxford. Then I changed into a pair of his jeans, which were too tight and too short, but would serve well enough.

I put my bloody clothes into the plastic bag with Roland's, then threw that and the duffle bag into the trunk of the Corvette. I drove his Mazda over the top of the mountain and down the back side. After half a mile, I turned off the road into the bush. I drove a quarter mile or so very slowly, picking my way between the trees. The terrain was rough, and the Mazda wouldn't have made it that far if I weren't going downhill. After wiping down everything I had touched, I left the car with the doors, trunk, and windows open beneath the dripping trees, hoping the rain would contaminate whatever evidence might have remained.

Then I walked back to my car through a drenching downpour. I placed a piece of gravel beneath Roland's phone and ran over it backwards and forwards so no one could possibly track its location. Then I put it in the trunk with the clothing and the gun. I headed down the mountain and turned south toward San Francisco. I wanted to go as far as I could from the scene of the crime, to ditch the evidence where no one would look for it, to find a fresh change of clothes, and to clean the Vette, inside and out.

The bag of bloody clothes, minus the gun, went into a dumpster behind a restaurant in Yountville. Roland's wallet and phone went into two other garbage cans down the road in Yountville. I washed and vacuumed the car. I pulled up the lining of the trunk and shampooed it, then vacuumed everything underneath, and scrubbed it down twice with a wet, soapy rag. Then I headed into the city and parked in a garage off Market Street. I had three drinks at a bar in North Beach, took a long walk through heavy rain past Fisherman's Wharf, through the Presidio, and then dropped the gun and the sixty-thousand-dollar watch off the Golden Gate Bridge. By then it was dark.

I spent the night in a hotel in the Tenderloin, sleeping past noon the next day. When I started getting hungry around four, I left my room to find the streets of the city surprisingly hot beneath the glaring sun. I bought a shirt and a pair of pants that fit, some underwear and socks, and a new pair of shoes. I wrapped Roland's clothes in the bag I'd gotten from the store and stuffed them into a garbage can on Eddy Street beside a nodding junkie.

Then I had a heavy meal of steak and potatoes and scotch and beer. I returned to the hotel at dark and slept for twelve hours.

I awoke late the next morning to a text from Marilyn.

"Where are you?"

35

As I left the hotel, I replied to Marilyn's text, saying I was out on a job. Ten seconds later, she called.

"Johnny, come visit. I can't stand being alone."

"How was the funeral?"

"What kind of question is that? Have you ever *been* to a funeral?"

"Yeah," I said. "I mean, like, did you hold up OK? I was thinking about you."

I only realized that was a lie after I said it. I had actually spent the past two days obsessing over whether I had gotten rid of all the evidence, whether I had left any clues or loose ends that I'd have to explain later. I hadn't thought of Marilyn at all, except a couple times when I was drunk. And even then, I wasn't thinking about her at the funeral. I was thinking about her body next to mine.

"Why's the traffic so loud?" she asked. "Where are you?"

"I told you, I'm on a job."

"In the city?" Her voice sounded funny when she said that, like she was drunk.

"No. Have you been drinking?"

"A little. Come back. I miss you."

"It'll take me a while to get up there."

"Up? So you are in the city."

"I'll see you in a while," I said.

The conversation bothered me throughout the long, traffic-choked drive across the bay. Why did she grill me like that? What difference did it make where I was? I don't think she had ever cared before.

149

Then another part of me said, She didn't grill you. She just asked where you were. If you didn't feel so damn guilty, you wouldn't be making a big deal out of this. Get a hold of yourself, Johnny Boy. Stop acting like you have something to hide.

"But I do have something to hide."

Well you don't have to say it out loud. Look at yourself, John. Look!

My eyes went to the rearview mirror.

You look guilty.

"No I don't!" I said aloud.

I had to turn on the radio to distract myself.

Traffic thinned out when I left the interstate in Vallejo, and the rest of the drive went quickly. The air was hot and dry, so I had the top down, switching from station to station, checking the news channels to hear whether anyone had found the body by the overlook. There was no word of it yet. When I stopped for gas near Rutherford, I checked the news on my phone. Nothing there either.

As I rolled into town, I saw a couple of vultures circling the overlook. It wasn't unusual to see one or two near the hilltops, gliding on the drafts that rose up off the slopes, but the sight of them made me think of the body below. It had been shot, stripped, and rained on. The past two days had been brutally hot, which meant it would be decomposing quickly and it probably smelled horrible. The vultures had found it, and probably the crows as well, along with whatever insects and animals lived in those hills.

Two more days of this heat, I thought, and there won't be any meat left on him. At least that's how it worked in the murder mysteries I read in prison. I strained my eyes to see if there were any vehicles parked by the overlook. All I could see was one yellow car crawling slowly up the hill.

When I turned my gaze forward again, I saw a police cruiser parked in front of my apartment. I slowed to see if it was who I thought it was, and there was Lou Eisenfall coming out of the building. He saw me, so I stopped.

Play it cool, I told myself. John Manis cool.

"Hey, Lou."

"Just the person I wanted to talk to." He walked up beside the Vette, and I gave him a quick once-over glance to gauge his mood. He seemed pretty calm. "You have a few minutes to come into the station? I want to ask you some questions."

"Sure, Lou."

He got into his car and I followed him to the station, the tension in my nerves rising with each passing block. This won't be about Roland, I told myself. They haven't found him yet.

But how do you know that, I asked. What if they found him an hour ago and they're withholding it from the news so they can talk to you first?

No. If they found him an hour ago, there'd be cop cars up on the mountain. Besides, you saw what a hard-ass Lou was at Marilyn's the other day. When he thinks he's onto something, he gets aggressive. He starts prodding and bullying. He was at ease just now. Just stay calm, Johnny Boy. That's all you have to do.

By the time I parked, my palms were sweating, my breathing was shallow, and my face was tense.

"Come in," Lou said, holding open the glass door of the police station.

On the elevator ride to the second floor, he asked if I'd like some water. I told him yes, while the voice of John Manis or Tom Gantry coached me to breathe slowly and deeply. As the door opened on the second floor, I was feeling a little calmer.

"Wait in here," Lou said, showing me into a small room. "I'll be right back."

He was so polite, he actually put me at ease.

The room had a grey carpet, a white table, two black chairs, and a window that looked east toward the overlook and the circling vultures.

Lou returned in a minute with two cups of water, a yellow legal pad, and a pen. He pointed to a tinted glass dome hanging from the ceiling and said, "That's a video camera. There's a mic in here too. I'm going to ask you some questions, and we're going to record the interview. Is that OK with you?"

"Fine with me, Lou."

"All right. You want to start by telling me where you were the night of Bastian's death?"

"Yeah. I was at a lady's house way up one oh one, near Cloverdale. You asked me about that the other day, remember?"

"I remember," Lou said calmly as he wrote a note on his pad.

"Where were you before that?"

"At Marilyn's."

"Uh-huh. And Bastian was there?"

"Yeah. He was already drunk when I left."

"What time did you leave?" Again, his tone was calm and even, like he was just gathering facts as a formality to finish out a report that no one was ever going to read.

"Around five thirty," I said. "Maybe a little later."

"Stop bouncing your leg," Lou said. "It makes me nervous."

"Sorry, Lou." I hadn't noticed I was bouncing my leg, but I stopped when he pointed it out.

"What time did you arrive at the job? At the house near Cloverdale?"

"I think it was around six thirty."

He noted that, and without looking up asked, "And what time did you leave?"

"Eight thirty. Maybe a little later."

"What did you do at the house? Between six thirty and eight thirty?"

"Talked to an old lady and her granddaughter."

He looked up at me. "Weren't you supposed to be fixing something?"

"Yeah, but that lady likes to talk."

Lou tapped his pen on the pad and let out a deep breath. "She was quite taken with you."

That startled me.

"The old lady?"

"The girl and the grandmother both," Lou said. "Why didn't you call a tow truck when you had a flat?"

My heart skipped a beat. How did he know I had a flat? The Lemonade Lady didn't even know.

How long had he been digging into this case, and how far had he looked? Because if he looked far enough...

Then a new thought struck me like thunder. If I hadn't been so preoccupied the past few days—saving my own life, taking someone else's, covering it up, and getting drunk—I would have connected the dots.

Marilyn had given Roland a pair of diamond stud earrings worth several thousand dollars as a down payment. A few days later, Bastian was dead and Roland was wearing his watch.

The thought shook me so hard I could barely breathe. And Lou was sitting two feet away. Paranoid, relentless Lou Eisenfall. Thank God he was looking down at his notes at that moment, because if he had been looking at me, I might have cracked.

I was about to break into a full-on panic when John Manis said calmly, "Whatever Marilyn did is her own problem. The only thing you have to worry about is Roland. You got rid of the watch and the gun and the phone. You got rid of the clothes. The body will be gone soon enough if this heat keeps up. And Lou isn't even looking at you. He's busy with his notes. If he truly suspected you, he'd be watching your face for signs of guilt. But he's not. So relax."

That kept me from panicking, but I wouldn't say I was relaxed.

"I didn't call a tow truck because I had a spare. I changed it myself."

"What time did you leave the gas station in Geyserville?"

Again my heart leapt. "How did you know I was there?"

Finally, he looked at me. "You have a very distinctive car. There aren't many aqua-green 1963 Corvette convertibles on the road these days. The station attendant noticed. He said your hands were dirty, like someone who just changed a tire. You went to the men's room and washed up."

"I left there... I don't know. Ten fifteen."

"That's what he said." Lou laid his pen down on the pad, leaned back in his chair, and put his hands behind his head.

"If you left there at ten fifteen and you were driving a few miles under the speed limit, you'd reach the spot of the crash at just the right time. The problem is, you left there at ten twenty-three, according to the station's surveillance video, and you'd have to be driving very fast to get to a point south of the accident, switch into a red car, then turn back north, chase down Bastian's Mercedes, and run him into the steamroller by ten forty-one. That was the time Bastian's car sent a signal that it had crashed. You'd also have to have known Bastian would be traveling that stretch of road at that time of night. And you would have had to know that well ahead of time, so you could plant the red car in the right place. And that just doesn't add up."

"No," I said, breathing a slow sigh of relief that I hoped Lou didn't notice. "It doesn't."

It would make more sense if someone had followed Bastian from town, maybe even from the restaurant where he'd been drinking. If someone was looking for an opportunity to cause an accident, they could have been following him for days, just waiting for the right time to strike. I didn't want to say all that to Lou, because I'd sound too eager to cast suspicion away from myself. Besides, Lou was obviously smart enough to have thought all that through.

Then he asked in a casual tone that caught me completely off guard, "Why didn't you stop at the crash?"

"What? I didn't see the crash."

"If you left the gas station at ten twenty-three and you were going under sixty miles an hour, you had to have passed the crash. Why didn't you stop?"

"I... I didn't see it."

"You didn't notice a crumpled white car wrecked against the back of a steamroller?"

"No, I..." I was on the verge of panic again. "I must have passed before it happened. I was going pretty fast."

"So you saw Bastian's car go by?"

"Maybe I did. I wasn't really paying attention to other cars."

"Why not? You have something on your mind at the time?"

"No. I just didn't have it in mind to make a note of every vehicle that passed by."

"Did you see the red car?" Lou asked. His tone was calm and reasonable, but his eyes were boring into me.

"I... I don't remember. I don't remember what I saw that night."

"But you didn't see the crash?"

"No."

"OK," Lou said. "What time did you get back to town?"

My heart leapt again. I had turned around and driven north after the crash, trying to avoid the emergency vehicles as I held Bastian's platinum bracelet in my hand. I waited several hours before returning. I drove by the crash scene just before dawn, and there were still two police cars there. Had they noticed my "very distinctive" car as I passed? I remembered seeing one cop standing with his back to the road. The other might have been in his car. I don't know.

"There's nothing to be nervous about," Lou said. "It's just a simple question. What time did you get back to town?"

"I don't know. It was late."

"How late? Past eleven thirty?"

"Yeah."

"What took you so long?"

"I uh... I stopped at the overlook for a while."

"Up there?" He pointed through the window toward the mountain where the vultures circled.

"Yeah. It was a starry night."

Lou rested his forehead in his hand and wrote a note on his pad, ignoring me for a few seconds. Then he put the pen down and said, "Look me in the eye and tell me you had nothing to do with this."

I looked him in the eye. "I had nothing to do with this, Lou."

He nodded silently as if he accepted my answer. Then he asked, "And Marilyn? What about her?"

"What about her, Lou?" Those words came out in a higher than normal voice, because again I was thinking of her paying Roland in diamonds and Roland having Bastian's watch.

"Did she have anything to do with this?"

"You were with her the night of the crash," I said with a hint of defensiveness. "You drove her home and you stayed twenty minutes at her house."

"That's not what I asked you," Lou said. "I asked if she had anything to do with this."

"How would I know?"

Lou watched me quietly for a few seconds, then let out a sigh. "That's not the answer I wanted to hear," he said. "I was hoping you'd look me in the eye and give me a firm no, like you did when I asked if you had anything to do with it."

36

Lou concluded the interview in a calm, professional manner, handing me his card and telling me to call him if I had any information to share. But the whole thing left me unsettled. As I left the building, I wondered why he had decided to go soft on me. He could have questioned me further about what time I got home the night of the crash, or any number of other things, but he didn't.

He could have poked a little harder when he saw me looking guilty, but he didn't do that either. And he had told me that according to the evidence he had gathered so far, he didn't think I could have been the driver of the red car. I had been through a couple of police questionings after I stole that money back in Illinois, and I was pretty sure it wasn't standard practice for a cop to say he has evidence that exonerates you.

Why would Lou do that? So I would think I was off the hook? So I would let my guard down? His words actually had the opposite effect. They made me paranoid that he had some surprise up his sleeve, that he'd spring it on me when I wasn't expecting it, just like all those questions I hadn't seen coming, like "Why didn't you stop at the crash?"

On the sidewalk in front of the building, the calm, confident voice of John Manis said, "He's got you paranoid, Tom."

"Hell yeah, he's got me paranoid." I said that out loud, then looked around to see if anyone had noticed.

"You have nothing to worry about," Manis said.

But I was there when Bastian died, I thought.

"But you didn't do it, so you have nothing to worry about."

It looks bad though, I thought. Me and Marilyn and all that money. A prosecutor could make a case—

"What do you care about appearances?" Manis interrupted. "It's the truth that counts, right, Tom? And the truth is you didn't kill anyone. The truth is, you are absolutely innocent."

Those words carried a sharp sting. *You didn't kill anyone. You are absolutely innocent.* I could see Manis sitting on the deck of the boat with his feet up on the cooler. I could see his easy smile as he followed those words with a tip of his bottle and a sip of cold beer.

I walked past the Corvette and kept going for two blocks because something else was bothering me. It had happened right at the end of the interview with Lou, as I stood to leave. Over his shoulder, through the window behind him, I saw a black car coming down the mountain from the overlook. Lou's prodding insinuations had got me paranoid about Marilyn, and I wanted to know if that was her Mercedes coming down the road. If it was, she would be turning onto Main Street in a minute or so, and I'd be there to see her.

Lou had me so riled, I was ready to jump in front of her car, make her stop, haul her out, and pepper her with questions.

"What were you doing at the overlook, Marilyn?" Or better yet, ask it the way Lou would ask it—which is to say, throw in a couple of suggestive, incriminating details that tell her you know more than she expected you to know. "Who were you meeting at the overlook, Marilyn? And how much did you pay him this time?"

My phone chimed just as I stopped at the intersection where the black car would be appearing in a few seconds.

It was a text from Marilyn. "Where are you?"

"Where are YOU?" I texted back.

The black Mercedes rolled up to the stop sign across the street. It was her, and she had her phone to her ear.

My phone rang.

"Marilyn?"

"Johnny, I'm scared."

"Scared of what?" I asked as I watched her turn and drive past me.

"Roland didn't show up."

"What?" That comment caught me as much off guard as any of Lou's questions. I was about to ask who the hell Roland was, because she had never mentioned his name before.

Before I could ask, she said, "That's not like him. Something is wrong."

"Who the hell is Roland?" I demanded.

"A very dangerous man. That's why I'm scared. And you should be too. He told me he was going to kill you."

Now I was completely lost. "Who the hell is Roland? Why would he want to kill me? And why did you give him a pair of diamond studs?"

"Please don't yell at me," Marilyn said.

The line went quiet for a few seconds, and then she said in a smooth, cool voice, "Do you remember I told you there was a reason I left San Francisco? Well, he was the reason."

She paused, and when she spoke again, the calm slipped away and I heard in her breaking voice the creeping panic that I had just barely escaped in my interview with Lou. "Johnny," she said, "please come to my house. I'm really, really scared. You have no idea what that man is like."

Actually, I had a pretty good idea of what he was like. And if Marilyn was wrapped up in some kind of trouble with him, she had plenty of reason to fear.

"OK," I said. "I'll be up in a little while. Have you talked to Lou?"

"No," she said. "Why would I talk to Lou?"

37

When I arrived at Marilyn's twenty minutes later, she was standing at the kitchen island drinking iced bourbon from a tumbler, her keys and purse on the counter beside the liquor bottle.

"You want to pour me one of those?" I said.

"Why don't you start with a double," she said. "So you can catch up with me."

She took a glass from the cabinet, filled it with ice and bourbon, then handed it to me. As she refilled her own glass, I said, "So who's Roland?"

She stood with her shoulder to me, looking toward the sink. "One of my mistakes." She took a deep breath, followed by a sip of her drink.

"Why'd you give him the diamonds? So he'd kill Bastian?"

"So he *wouldn't* kill Bastian," she said angrily as she turned her dark flashing eyes on me. "What kind of person do you think I am?"

"You told me you were horrible."

"Don't use that against me." She put her hand up as if to ward off a blow. "Don't. That's not fair."

"You said, 'You have no idea how horrible I am.' Those were your exact words."

"*You're* horrible," she said. She threw her drink in my face. "You're a horrible person to come into my house and talk to me like that. Get out of here."

I wiped the liquor from my face with my sleeve. "Not until you tell me who Roland is."

She folded her arms tightly across her chest and glared at me.

"Come on," I said. "If you're so scared of the guy—"

"All right," she said in a tone of forced calm. Her body was tense as she tried to smooth over the anger she was still feeling. "All right. Come into the living room and have a seat. This is going to take a while."

She refilled the ice in her glass and carried it and the bottle into the living room. She sat on one white couch, I sat on another to her right, and we put our drinks on the glass coffee table.

"You know Bastian and I lived in San Francisco," she said.

"I know."

"I liked it there." She looked down and smoothed out her short black skirt. "But it was too easy to get into trouble."

"What kind of trouble?"

She kept her eyes fixed on her drink. "The kind of trouble Bastian and I liked to get into. Sex. You know."

Then she looked up at me. "We both slept around, though he did a lot more than I did. I've always been picky. He wasn't. And I got jealous. He didn't."

"So where does Roland come in?"

"We met him at a club," Marilyn said. "Not a nightclub. Like a swinger's club. A clothing-optional house party, where the longer the party goes on, the more optional the clothing becomes."

Her eyes seemed to drift for a moment as she recalled the scene. "He was good looking," she said. "And he was charming."

"Charming?" I said. "Roland?" I shouldn't have let those words slip out with that incredulous tone, but I just couldn't see anyone ever applying the word charming to a man whose eyes showed nothing but anger and hatred.

My tone took Marilyn aback. "Why do you sound so shocked? Do you think I'd be interested in a man who was dull or stupid?"

"No... No." I shook my head, trying to shake out the image of Roland's hardened eyes.

"Well, he was charming. And he was quite taken with me."

"Who wouldn't be?" I said.

She ignored that comment. "He followed me around the house. Followed me to the pool out back. He talked and joked. He looked at me the way you sometimes look at me. Smitten, you know?"

"Is that how I look?"

"Sometimes." She picked up her drink and took a sip. "Anyway, Bastian noticed, and I could tell he didn't like the guy. Normally, Bastian didn't care what I did, which hurt me early in the relationship, and hurt much more after a year of marriage. But this guy got to him. He really bothered Bastian, and I liked that. Roland and I had sex by the pool. Bastian watched for a few seconds from the patio door, then turned and went back inside.

"Later that night, Bastian and I had sex. He was really charged up. Anger, jealousy, hatred, fear of losing me. I could feel it all in him. It was a hot, hard, punishment fuck, and it really turned me on.

"Afterward, he said to me, 'Don't ever have sex with that guy again.' And I said OK.

"I didn't think I'd see him again, so I didn't care. But I wound up seeing him here and there around town. I'd come out of the grocery or the pharmacy and he'd be on the other side of the street. Or I'd be picking up my order at the coffee shop and I'd turn to see him at the register. I never spoke to him. Never even said hello.

"Then one day, I ran into him near Washington Square. He was wearing black slacks and a blue button-down shirt. When I looked at him, I felt a tingle. A thrill. It was physical. That surprised me. Does that ever happen to you?"

"Oh, yeah," I said, picking up my drink. "That's the source of all trouble for men."

"Well it was a strong feeling, and he turned and looked at me just as it was at its height. Maybe it showed in my face, I don't know. But something encouraged him. He walked up and said hello, and we stood there talking for a while. Again he was charming.

"Bastian had been traveling a lot on business around that time, and I had been imagining all sorts of horrible things about him. He's having an affair, I told myself. And you have to understand, that's different than just screwing someone. He didn't remember the women he screwed, but anyone he took to bed more than once obviously mattered and was a threat.

"I told myself, He's been away too long. He's with some woman in a hotel. They're waking up together day after day, having breakfast in the room so they won't have to bother getting dressed. They're in love and they can't stand to be apart.

"I had no evidence of that, but the thoughts were driving me mad. And now here was the man who could bring Bastian back, the handsome, charming threat who inspired my husband to fuck me with real passion.

"He asked if I'd like to have a drink, and I said yes because I knew Bastian would be returning in a few hours, and I knew he'd ask me what I'd been up to and where I'd just come from. I could tell him I'd been with Roland, and then watch him go through some of the agony I'd been going through.

"Well, Roland and I had our drinks, and we went back to his place, and it was obvious where things were headed. Before our clothes came off, I got a text from Bastian that said he needed one more day in New York and would return tomorrow. That upset me, not just because it threw off my plan of coming home late and having him ask me where I'd been, but because he should have been in the air by then. If he needed extra time in New York, why did he wait until after his plane had left to tell me he wasn't coming? In my mind, it just confirmed he was hiding something. He had a new lover, and it was going so well he had missed his plane and couldn't come home."

She drank the last drops of liquor from her glass and swished the ice around.

"Roland could see I was upset. He lit a joint and asked what was wrong. I told him I was so angry with my husband, I wanted to kill him. I didn't notice Roland was fiddling with his phone."

"His phone?" I asked.

"Yes. He was holding it in his lap, and he asked me about killing Bastian. Why did I want to kill him, he asked. Because I walked into the wrong marriage, I said, and I did it with my eyes wide open. Because Bastian was always breaking my heart. Because he had introduced me to a life I couldn't leave—I meant the money and the comfort, not the swinging and the sex. Because he made it so miserable for me to be where I had wanted my whole life to be.

"How would you kill him, Roland asked.

"Oh, I don't know, I said. He drinks a lot and he drives too fast. All it would take is a simple accident.

"I said all that in jest. I mean, I was angry, and we had been drinking and smoking pot, and we went off on this fantasy about killing Bastian, and Roland recorded the whole thing on his phone."

"Did you sleep with him?" I asked.

"Yes. I was upset."

She set her glass on the coffee table and poured another shot of whiskey.

"You want some?"

"Sure." I set my glass down and she filled it.

As she screwed the top back on the bottle, she said, "The problem with men is they think everything is about them. If the sex is intense, a man thinks it's all his doing. He thinks it's because he's the best lover in the world. He never stops to think that we bring our own emotional burdens to unload, that sometimes the fire they feel in us was burning for years before they came along."

She paused for a moment, and I took a sip of my whiskey. I was less angry with her now than I had been when I came in. I was actually starting to pity her. I couldn't say she was completely blameless in the mess she'd been describing, but I couldn't judge her either. I had done worse things with worse motives.

Her intelligence and articulateness moved me, as did her willingness to admit that she had acted out of jealousy and spite. Most people would try to cover up that part. They'd keep pouring the blame on someone else to make themselves look like the victim.

"I didn't think I'd see Roland again," she said. "But then he started calling. I don't know how he got my number because I never gave it to him. I told him not to call, and he started showing up everywhere I went. At the grocery store, the coffee shop, at the bar, even on the corner by our house. It was too much for coincidence. He was stalking me. And it struck me then that he'd been stalking me before. That's why I had kept seeing him around town. Our run-in at Washington Square wasn't pure chance. He had been putting himself in position for it to happen."

She paused for a moment and stared in thought at the coffee table. Then she said slowly, "I had a feeling..."

I waited for her to continue, but she just kept thinking until I prodded her. "You had a feeling about what?"

"Well," she said, looking up at me. "Sex with him was intense. Very intense."

I understood that. I'd been with her enough times to know what she was like.

"And I think some people aren't used to connecting on that level. Some people are lonely, and when they have an experience like that, it affects them deeply. I had that feeling about him. That he'd been a loner, and I'd pierced his shell. I hit on some depth of feeling in him that no one else had gotten to, and it shook him. And then..."

She said he went on calling her, following her, and pleading with her on the few occasions when she actually confronted him. She'd tell him to go away, and he would remind her she wasn't happy in her marriage. They could run off together, he said. They could be happy.

She told him she'd get a restraining order if he didn't leave her alone, and in response to that, he showed her the video he had recorded of her talking about killing Bastian.

"I told him that was just drunk talk," Marilyn said. "Stoned talk. It doesn't mean anything to anyone."

"It means more paired with this," he said. Then he showed her a video of them having sex.

"I was shocked," she told me. "Because it meant he had a camera set up somewhere in his bedroom to record everything we had done. I remember looking at him and thinking, What kind of pervert is this? And he just stared right back at me with this look like, Well what did you think you were getting into? And there was a hardness in his eyes I hadn't seen before. It was like the mask of his charm slipped away all at once. There was something really wrong with the man."

I knew exactly what she was talking about. I had seen that hardness the first time I'd met him, and it told me right away something wasn't right.

"It finally dawned on me. That's why Bastian didn't like him. He was the kind who'd pour on the charm for a woman but wouldn't bother for a man. A man could see right up front who he was."

Roland continued to stalk and harass her.

"In subtle, disturbing ways," she said. "Like I'd be out shopping, and when I got back to my car, all the bags I'd left on the back seat would be dumped out on the floor. And Roland would be sitting on a bench across the street, smiling quietly to himself. He wanted to get under my skin, and he did, to the point where I just didn't want to be in the city anymore. I wanted to leave.

"Bastian had been building his dream house up here, a place I had no intention of ever going because I always thought of Napa Valley as a place for middle-aged winos to go soft. But when the house was finished, I said, Let's go. Let's get out of here. I don't ever want to come back to this city."

Roland showed up a few months later with a proposition. Give me ten thousand dollars and I'll leave you alone forever. Marilyn gave him the money and didn't see him again until a few weeks ago, when he wanted more money.

"I told him no, and he said, Well then, I'm going to kill Bastian."

"What?" I said.

"That's what he told me. He said, I've been watching you, more than you know. Everyone in town knows what kind of marriage you have, and everyone knows you're too weak to leave. You're the kind of coward who would kill your husband before you'd leave him, because all you ever wanted was his money. So tell me what happens if Bastian dies in a suspicious car accident and then I release those videos I showed you?"

Marilyn took a deep shuddering breath and said, "I could see in his eyes that he had thought it all through. I mean, thought through actually killing my husband. My blood ran cold. Then he laughed and slapped me on the shoulder and said, Hey, just kidding, Marilyn. But I do need some money. How about another ten thousand?"

She shook her head. "I didn't know what to do. I had naively taken ten thousand in cash from the bank last time he'd asked, and when you take out that much at once, they fill out a form that goes to the IRS. I remember standing there in front of the teller thinking, Should I change it to nine thousand and get the rest tomorrow? Then I told myself, No. That would look suspicious. You see, I was already thinking like a guilty person. I don't know why."

She took a deep breath and let it out, then sipped her drink and put it back down on the table.

"The earrings you saw me give to Roland were the compromise. They were worth more than ten thousand. The deal was, I give him the earrings, he gets them appraised, and if they're worth ten thousand, he gives me the videos.

"Well, I gave him the earrings, and I immediately felt stupid. I said to myself, What difference does it make if he gives you the videos? He could have a thousand copies. And who says he'll go away? He's obsessed. He'll come back and blackmail me again. I need to go to the police. I need to get out of this. But part of me was still scared about that video. Maybe because there was a grain of truth to it. Maybe because I know Lou Eisenfall so well. He's always ready to believe the worst about anyone. And what if Bastian saw the video? Would he divorce me? If he did, how would that video look in court? He could push me out on the street with nothing."

She stared toward the patio doors and the pool out back and drifted into thought.

"And then..." she said slowly. "Then..." She turned and looked at me. "Bastian died in an accident, just as I had described in the video. Only he had some help. Someone hit him first and made him crash, and I swear to God I would not put it past Roland to do something like that.

"You saw what state I was in after it happened. Do you know what was going through my mind? I could have stopped that. If I had reported Roland when I had the chance, if I had gone to the police and just told them he was blackmailing me, this wouldn't have happened. If I hadn't been such a coward, my husband would still be alive. He wasn't the best person in the world, but he certainly didn't deserve to be murdered.

"And look at the position I'm in now. My husband is dead, and Roland the blackmailer has a video of me describing the event before it happened."

She crossed her arms and bit her lip.

"He was supposed to meet me at the overlook today with the videos."

Her eyes began to tear up as she smoothed her skirt again. "But I don't know where he is," she said with a shaky voice. "I don't know what he'll do next. I just don't know." She looked at me desperately. "You saw the way Lou spoke to me the other day. You heard the things he said. If Roland shows him the video... John, I'm terrified."

I got up from the couch I'd been sitting on and took a seat beside her. As she leaned into me and rested her head on my shoulder, I could feel her shaking.

I put my arm around her and said, "Don't worry about Roland."

"Jesus, John, how can you say that? Put yourself in my shoes."

"He won't bother you again."

"That's what you think," she sulked.

"That's what I know. His phone is gone too. So there are no videos anymore."

"John?" She turned and stared at me wide-eyed. "What are you talking about?"

I told her.

<h1 style="text-align:center">38</h1>

Marilyn and I barely left the house for the next three days. We sat around the pool, we drank, watched movies, and ordered in food. Marilyn was drunk before dinner each night, and I kept having the same nightmare.

In the dream, I sat on the wall by the overlook. John Manis came up from behind and surprised me with a friendly hello. I turned and shot him. He looked at the wound in his chest and said, "Why'd you do that, Tom?"

I shot him again and then dragged him down the hill.

As I dug his grave, he said, "I don't understand why you're doing this to me. I'm not even dead."

I shot him four more times and buried him.

He kept coming up out of the ground, like a tireless beetle digging its way out of a mound of sand.

"Tom, why are you treating me like this? What did I do wrong?"

Each night, I woke in a sweat and couldn't go back to sleep.

By the evening of the third day, as Marilyn and I sat on the couch in the living room, I was dead tired and on edge.

"You want a drink?" Marilyn asked.

"No thanks."

"I think you could use one."

She curled up and rested her head on my chest. "Turn on the TV."

"The remote's all the way over there," I said. It was on the coffee table, four feet away.

"Mmm." Marilyn closed her eyes. "You have a fast heartbeat," she said with a yawn. "A very fast heartbeat. Are you..." She rubbed her hand over my crotch.

"No," I said.

"Oh."

I stared out toward the pool, wondering when they'd find Roland. I even thought a few times about going up the mountain and burying him. Manis, at least, was under the ground. No one was going to stumble across his remains.

Poor Manis.

Oh, God. Poor John Manis!

"Tell me again how you killed him," Marilyn said.

I killed him. He didn't deserve it, but I killed him.

Marilyn lifted her head. "Jeez, John, your heart is going to pound right out of your chest."

"It was an accident!" I said.

"No it wasn't. You said you shot him."

"No, it was an accident! I didn't mean it. I swear to God!"

"You don't have to feel bad about it." She cupped her hands around my face. "He was going to kill you. You had every right to do what you did."

"He never did me wrong. Not once!"

"Stop yelling! What's the matter with you?"

"I have to get out of here." I pushed her away and leapt up.

"Where are you going?"

"I don't know. To town."

I was out the door in seconds.

As I started the Vette, she called from the front steps, "Johnny, be careful!"

39

I parked the Corvette in front of the apartment and got my mail from the box—bills for utilities and auto insurance. A new credit card with a five-thousand-dollar limit. I dropped the mail on the kitchen counter and picked up my appointment book as the old fridge rattled to life.

I scanned over the entries for the past few weeks, noting all the thirty-minute blocks I had penciled in and left undone. I had not exercised. I had missed a dozen apartment cleanings and four car washes. I had skipped evening study hours when I should have been learning about computer viruses and smart TV remotes. I had not shopped or cooked. The whole calendar was riddled with lies.

After I erased the contents of all those blocks and wrote in what I had actually been doing, my calendar looked like the notebook of an infatuated schoolboy compulsively scrawling out the name of his beloved.

Marilyn.
Marilyn.
Marilyn.
Marilyn.
Marilyn.
Marilyn.
Marilyn.

I debated whether or not I should write in Roland's murder, but there was a problem. I couldn't remember exactly what time I'd killed him. I knew it happened on the day of Bastian's funeral, and it was probably around lunch time. I had lunch penciled in for a solid hour that day, but I didn't eat it. No wonder I'd felt so out of sorts. I put a star next to the next seven lunch entries on the calendar, so I wouldn't forget. Hopefully no one else would get killed.

When the compressor in the fridge cut off, the apartment was deathly quiet. I had to get out.

So I walked down the street to The Bohemian Sage. Because maybe Marilyn was right. Maybe I did need a drink.

<h1 style="text-align:center">40</h1>

I walked into The Sage, and who did my eyes fix on? Jennifer, the blonde-haired woman with the sweet round face. The one who almost ran me over and then wouldn't let me into her house. The guy sitting with her turned his giant bald head to look at me. I assumed that was her husband, Edgar. He must be intelligent, I thought. With a head like that, he must be full of ideas. I waved hello and she stiffened.

I went to the bar and ordered a beer and a burger. The beer came first, and as soon as I got the glass to my lips, Lou Eisenfall walked up. He was out of uniform, wearing an ill-fitting brown suit.

"Have a seat, Lou."

"Did Marilyn turn in that insurance policy yet?"

"I don't know. We haven't talked about it." I drank two long sips of beer.

"You've been over there three days and you haven't talked about it?"

"How do you know I've been there three days?"

"How do I know anything?" Lou asked.

"You're a busybody, Lou. You go poking around in other people's business."

"You know the coroner still hasn't ruled on the manner of death," Lou said. "The cause is blunt force trauma from the impact, but the manner could be accident or it could be homicide."

"What's that have to do with me?" I sipped my beer and looked away from him, toward the liquor bottles behind the bar.

"It's unusual for a case to go this long without a ruling," Lou said. "You know what that tells me?"

"What, Lou?"

"It tells me there's some conflict going on. Like the coroner wants to rule this an accident but the insurance company wants it ruled a homicide. Because a homicide will lead to an investigation that might save them ten million dollars. You know beneficiaries don't get paid if they murder the policy holder."

"I don't know why you're telling me this, Lou." I drank half the beer.

"It's also unusual for a beneficiary to hold on to the policy for so long after the death. It's almost like she's waiting to see how the coroner rules before she tries to cash in."

"Sounds like a lot of weird stuff is going on in your world."

"Dammit, John. This is serious. What the hell's wrong with you?"

"You're the one who's all worked up." I said. "Not me." I drained off the rest of the beer and waved to the bartender for another.

Lou looked at me closely, the way he'd done the first time we'd met. I must have had dark circles beneath my eyes from all the nightmares.

"You having trouble sleeping?" he asked.

"No."

"You taking any drugs?"

"You mean drugs? Or meds?"

His eyes narrowed. "Something's not right with you, John Manis. I've known it since the minute we met. You practically knocked me down, remember? And every time I've seen you since, you've looked nervous, out of sorts. You ever been hospitalized?"

"Huh?"

"You know what I'm talking about. You have a history of mental illness?"

"No, Lou. Jeez, what a thing to say." The bartender slid me a new draft, and I took a long sip while Lou watched me closely.

"Anyone in your family?"

"You leave my mother out of this."

"OK, John." He nodded slowly. "I want you to pass something along to Marilyn. I want you to tell her that no matter what the coroner rules, the insurance company will investigate the minute she hands in that policy. They won't let go of ten million dollars without a fight. They have a lot of resources, their investigators are tenacious, and they aren't bound by the same rules as law enforcement. If you think talking to me is uncomfortable, wait till you have them up your ass."

"Why don't you tell her that, Lou?"

I saw him smile for the first time. "Oh, I want you to tell her. It'll have more impact if she hears it from you. Fear and distrust are cancers in the love nest. They eat away at you."

"Is that all you have to say?"

"That's all."

"Then leave me alone."

He turned and walked away.

When my burger came a few minutes later, I saw him talking to Jennifer by the restrooms. They stood close, as if exchanging confidential information. She looked at me twice and quickly looked away.

41

I had four more beers at The Sage, then I went home and ate six Benadryl and slept straight through till the next afternoon. No dreams. Just a black, timeless sleep, like death.

When I returned to Marilyn's around five that day, I found her in a white bikini on a canvas lounge chair beneath the poolside umbrella. She was sipping a piña colada and casually turning the pages of a fashion magazine.

"Hello, Johnny," she said without looking up. "It's hot out here, isn't it?"

I sat in the chair beside her, and before I could answer, she said, "Did you bring a bathing suit?"

"No."

"Well you can swim in your underwear then. Or in the buff. You're not shy, are you?"

There was a strange coolness in her voice. Maybe after a day apart, she had finally detached and wasn't ready yet to return to the smothering mutual dependence of the days before. I wasn't ready to go back there either, and it was actually nice to see her so indifferent. It made me feel like I'd have to work to win her back.

"Has Lou been questioning you?" I asked.

"Why?"

"He seems to think you killed your husband."

"He thinks *you* killed Bastian," Marilyn said without looking up from her magazine.

"What makes you say that?"

"He told me so."

"When?"

"When he interviewed me this morning."

177

"Wait," I said. "Did he do a formal interview? Like, video recorded and all that?"

"Yes. At the police station."

"He made you go down there? Like a criminal?"

"No," she said as she set her drink on the table beneath the umbrella. "He wanted to interview me here, and I told him I didn't want him in my house. So I talked to him at the station."

"Did he accuse you of killing Bastian?"

"No," she said as she returned her attention to the magazine, "but he told me you were present at the crash."

"What?" I asked incredulously.

"That's what he said. How come you never told me you were there?"

"I wasn't," I lied. "Did you believe Lou when he said that?"

"No."

I tried to picture Lou and Marilyn in that little room with the video camera and the window that looked out on the mountain. Would Lou have said that on camera? That I was present at the scene of the crash? And how would Marilyn have reacted when she heard that? I was full of questions, but the one that came out of my mouth was, "Was your lawyer with you?"

"No," Marilyn said carelessly.

"Why not? I thought rich people always had their lawyers present when they talked to cops."

Marilyn laughed. "Rich people? Is that who I am to you?" She put the magazine down in her lap and said, "I didn't bring a lawyer because I didn't have anything to hide. Bringing a lawyer would make me look guilty. You know how Lou thinks."

Then she turned to me and said, "So where were you the night of the accident?"

"Coming back from The Lemonade Lady's house. Remember? I left here at five thirty."

"Yes, but Lou said you were on the road at the time of the crash, which was very late. What were you doing with The Lemonade Lady that took so long?"

"Seducing her granddaughter," I said. "I also had a flat."

"But, wait." She sat upright now and looked at me. "You *were* on the road at the time of the accident?"

"I was on that road. It's a long road."

She studied my face in a way that made me uncomfortable. "You're evading me. How come you never told me before that you were out there that night?"

"Oh my God! Are you accusing me of killing your husband?"

Still watching me closely, she said in a calm, measured tone, "I didn't say that. And no, I don't think you killed him. But it's funny that your mind jumped right to that. That's how a guilty person thinks. You know, I've had this sense ever since I met you that you're hiding something, and to be honest, I don't care. If you have secrets, you can keep them. I have my secrets too. Who wants to know everything about their lovers anyway? It kills the mystery."

She stood and carried her empty glass back to the house. "I'll have Esme mix you one," she said as she went inside.

I took off my shoes and socks and rolled my pants up to my knees. I sat on the edge of the pool with my feet in the water, remembering that Lou had wanted me to talk to Marilyn about the insurance policy.

But why should I tell Marilyn what he said? He was just trying to drive us apart. He said himself he wanted to sow distrust, to plant a cancer in the love nest.

For a moment, I wished I had Roland's gun back, so I could shoot Lou Eisenfall.

Then John Manis said, "Look at yourself, Tom. What kind of person thinks thoughts like that? Are you going mad?"

"I don't know," I said aloud. "Maybe I am."

"What's that?" Marilyn asked. I turned just in time to see her holding out a fresh piña colada. "Did you say something?"

"No," I said. "Just mumbling."

But I couldn't shake the image of Lou, and I couldn't stop the festering doubts he had planted in my mind. How had

Marilyn slid so easily into a relationship with me? Manis shot back, "How did *you* slide into it?"

And how can she be so at ease after losing her husband, I wondered. I told myself, She's not at ease. She drinks in the middle of the day. She's clingy. She's wild in bed, like a person who's not fully in possession of herself. Like someone who's suffered a great shock and is trying to distract herself from the pit of grief she's afraid of falling into. Like Johnny Manic at the tables in Vegas.

"What in the world is going through your mind?" Marilyn asked. She watched with curious fascination as she waited for me to answer.

"Oh, secrets," I said. "Let's all keep our secrets."

"But I want to know that one. I want to know what made that look cross your face."

"What look?"

"I can't describe it," she said. "But tell me."

I didn't want to tell her. My doubts were private, and I would resolve them on my own. To even suggest to her that I might believe an ounce of Lou's innuendo would have been a betrayal. It would have wounded her, and she was a person I could never bring myself to hurt.

"Come on," she said playfully. "I'm waiting." She smiled and sipped her drink.

My mind raced backward through a number of scenes: her at the bar with Bastian the night we first talked, her in the grocery store on my first day in town, Roland spitting sunflower seeds at the overlook. They were random thoughts that flitted away before I could catch them. Then my brain settled on the image of that curious word etched in platinum and I said casually, "What did the inscription on Bastian's bracelet mean?"

A look of shock came over her face, followed immediately by a hot, murderous look, which she quickly covered over with a smile. "How... How do you know there was an inscription?" she stammered.

"I saw it," I said, pumping the straw up and down in my drink. "In the bar, the night we met."

She shook her head, her wide, unblinking eyes fixed on mine. "No you didn't," she said coldly. "The inscription was faint, and the light in there was too dim. Besides, it was on the inside of the bracelet."

She was right. The etching was faint. I had to shine the flashlight from my phone on it before I could read it.

"Oh," I said. "Well the bracelet flipped over when he was talking to me. I thought I saw an inscription."

"Oh," she said softly. And then in a whisper, "Maybe you did. I never knew what it meant."

She seemed to drift away then. She detached from me, and we drank our piña coladas and stared at the rippling pool in silence.

A few minutes later, she stood and said, "We've been spending a lot of time together, and I think we need a break."

"I was thinking the same thing," I said. "I have a couple of jobs to catch up on, so I'll be busy tomorrow." That was a lie. I had nowhere to go and nothing to do but sit around and think of her.

"OK," she said. "Sorry I'm weird. I have a lot on my mind these days. I can't even process everything that's happened."

"You don't have to explain."

She gave me a kiss goodbye and walked into the house.

42

I spent half the night thinking about Marilyn's reaction to the bracelet, Marilyn and I getting on each other's nerves, Marilyn's insurance policy, the suspicions Lou had been stoking, and Marilyn all alone in the great big house that she was about to lose.

She had said her worst fear was that her world would be pulled out from under her, and she must have known it was happening. Lou had told her that Bastian had piled up debts against his businesses and properties. She knew the IRS was after him for back taxes and penalties. The only thing she didn't know yet was that Bastian hadn't been paying the mortgage on the house here or on the house in San Francisco.

Knowing she'd have to sell off his businesses to get out of debt was one thing. Having her house taken away was another. The first was an annoyance. The second, to a woman like Marilyn, would be the ultimate outrage.

It was Esme who called me that afternoon, asking in Spanish, "Please señor. Ms. Marilyn needs someone to calm her." I could hear Marilyn yelling angrily in the background. Male voices were trying to reason with her, to no avail.

On the six-mile drive to her house, Manis taunted me in a cool, smug voice. "It's easier to get wrapped up in someone else's problems than to deal with your own."

"They're *our* problems now," I said.

"She's more exciting than roulette, isn't she?"

"Shut up, John."

When I arrived, two men in suits were leaving. The green Jaguar parked beside Marilyn's Mercedes was the same one I'd seen the day Marilyn and Lou and the lawyer and insurance agent were discussing the insurance policy. In the dining room, I found its owner, Marilyn's lawyer, calmly explaining the situation to her while she stood red-faced, with her arms folded tightly across her chest like a petulant child who had just had a tantrum.

"They're not going to foreclose on a property like this," the lawyer said. "With the amount Bastian owes on this place, the last thing they want is a short sale."

"Why the hell didn't he pay the goddamn mortgage? Did he forget?" She shot me an angry look. "For six months?"

"I don't know what Bastian was up to," the lawyer said. "We're still figuring that out. But I don't want you taking your anger out on the appraisers. That's not productive. They're here to help you."

The lawyer explained he had been working with the bank to arrange the payments that would prevent foreclosure. The appraisers were looking at the art work, the silver, the furniture, the jewelry—everything that could be sold at auction to raise enough cash for monthly payments while the house sat on the market waiting for a buyer. The plan was to hold out as long as possible for a fair price, instead of dumping the place and losing millions.

From a financial perspective, it made sense. From Marilyn's perspective, it was insulting and terrifying. She would have to watch strange men come into her home and remove all her beautiful possessions, one by one, until at last, she was left all alone in an empty house. Then they'd remove her too, and she wouldn't have a penny to her name, because all the money from the home would go to pay Bastian's debts and back taxes. I couldn't imagine a more dire and horrifying prospect for her.

She listened for several minutes—arms crossed, frowning, and with increasing impatience—as the lawyer explained all this in a calm, rational tone.

"I know what's happening," she exploded. "I'm not a child, so don't treat me like one."

"You know I respect you, Marilyn," said the lawyer. "I'm telling you what you already know because you need to be reminded that there is a plan here. That there are rational players involved, and we are looking out for your interests."

"This is the best you can do?" she demanded. "Take apart my house and leave me with nothing?"

"It could be worse," the lawyer said. "You could end up with a mountain of debt. That's what we're trying to avoid."

"It couldn't be worse," she insisted. "It couldn't possibly be worse! Get out, will you? Leave me alone."

She turned and poured herself a glass of bourbon from the sideboard.

The lawyer said to me, in a low voice, "May I speak with you outside?"

We went out on the front step and talked by the open door while Marilyn stomped up the stairs.

"Look," he said, "Bastian was a friend of mine for many years. He wasn't the best husband, but he was a good friend. I don't know what he was doing with his money before he died, but he left Marilyn in a bad situation. She's a passionate person, as I'm sure you know. I can't say I approve of your relationship with her, or even that I like you. But I do care about her, and you're the one person who might be able to soothe her now. Keep an eye on her, will you?"

We could hear her upstairs cursing and stamping around the bedroom. It sounded like she was tearing the place apart.

"Let her indulge her anger," he said. "If you tell her she can't do something, she'll just get angrier."

"I know all about that."

"But don't let her do anything she'll regret."

"Was all that stuff true that Lou said? Did Bastian really borrow ten million against his businesses?"

I knew the answer, of course, but I wanted to know what the lawyer knew. He must have been digging into Bastian's finances since the death, and he probably had access to more material than I had.

"He borrowed heavily. He leveraged everything."

"Why?" I asked.

"We don't know. But it looks like he moved all the money into a cryptocurrency called Ethereum. I don't know why he would do that, unless he was planning on running away or something. The only advantage of a cryptocurrency is that it lets you keep your money beyond the reach of governments and banks. And you can spend it anonymously."

"So how do you get it back?"

"If we do manage to get it, it'll go right back to the banks he borrowed from. If we can't get it back, we'll sell off the properties and businesses to cover the debts. I haven't gone over all the plans with Marilyn yet. She's not in a state to hear it."

We heard something smash upstairs and Marilyn grunted and cursed.

The lawyer waved his hand toward the source of the noise and said softly, "This is my worst-case scenario right here. A situation like this with a client like her. If I do everything in my power, the best possible outcome is she's left with nothing, and she'll hate me for that forever."

We chatted for a few minutes more and before we parted, I slipped in my final question.

"How'd you find out about Ethereum? This cryptocurrency account?"

"We have his laptop," the lawyer said. "His browser history showed a number of visits to a site that manages Ethereum accounts."

The browser history! Why hadn't I thought to look there?

If I had known that, maybe I could have gotten the money back. Maybe I could have spared Marilyn all this grief.

And then she would love me.

43

When the lawyer left, I went up to the bedroom and found Marilyn standing beside the dresser, running her fingers through her long black hair in a daze. She had pulled all the clothes from the closet and strewn them across the floor. The drawers from the nightstands had been pulled out and overturned, and one of the bedside lamps had been smashed against the wall, leaving a gouge in the drywall and a pile of broken glass.

"Are you done?" I asked.

"I'm done *for*," she said.

"What the hell were you doing?"

"Counting up my life's worth. How much do you think the appraisers will get for this at auction?" She pointed toward the heaps of clothing on the floor.

"I think you need to take some time and collect yourself."

"I think you need to go fuck yourself."

"I don't like that tone," I said.

"Then go find some other whore to screw." The hollows beneath her eyes were dark with exhaustion, but I could see her anger building like a towering thundercloud threatening to explode.

"You know, if a guy talked to me like that, I'd hit him."

"Then hit me!" She gave me a shove. "Hit me, you pussy. Put me in my place!"

She took a wild swing at me and missed. She put so much force into it, she spun herself around.

I was behind her now. I wrapped my arms around her, pinning her arms to her sides, and I squeezed as hard as I could, lifting her off the ground. She thrashed and kicked for a while, and if I hadn't been so charged with anger, I wouldn't have been able to hold on to her.

I squeezed until her thrashing became weak and desperate, the product of fear instead of rage.

"Let go of me," she gasped. "Let go! John, you're hurting me!"

I kept squeezing until I heard real panic in her voice. "John, stop! I can't breathe."

Finally, I let her go, and the second her feet touched the floor, she spun around and slapped me as hard as I've ever been hit. It left a bright, stinging red mark across my cheek.

Then she smiled and said, "How does that feel, Johnny?"

She walked back to the dresser and poured a glass of bourbon. I watched her sip from it, thinking, This woman is crazy. She's either been pushed past her breaking point, or she's just plain crazy.

She walked back to me and, taking the glass from her lips, she pushed it to mine and said with a smile, "Bottoms up!" She dumped the contents of the glass—about an ounce—into my mouth, and I managed to get it down without choking.

"I know you think I'm crazy," she said. "But I like that you take it all in stride."

"I am not taking this in stride," I said.

"You're doing a great job." She smiled and hugged me and said into my ear, "I mean truly. No one else would put up with me, so thank God for you."

"I think you need to get out of here for a while. Get a change of scene. You have too much on your mind."

"I think you're right," she said.

"You want to take a trip?"

Her face lit up, and she said, "You know what I want to do?"

"What?"

"Let's sell some of Bastian's stuff and go on a honeymoon."

"What are you talking about?"

"The banks are going to dismantle this place and throw me out. If I'm going to lose it all anyway, why not have some fun? Like cooking one last feast over the embers of a ruined life."

"I think you're being a little dramatic. Your life isn't over."

"It might as well be." She shrugged as she poured another shot of bourbon. "But I like the idea of getting out of here for a few days. You're right. It'll do me some good."

She took a sip and held the glass toward me with a look that asked if I'd like some. I took it.

"And," she said, "I like the idea of making Bastian pay for our vacation."

She looked toward the closet and said, "We can sell some of his cuff links, or one of those stupid watches he was so proud of. Just one of those could pay for a first-class vacation."

"You can't just sell those," I said.

Marilyn looked at me for what felt like a long moment. "Why not?"

"Those things cost ten, twenty, thirty thousand dollars apiece. There aren't a lot of buyers in that price range."

"Just take it to a jewelry store," she said. "Sell it to them."

"They'll put it on consignment, and it'll sell in three months. Or six. Or never."

"Well that does me no good," she said as she sipped from the glass. "I want to go now."

"If you want to sell it today, you have to hock it, and you don't want to do that."

"Why not?"

"Because you'll get ripped off. They'll give you ten percent of the value, at best."

"Then let's add insult to injury," she said. "We'll sell one of Bastian's beloved watches at a ninety-percent discount to someone who doesn't deserve it."

"Why do you want to insult the man when he's already dead?"

"Why did he want to insult me by dying in debt?" she asked. Then she walked into the closet and opened one of the cherrywood drawers. She draped a platinum watch with a royal blue face over her wrist and said, "What about this one? How much do you think we could get for it? Enough for a nice hotel and some fancy dinners?"

"You don't want to do that, Marilyn."

"Don't tell me what I want to do," she said as she admired the watch. "This is actually a pretty piece."

"Lou thinks you killed your husband. If you go hocking Bastian's watches, it's not going to look good."

"Screw Lou," she said. "He can think whatever he wants."

"There are no pawnshops in town anyway."

"So, we'll go somewhere else." She looked at me as if I was supposed to tell her where. "Come with me, will you?"

The whole stupid idea was beginning to annoy me. I had already driven to San Francisco once with Bastian's bracelet in my pocket and my heart in my throat. And then I'd gone a second time with the watch Bastian was wearing when he died, and the gun I'd used to kill Roland. I was even more distraught that time. The whole stretch of road from the south end of town to the city was colored with fear.

The logical thing to do was to talk her out of this, and if I couldn't do that, I could tell her I wasn't going to participate. But her anger could flare up again at any moment, and I could see her anxiety about money ran miles deep, all the way back to the fears her mother had stoked in her in childhood. Those fears had come true once, when she returned from school to find her family evicted, and they were coming true again. Reasoning with her at that moment was pointless.

I was going to tell her that if she wanted to hock the watch, she'd have to do it on her own. But when it came right down to it, I just couldn't do that. I was the last person standing by her side in all this, and it felt cruel to abandon her.

"We're not selling that anywhere near here," I said.

"Then where?" Marilyn asked. "Where would you sell something like this?"

"In the city," I said. "Where there are millions of people and no one cares enough to ask questions."

"You know a place?"

"I'm sure we could find one."

"Then let's go to the city."

And with that, the anger and darkness began to lift from her troubled eyes.

I had no interest in hocking Bastian's watch, or doing anything to raise more suspicion from Lou. But on the other hand, Marilyn was calm. The idea of a trip to the city pleased her. And I thought of what the lawyer had said. Indulge her, but don't let her do anything stupid.

Hocking just one watch, among all her possessions, seemed like a fair indulgence.

"Ok," I said. "Let's go to the city."

Marilyn smiled. "Yes!"

She put the watch on her wrist, where it hung loosely while she pulled on a pair of flats. I told myself I'd talk her out of selling the watch during the long drive south, and we'd spend a day or two enjoying San Francisco.

As we left the room, I noticed that the only things she hadn't knocked to the floor during her rage were the items on the top of the dresser: the bourbon bottle, the glass, and the sealed envelope, still unstamped and unaddressed.

44

We pulled onto the main road in Marilyn's Mercedes a few minutes later. I was driving, because I had had only an ounce and a half of alcohol, while she had quite a bit more. I also didn't trust her behind the wheel when she was emotionally unstable.

Once we were on the road, she seemed surprisingly happy, humming along to the radio as we made our way south toward town. I wanted to build on her good mood and give her more reason to hope.

"Your lawyer thinks he knows where Bastian put the money," I said.

"I know," said Marilyn blankly, as she turned to watch the scenery outside her window.

"It's just a question of whether they can get into the account and get the money back."

She didn't say anything, so I added, "I'm sure there's a way."

"I'm sure there is," she said absently.

Her lack of interest seemed odd to me. I told myself it was because she had spent her emotions in her afternoon rage and didn't have enough energy left to get worked up. But still, all her fears were centered on money, and recovering the ten million Bastian had stashed would go a long way toward making things right. So why was she so indifferent?

I was about to add, "That's got to take a load off your mind," when a siren shrieked behind me. I looked in the rearview and saw the flashing lights of a police cruiser.

"Lou Eisenfall," I said. I held my hand up in front of my face, then breathed into it and sniffed to see if my breath still smelled like alcohol. It didn't.

As I slowed and pulled to the right, the car went roaring past.

"Well, for once it's not me," I said with relief.

But I spoke too soon. As we approached town, we saw a line of emergency vehicles with their flashers on, crawling up the mountain toward the overlook.

They had found whatever was left of Roland.

I took a deep breath and let it out.

Then another, and another, and another.

"You OK?" Marilyn asked.

Inside my head, lounging at ease with his habitual smile, John Manis said, "Of course you're OK." And then I heard myself say aloud, "Of course I'm OK."

As we passed the south end of town, I turned to see her looking at me, wide-eyed, somber, and worried.

She rested her hand on my leg and we drove on in silence.

45

By the time we reached Union, Marilyn's worry had turned to impatience. She was shifting in her seat, scanning through the radio stations, turning the radio off in frustration and then back on a minute later, as if she had forgotten. Every few minutes, she'd sigh, like our trip was some formal procedure she had to endure. I was glad when we finally reached the city and could get out of the car.

When we parked by the pawnshop, I said, "You sure you want to do this?"

"I'm sure," she said.

"You're going to get ripped off."

She shrugged. "The owner of that watch is no longer around to wear it. So why should I care?"

"You should care because if you sell it properly, you can get ten times the price."

"Don't lecture me," she said. "I'm not going to wait six months for the money."

"All right," I said with a sigh as I opened the door. "Come on then."

"I'm not going," Marilyn said, looking at her fingernails.

"Come on. This'll take five minutes."

"You do it."

"All right then, you can sit out here by yourself."

She pulled the visor down and looked in the mirror as she ran her fingers through her hair. I got out and walked into the crappy no-questions-asked pawnshop where I had sold the bracelet.

The fat proprietor, whose greasy beard looked like it had been hocked by a down-and-out pirate two centuries ago, was slouched over the counter, flipping the pages of an old *Playboy* magazine.

"What can I do you for?" he asked without looking up.

"I want to sell a watch."

"A good watch?" He pried his eyes from the milky-white breasts of the suntanned model who had just pulled down her top. "Or a piece of sh—"

His eyes lit up when he saw the piece in my hand, and he blurted out, "Fifteen hundred. Cash money!"

"No way," I said. "This thing's worth way more than that."

We haggled for a while and finally settled on two thousand five hundred.

"You planning on coming back for this?" he asked.

"No," I said. "Keep it."

He slid it into his pocket.

When I returned to the car, Marilyn was in a better mood. I handed her the cash and she spread it in her hands like a Japanese fan. Then she put on a joking frown and said, "Why couldn't they give us crisp new bills?"

"Everything is secondhand down here."

"Let's go spend it," she said. "I'm hungry."

We ate at an Italian place in North Beach, then we drove up California Street and checked into the Ritz. Marilyn charged the meal and the hotel on her credit card.

"You didn't need that cash," I said.

She smiled. "But it helped my mood."

That was true. She was starting to act more like her old self, like the weight of her worries had been lifted.

Her spirits continued to brighten as we walked along the bay in the late afternoon. She was laughing, almost giddy, and her steps were light like a teenager's. When she saw an old three-masted sailing ship coasting across the bay, she pointed at it and said, "Look at that one, John. Have you ever seen one actually sailing before?"

And she loved the hotel. She loved the way the staff greeted her by name in the lobby. She loved being served in the restaurant by men in tuxedos, and she loved to undress in a bedroom that wasn't hers. She drank only two glasses of wine with dinner, and instead of going out after, she wanted to go back to the room. Her cheeks were red, her eyes were lively and alert, and she was playful.

I tell you, when Marilyn was on, no one came close to her. I put up with a few days of bitchiness, and then she repaid me in spades, in a way no other woman could match.

46

We had breakfast delivered to the room the next morning and sat at the table by the window watching the local news, which included a short segment on Roland. A reporter standing near the overlook described how two hikers had come across the remains. The skeleton had been picked clean by vultures, crows, and insects, and some of the bones had been carried away by raccoons and other animals. Police had no idea who the man was or how he died, but they thought the death was recent, and it was suspect, because the man had no clothing or other possessions.

I turned the TV off and tried to remember where I had shot him. Once in the chest. The bullet went in below his sternum. I remember seeing the wound when I stripped him down. It didn't come out through his back, so it's possible it left no mark upon the bones, and if only the bones remained the coroner may never know it was a murder.

But the bullet inside his body must be on the ground somewhere near the scene. And he had shot himself too during our struggle. The gun went off beneath his chin, shattering the left side of his jaw. If they found the jawbone, they could probably figure out the damage had been caused by a gunshot.

"A penny for your thoughts," Marilyn said.

"Oh, you don't want to know," I said.

"You look worried," she said. "You need some distraction. And you're in the right city. Have you ever been to the Legion of Honor?"

"No."

"Well then let's go."

We took a Lyft to the western edge of the city and spent the day looking at art and the incomparable views of the Marin Headlands and the vast Pacific. We had a long, late lunch at an outdoor cafe: Caesar salad, curried chicken, and white wine. Marilyn was smiling, her posture relaxed and easy, and when she did slip into thought, I could tell she was thinking of pleasant things.

"Have you ever had a massage?" she asked as we finished lunch.

"Are you going to give me one?"

"No, I mean a professional massage. From a spa."

"No," I said.

"Well I want one. Care to join?"

"Sure."

We spent the late afternoon in the spa, where I learned from the masseuse's hands that I was more tense than I had thought. Marilyn and I left relaxed and a little sleepy. Then we dropped six hundred dollars on dinner.

The second night in the hotel was just like the first. Passion. Bliss. Sleep.

The following morning, as we ate breakfast in the room, Marilyn said, "We should go back."

"I don't want to go back," I said. "I like it here."

She sipped her coffee and looked through the windows at the buildings across Pine Street. "It's expensive."

"So?"

"So I don't see you paying for anything."

I looked out at the city for a while, not wanting to look at her.

"Something wrong?" she asked.

"Why'd you have to spoil the mood?"

"It's just reality," she said as she laid her coffee cup on the saucer. "Everybody has to face it sometime."

"We don't really though."

"Yes, we do."

We checked out at noon and pushed through traffic for almost an hour before making it onto the open road. I was deliberately driving slowly because after our little honeymoon and a taste of the old high life, I was in no hurry to see my depressing apartment again. Marilyn didn't notice how the cars sped past us because she was busy looking at her phone.

She was quiet for so long, I finally asked, "What's so interesting on that screen you're staring at?"

She didn't respond, and when I turned to look at her a few seconds later, her back straightened and she laid the phone face down in her lap. "The coroner made his decision," she said. "Bastian's death is a homicide." Then she turned to look out her window.

For the next few seconds, neither of us said a word. But my pulse was creeping up, and my stomach was beginning to tighten. I pictured Lou coming after Marilyn. Lou connecting her to Roland and Roland to me.

"So what does that mean?" I asked.

"I don't know," she said.

"Does it..." I couldn't ask.

"Does it what?" she said, turning to face me. "Does it make me nervous? Is that what you were going to ask?" She waited for a second, and when I didn't respond, she said, "Boy, Lou really got to you, didn't he? Let me ask you something, John."

She touched my shoulder and said, "Look at me."

"I can't," I said. "I'm driving."

"You can look at me for just a second. Look at me!"

I turned and looked her in the eye.

"Do you trust me?"

She waited as I stared at her, then she repeated, "Do you?"

I told her I did.

"Then why do you ask me questions like that?"

"Lou got under my skin with all his questions and insinuations."

"Well you have to choose who you believe. He makes the same insinuations to me about you, but I've never doubted you for a second."

The rest of the ride was quiet, somber almost, with Marilyn sighing and scanning the radio stations for news about Roland.

The tension and unhappiness that had dissolved during our days in the city was gathering again as we returned to the pulsing center of all our troubles.

As soon as we arrived at her house, she went straight to the liquor tray, straight to the bourbon.

"It's early," I said.

She frowned and said, "I know." She put the bottle back on the tray without pouring anything. Then she tapped her fingers on the dining room table and thought.

"How long till dark?" she asked.

"Hours," I said.

"Damn."

"What's the matter?"

She stood quietly for a few seconds, thinking. Then she said slowly, thoughtfully, "Johnny, why don't you go home?"

Her coolness at that moment, the ease with which she pushed me away struck a nerve of insecurity deep inside me, of desperately wanting to be assured of her affection while fearing that it would never truly be mine.

"Marilyn, I love you." The words tumbled out impulsively, embarrassingly, like the awkward confession of a clumsy schoolboy.

"No you don't," she said matter-of-factly. "You're just lost, and I'm the only thing around."

"No, I think I do."

"Well you shouldn't." She turned and walked toward the stairs. "Now leave me alone. I have work to do."

As I pulled out of her driveway, I wondered what kind of work she could be talking about. She didn't have a job. She didn't do laundry or cook or clean the house. Esme took care of all that. And she didn't seem to have a single friend. I don't know why that didn't occur to me until then.

When I got to my apartment, Lou Eisenfall was parked out front. He didn't seem to care when I parked in front of him. He just sat there looking troubled.

"How you doing, Lou?"

"Not too good, John."

"You here to talk to me?"

"Not now." He seemed lost in thought. "You know they ruled Bastian's death a homicide?"

"Yeah, I heard."

He turned his eyes up toward me and said, "You know what that means?"

He waited a second, then he said, "It means I can start getting search warrants."

47

Nightmares woke me before midnight. Me shooting Manis up at the overlook and trying to bury him. I lay in bed till dawn, staring at the ceiling and listening to the voices. His and mine. Mine and his.

I went to the coffee shop when it opened at six thirty.

I sat at a table by the window and watched Marilyn's black Mercedes drive by.

Six forty-two. What is she doing up this early?

I texted her and got no response. An hour later, my call went to voicemail.

What did she mean she had work to do?

She didn't respond to my texts at eight or eight thirty or nine.

Why had she asked me to leave? Had I done something wrong?

"That's the part that hurts the most," Manis said. "Not knowing what you did to deserve it."

Go ahead, John. Rub it in.

"I have to catch you while you're listening," he said. "Otherwise you don't hear me."

At nine fifteen, I drove to her house and Esme answered the door.

"Where's Marilyn?" I asked in Spanish.

"She went to the city."

"You mean town?" I asked, pointing south toward town.

"No, señor. The city. San Francisco."

"But we just came from there yesterday."

Esme shrugged.

I drove back to town and went into the grocery—to get a sandwich, I told myself. But the way my stomach was churning, I knew I couldn't have eaten.

I went to the grocery because I thought somehow Marilyn would be there. I'd see her in the produce aisle, as I'd done my first day in town. Or I'd find her by the deli counter, or at the end of the cereal aisle. It didn't matter that her car wasn't in the lot outside.

None of the women in line at the checkout were Marilyn. And she wasn't getting coffee or a sandwich. She wasn't looking at apples or cherries. She wasn't buying meat or fish. I threaded my way through the interior aisles, past the canned vegetables, cereals in boxes, and other things she didn't eat.

There was no Marilyn. Only an empty town with an empty apartment where I couldn't sleep, and a grocery that had lost its soul. Lou had found Roland and I had killed Manis and the news wasn't saying anything about who knew what. Marilyn's ghost haunted the empty aisles of the store, and some damn kid was crying and crying and crying and no one was listening to him.

I followed the cries to the bakery, and there was a three-year-old boy standing in front of the cake display with his face pressed up against the glass. He was sobbing and leaving a trail of snot down the front of the case because all he wanted was a cake, but no one would listen to him except the woman behind the bakery counter with the red scrunched-up face who was at the end of her rope because she just wanted him to shut the hell up.

I grabbed the kid by the arm and turned him toward me and said, "Hey, kid, what's your name?"

And he said, "Mason."

"How old are you, Mason?"

"Three."

"Which one of those cakes do you want?"

He pointed to the chocolate one. The biggest one in the case, naturally.

I told the cake lady to box it up and give it to him, but as soon as she started folding the white box into shape, the mom came stomping over and said in this rude snippy tone, "Excuse me? What are you doing?"

It was Jennifer. The round-faced woman with the white Range Rover.

"I'm buying your kid a cake."

She swooped down and scooped him up and said, "No you're not," and she started walking away fast.

I followed her, and she walked even faster.

"Where are you going?" I asked.

She went past the register, out the door to the parking lot.

"You left your cart," I said.

She hit the button on her key fob, and the hazards flashed on the Range Rover and the door locks clicked. She opened the back door and stuck the kid in the booster seat, and then she whipped around and said, "Get away from me, you creep!"

"I was only trying to help."

She turned and started buckling the kid, and I said, "You know, a lot of problems in this world aren't solvable. Hunger and war and disease and Roland and John and Marilyn. But that was an easy one. The kid just wanted a cake, and he was crying, and the cake lady was getting annoyed. I thought I could do everyone a favor."

She slammed the door and I followed her as she ran around to the driver side and got in.

"It's not often you can solve so many problems just by buying a cake," I said.

She gunned it backward and almost rammed into Lou Eisenfall's cop car, which was just pulling into the lot. They both had to hit the brakes to avoid a collision.

I ran up to her door and yelled, "When you see a chance to make things better, you have to take it." I wouldn't have yelled if she had rolled down the window. I had to make sure she understood me through the glass.

"Because some things aren't forgivable," I shouted. "Some things can never be undone."

She got the car into drive, and as she pulled forward, she rolled down the window and shouted, "It's ten a.m.! Nobody eats chocolate cake at ten a.m.!"

"Really, lady? Is that what this is all about? Because by the way you reacted in there, I thought maybe it was me."

Lou Eisenfall pulled into the spot she had just left, and when he got out, he said, "What the hell was that all about?" He looked angry.

"I don't know," I said. "I tried to do her a favor but she didn't like it. What are you doing, Lou?"

He grabbed me by the arm and yanked me back toward the store.

"We're going to talk to the staff," he said, "and then I'll talk to Jennifer and get her side of it."

"Her son's name is Mason," I said.

Lou talked to the cake lady and the store manager, and an old woman who'd been by the bakery display when it happened. They gave him the story exactly as I just gave it to you.

I said, "Now, Lou, I know you weren't coming here to see me, because you couldn't have known I was going to be here. Unless you have some kind of telepathy. Do you, Lou? Are you a mind reader or a clairvoyant?"

He shook his head, looking tired and annoyed. "Shut up, John."

"Seriously though, why were you coming here?"

"To get a sandwich."

"What kind?"

He grabbed my arm and spun me around so we were face to face. His jaw and fist were clenched like he wanted to hit me.

"Goddammit, you fucking lunatic, I want you to get the hell out of this town."

"Why, Lou? I like it here."

"What the hell do you think you're doing with Marilyn?"

"I'm banging her, Lou. We're having a great time."

"Jesus, John! Watching you two is like watching a train wreck in slow motion. You're both crazy. Especially you."

I shrugged. "Everyone's entitled to their opinion."

"You know I'm watching you."

"Yeah, you told me."

"You know what the problem with the law is?"

"Oh, there are lots," I said. "Lots of problems."

"Well the one that's bothering me right now is that I can't do a goddamn thing about either one of you. It's damn near impossible to get a person involuntarily committed in this state. You practically have to wait for them to kill someone. And that's what I'm afraid of, John."

"That sounds pretty scary, Lou. You think I'll do it? You think I'll actually kill someone?"

His whole face got red, like he was going to blow his stack. But somehow he kept a lid on it.

"I'm going to tell you something, John, and I want you to listen."

"OK."

"If I ever have to respond to a call about you..."

He looked around to see if any customers were in earshot.

"Yeah?" I said.

He leaned in. "If I ever have to respond to a call about you..."

"You already said that part, Lou."

His voice was trembling and his breath smelled like coffee. "I'll shoot first and ask questions later. I don't care if you're pissing on a tree or playing your music too loud. You're the kind of problem that only gets worse, and I don't like problems. Do you get me?"

"Thanks for the tip, Lou."

His anger was starting to come down, but he was still tense when he said, "I'll give you another tip while I'm at it. Stay away from Marilyn Dupree."

"You already told me that, Lou. You've told me like three times."

"When I told you before, it was for her sake. This time, it's for yours. She's smarter than you, John."

"You think?"

"She is. And when she's done having her fun, she'll toss you aside."

I thought about that for a second. "Well, that's logical," I said. "What's the point of keeping someone around if they're no fun anymore?"

Lou watched me for a moment, and I could see he was trying to calm himself. I guess that's something you have to learn as a cop, because cops have to deal with a lot of criminals, and criminals are assholes.

He said in a nice even tone, "Get out of here, John. I don't want to look at you."

I stood there for a moment watching him.

"Lou?"

It took him a couple seconds to respond. "What?"

"You look troubled."

He let out a sigh and said softly, incredulously, "*I* look troubled? Get out of here, John."

I left there feeling sad. Lou Eisenfall was the face of law and order, the guy who kept the world in line, the guy who didn't get rattled by emotion. Only now he was upset. Bastian was murdered and Roland was murdered and he hadn't even learned about Manis yet. A madman was running around his nice quiet town. A madman wearing a suit that didn't belong to him was going into all the houses in town, playing Mr. Fixit, and who knew who he might kill next?

How'd you like to have Lou's job, I asked myself. What do you think it's like to be him right now?

I hated myself for ruining everything.

No wonder Marilyn ran away.

48

I don't remember how I frittered away the hours of the day.

I do remember that a heavy burger and a whole bottle of Burgundy and six Benadryl couldn't put me to sleep. I do remember how long and miserable the night was. I remember hearing on the news that the cops had a warrant to search Marilyn's house. And they were still trying to put together the pieces of Roland. His skull and jawbone were gone, carried off by animals, and that meant the cops hadn't seen the gunshot wound and didn't know yet that he'd been murdered.

But I had a feeling Lou knew. I had a feeling he sensed it.

His car was in the lot in front of the grocery store the next day. So was the white Range Rover, and a second police cruiser.

I went in to get coffee and a croissant. I don't remember what time it was, because it's hard to keep track of time when day and night run together and the voices are the same, hour after hour after hour. When you're gambling in Vegas and there are no clocks, when you're killing Roland or trying to find John Manis's body in the night-darkened sea, when you're in love with Marilyn and she runs away, you never know what time it is.

And so what if Lou and Jennifer and that big muscular cop are sitting together at a table by the checkout? So what if you catch them glancing at you now and then? I can sit at a table too. I can eat my croissant and drink my coffee and not even care what they're talking about. Even though I know they're talking about me. I know just like a dog knows when its owner is about to leave. It's an intuitive understanding. We are in a set piece. This is all staged, and it's about me. And if Jennifer wants to walk over here and say something, that's her business. She can do whatever she wants. Jennifer, the psychiatric nurse with the blonde hair and the round face, who doesn't like me.

"Hello, John. Do you mind if I sit?"

"Suit yourself," I said indifferently.

Lou and the other cop were watching. They weren't looking directly at us. They were pretending to talk and look at each other, but I could tell they were paying attention.

Jennifer said, "Did I upset you yesterday?"

I tried to look away from her, but she had a kind face. A kind and gentle and welcoming face.

"I'm sorry if I did," she said.

"Are you?"

"I'm sorry I called you a creep."

I looked over at Lou. He was watching now.

"But you do think I'm a creep," I said. "I can tell. You thought I was a creep when you almost ran me over, and you thought I was a creep when I came to your house. I waved to you in the restaurant and your whole body stiffened and you didn't wave back because you think I'm a creep."

She took a breath, like she was unsure what to say next, and she flattened her hand on the table and started rubbing the surface.

"John," she said softly. "That day I almost hit you on the road... Where were you? What were you thinking when you wandered out into the lane?"

My pulse began to rise. "I... I don't know what I was thinking."

Her gentle eyes fixed on mine, and again I had the sense, as I had had that first day, that she could see inside me.

"When you came to my house," she said, "you stood on my porch, and you whispered something."

She paused and watched. My chest tightened and my breathing became shallow. My back and armpits moistened with sweat. She *could* see inside me.

"Do you remember what it was?" she asked. "What you said?"

I shook my head no and my hands began to tremble. What did she see? What was she getting at? She was getting at something. I could feel it, and I had a scary sense of where she was going.

"You said, Shut up. Do you remember?"

Again, she paused and watched me. She knew me. This woman knew me. She was sending a searchlight into the darkest corners of my brain, probing, because she knew there was something down there that had to come out.

"You were talking to someone who wasn't there."

In a sudden flash, I saw John Manis—not as he was in life, at ease and amused with the world—but as he was now in death. Rotted through, eaten by insects, his darkened, leathery skin collapsed upon the bones and pierced by the roots of weeds that rose into the dappled sunlight of the forest floor.

My throat began to tighten, and she watched me quietly the way she had at her house. Hands, eyes, breathing, eyes. Going through her clinical checklist.

Then she said, "I know I upset you yesterday, and I apologize. It's not fair to judge a person for things they don't understand. I don't think you understood how I was feeling when you approached my son."

"You seemed pretty pissed off." My voice was quavering.

"I felt threatened," she said.

Then calmly and patiently, she explained, looking me in the eye the whole time to make sure I got it.

"I want you to try to see it from my perspective. I was here with my child."

Why did she have to look me right in the eye? Why did she have to be so direct? So patient? So unrelenting?

Had Manis's mother been like this? Had she taken him along on her errands? Strapped him into his booster seat? Worried over him?

"He's three years old," she said. "He's innocent and vulnerable, and when a man approaches him—" She broke off midsentence with a look of alarm. "What, John? What is it?"

"Oh my God!" The panic rose from deep in my gut. All of it was coming this time. Everything I'd been pushing back for months and months was welling up at once, and there was no stopping it.

"What? What's wrong?"

"Is that how I made you feel?" My voice had risen a full octave, and I could see she was as scared as I was.

She looked worriedly at Lou, and then back at me. She took a deep breath to calm herself, and she said, "Is *what* how you made me feel?"

"Like..." Jesus, the walls were closing in. "Like... I would hurt your child? Is that what you see when you look inside me? That I would hurt someone's child?" My heart was pounding and I was yelling just so I could hear my own voice above the thundering rush of blood in my ears.

"Well, no," she said. The fear was rising in her eyes too. "Not right there in the middle of the store." She looked back at Lou and the other cop. "Not with all those people around, but—why did you ask that? Why did your mind go straight to that?"

"Why did *you* ask it?" I shouted. "Because you know! Because you have a crystal ball and you can look inside me. Because you see everything, don't you?" I leapt up and pointed at her. "Why would you say that?" I screamed. My chair went over backwards with a bang. Her body stiffened, and her eyes went wide with terror.

"Who says things like that?" My voice broke as I screamed. "Hurt an innocent person? Do you think I'm a monster? Jesus Christ, it was a fucking accident!"

Lou and the other cop bolted up out of their seats, and Jennifer's face went white, but as scared as she was, as scared and terrified as she was, she took my hand in hers, and she said, "Lou has someone he wants you to talk to."

And then Lou and the big guy were standing beside her, their faces full of uncertainty and fear, and Jennifer looked me in the eye, and she was filled with terror, and she gathered all her courage, and she said, "Will you go?"

And I said yes.

Because no one has ever been as nice to me as Jennifer, who held my hand and looked all the way down inside me and saw everything and didn't hate me.

49

The hospital was orderly and immaculate. There was no dust anywhere. No untidy stacks of folders at the nurses' station. No extraneous noises. No flickering overhead fluorescents.

They had a process for intake, complete with a checklist. Empty my pockets. Give them my belt and shoelaces. They took my vitals. I talked to a nurse, then another nurse, then a doctor. They showed me to my room, where the floor was spotless and the bed was neatly made.

The nurses and orderlies wore color-coded uniforms. Nurses in light blue, orderlies in green. They worked on orders doled out by a computer every fifteen minutes. There was a time for morning meds and a time for evening meds. A time for breakfast, lunch, and dinner—all preordained and executed with clockwork precision. Everything was engineered to put me at ease.

When they brought me in, my heart rate was one forty-four. After two hours, it was down to seventy-six.

The doctor was a soft-spoken black woman with a short Afro. She was just a few years older than me, but her calm, confident manner made her seem like a wise elder. We met several times over the next three days.

"You were agitated when you came in," she said.

"I wasn't doing well."

"You seem better now."

"I feel better. Things out there were out of control."

"Tell me what's going on."

All I could talk about was Marilyn, and after twenty minutes of that, the doctor said, "What was going on before Marilyn?"

"Well, I was in Vegas." I told her I'd gambled away a lot of money. I told her about the times I'd stayed at the table forty or fifty hours straight, playing the showman. I'd gather a crowd. I'd brag about how I was going to beat the odds. They groaned when I lost and cheered when I won. I told her I bought a Corvette at two a.m. between two epic stints at the roulette wheel.

"Did you recognize your behavior at the time as compulsive?"

"Recognize? Ha! Doc, I lived it."

"Why craps?" she asked. "Why roulette?"

"They were the most exciting."

"But those are games of pure chance. Why not poker or blackjack? The games where you can employ some strategy?"

"I don't know, Doc. I never even thought about that."

"You felt the need to take a risk?"

"Well, yeah. That's what gambling is."

"But you didn't want to be in control, like a card player who can choose to fold or double down. What happened before Vegas? What got you into that state?"

I started getting uncomfortable. "Well, there was New Orleans."

All I could tell her was that I gambled there, because that's all I remember.

"How did you get to New Orleans?"

She could see I was getting more tense.

"I drove there. From Miami."

I told her about Miami. Nice weather. Nice beach. Lots of rich people partying late at night.

"And before Miami?"

My chest began to tighten.

"I was on a cruise ship."

Long pause.

"Go on," she said.

"I, uh... I'd been in Central America. I got sick of..." I looked at her to see if she was judging me, to see if her eyes were drilling into me like Lou's, or if they were soft, like Jennifer's.

She was warm and attentive, waiting patiently.

"I got sick of the heat and the insects and being poor. Barely scraping by."

"Poor? But you had all that money from selling your mobile games."

"Yeah, I mean like..."

Whose story was I supposed to tell? Mine? Or John Manis's?

"I mean, like, poor in spirit, you know?"

"You were lonely?"

"Yeah."

"Like in Vegas when you were gambling away all your money?"

"Yeah, I... How did you know I was lonely in Vegas?"

"In all the stories you told, you never mentioned the names of other people."

"I don't remember their names," I said. "Maybe they didn't have names."

"Go back to Costa Rica," she said. "Tell me what happened there."

My pulse shot up and my throat began to tighten. I could feel my face twist into a look of distorted horror.

50

I was aware of Manis's existence before I met him, though only in a vague and abstract way. I had twice caught glimpses of him on the streets of San José. Once he was going into a restaurant. Once he was coming out. Both times he was dressed well. Collared shirt and dark slacks. Each time, he had a different woman on his arm. And both times, he turned to look at me just as I was turning to look at him.

In the weeks before we met, I must have been lurking somewhere at the back of his consciousness in the same way he had been lurking at the back of mine. Why else would he have chased me down that afternoon in front of the shops and restaurants on Paseo Colón?

His face was flushed and sweating, his smile broad and lively. "You American?" he asked.

"Yeah."

The two of us stood there staring at each other, but it wasn't awkward. We were too fascinated with our own mirror images to have felt the clumsy silence of strangers who didn't know what to say to each other.

Both of us, I think, were playing that old game from children's magazines, where two supposedly identical drawings appear side by side and the reader is challenged to spot the differences.

Manis stood upright, with perfect posture. Not rigid, but at ease. He had a ready smile and he looked you in the eye when he spoke.

I stood with shoulders stooped, didn't smile without a reason, and didn't look people in the eye unless I had to. Those were the products of being on the run for so long. I didn't mean to come off as unfriendly. I just didn't want to draw attention to myself. I didn't want to be noticed at all.

"You've been around awhile," he said. His broad white smile projected confidence. His eyes, blue like mine and betraying obvious curiosity, showed a friendly and playful spirit.

"Yeah. I work at a little B and B over..." I pointed toward the east end of town as I trailed off.

"Where you from? What part of the States?"

I hesitated. I never felt safe giving out details that curious people might someday piece together. I could have responded with some random place like New York or Oklahoma City, but what if he turned out to be from there? He'd ask what I thought of such-and-such restaurant or the bar on some corner.

"Illinois," I said.

"Ah. Never been there. What's your name?"

I had stuck with Tom at the bed and breakfast because I was used to answering to it, though the old couple who owned the place called me Tomás.

"Tom," I said.

"John," he said. We shook hands and examined each other once again.

I stood up straight now, conscious of my habitual slouch in the presence of my better self.

"You're an inch taller," he said, just as I was noticing the fact. "And..." He showed me the thick scar around the pinky of his left hand. "Bet you don't have that."

There were other subtle differences. His ears were bigger. He had a bare spot between his lower lip and chin where I had to shave.

He was smiling, mischievous, delighted, and supremely confident.

"You want to play a joke?" he asked. And I thought, yes, that's it. You look like a practical joker. Like someone who thinks the world is full of fun just waiting to be had.

"You'll need a haircut," he added. "To match mine."

We went to a bar up the street and he laid out his plan over a couple of beers. I would dress like him in slacks and a new collared shirt which he had at home with the pins still in and the one-hundred-thousand-colón price tag still attached. I'd go meet his date at the restaurant. She and I would talk for five minutes while he watched from afar. He wanted to see how long it would take her to figure out I wasn't him.

His enthusiasm and sense of mischief were contagious, but...

"How long have you known this woman?" I asked.

"Since yesterday."

She was a tourist passing through.

"I don't know," I said. "What if it falls flat? What if it pisses her off or creeps her out?"

"Oh, come on," Manis said. "It's just a game. And I'll buy you dinner after. A good dinner."

"All right," I said.

An hour later, in his apartment, he nodded toward the slacks and shirt draped over the couch. "Try those on," he said. "It's practically what I was wearing yesterday when I met her."

I took the clothes into the bathroom and changed. When I came out, he asked, "Is that really what I look like?"

A glance in the hallway mirror reminded me to straighten my posture. "Pretty much."

I looked my reflection in the eye, unconvincingly, then turned and found it was easier to look Manis in the eye because his eyes were so much more confident.

He picked up his phone and made a quick call. "Are we still on?"

I heard her say yes.

They chatted for a minute, and he made her laugh. His voice was a little deeper than mine and had an easy cadence. Would she notice the difference when I spoke?

On the way to the restaurant he gave me some background. Where they had met the day before. What they'd talked about, what she looked like, so I could recognize her. Then Manis turned off a block before the destination and left me on my own.

She was waiting at the front of the restaurant, just inside the door. She smiled when she saw me. She was young, maybe twenty-three, with dark hair and clear blue eyes.

"I didn't want to go in," she said. "The only place to wait is..." She nodded toward the bar, which was full of men.

"Sorry," I said. "I hope I haven't kept you waiting."

"I just got here a minute ago. And I'm starving," she added with a smile. Then there was a little look, a subtle double-take, as if she might have wondered whether I was really the man who had charmed her yesterday.

I reminded myself not to slouch, and maybe I overcorrected. Maybe I stood too straight and looked stiff. A cloud of worry crept into my mind. What if Manis doesn't show up for ten minutes? Or fifteen? Or twenty?

"Where are your friends?" I asked after we'd been seated. Manis had told me she was traveling with three other women.

"At the park." She flashed a shy smile, then picked up the drink menu and studied it like a college student preparing for exams. "They're meeting us for drinks after." She looked at me over the top of the slim, leather-backed menu. "Remember?"

No. Manis hadn't told me that part.

"Oh, right."

I wasn't as smooth as John Manis. I wasn't putting her at ease.

I turned and scanned the bar, searching for my own face. Then I looked toward the entrance, through the big glass windows to the stream of pedestrians passing on the street outside. Was he going to abandon me with her? Was the joke on both of us?

I checked the clock on the wall, and would keep checking it every twenty or thirty seconds. This unassuming young woman would never guess that someone would play a trick like this. The joke that had seemed mischievous and funny when presented with Manis's enthusiasm now seemed juvenile, offensive, and disrespectful. I regretted ever having agreed to it.

We'd been together for about a minute and a half. If Manis didn't show up in three and a half more, I would tell her what I'd done. It would be uncomfortable for both of us, but let the shame fall on me instead of her. I could pay for her drink and go home with my tail between my legs, and she could meet up with her friends at the park and give them all a creepy story to take home.

The waiter took our drink orders. Beer for me. Vodka tonic for her. And then, mercifully, John Manis swept in, his delighted smile and vibrant energy changing the atmosphere at once.

"Christ, you're awkward!" he said with a laugh. He meant me.

The woman started, as if a jolt of electricity had just come up through her chair. "You?" She looked back and forth between the two of us, astonished and confused. For a moment, I thought she'd be angry, but Manis's warm laughter made her smile.

"I told you I'm never on time," Manis said. "So I had myself cloned."

"Oh my God!" The woman dropped her head into her hands and laughed. "I swear, every time I go on vacation, I find the weirdo."

"Which one?" Manis asked. "Me? Or placeholder John?" He pointed at me like I was a piece of furniture. I don't think he meant to be rude. His attention was on the woman.

"Both of you!" She was still laughing off the clumsy tension of our meeting.

Thank God the woman is good-natured, I thought.

"He's the weird one," Manis said with a nod toward me. "How do you ever manage to get a date when you're so stiff?"

"I don't," I said.

"You just need practice," Manis said as he pulled out a chair for himself. He sat a few feet out from the table, leaning back with an easy smile. "A little confidence, a little charm carries the day."

"That's the difference!" the woman said with a snap of recognition. "That's what I couldn't put my finger on."

"That I'm not as outgoing?" I asked.

She shook her head. "No. It's the whole aura. It's just... everything."

I don't think she meant it to sting, but it stung, and Manis noticed. There was no mistaking her preference for the real John, or her unintentional denigration of placeholder John. I read a note of triumph in his eyes.

51

Six months after we'd met, Manis and I were sailing north on a thirty-four-foot sloop along the Pacific coast of Costa Rica. We had just dropped off two women, American tourists, at a yoga camp, and had a ninety-minute sail back to the town where we had rented a bungalow.

A fight between Manis and his tourist girlfriend had left him in a sour mood, and he was taking it out on himself with drink.

"Why are we hugging the shore?" he asked as he opened a beer from the cooler.

"Because it's getting dark, and I can't navigate if I can't see land."

"Screw navigating," he said. "Let's head for the open seas."

"No way."

The thickening clouds had blotted out the sunset, and the air was growing heavy. I was annoyed with Manis for getting drunk and leaving me to manage the boat alone. A moist breeze was rising, and I would have appreciated a reliable deckhand. Manis had taught me to sail in the first place, and was more capable than me, but he was in no state to help out that night.

So I stayed within a half mile of shore and kept us on a broad reach with a southeast wind, hoping to get back quickly to the bungalow, where Manis could pass out and I could have a break from his drunken provocations. We'd been on each other's nerves for the past few weeks, as any two people would be after spending too much time together.

The novelty of having a twin had long since worn off for both of us, and we had begun to define ourselves more by our differences than by our similarities. We knew that our months together were coming to an end. We just didn't get to talking about it until that night.

"You know, I'm thinking of shipping out," Manis said as he sat drunk in the cockpit in front of me. His body was relaxed, but his face was dark and sullen.

I knew he'd be leaving Costa Rica at some point, and the thought had caused me some anxiety. Life after Manis would be as boring as it had been before him. I would miss the evenings out, the food and wine he paid for, the company he attracted, and the lively energy of his charm. Manis was the kind of person who could strike up a conversation with anyone and keep it going throughout the evening. He was the guy who'd propose a spur of the moment trip to strangers and get them to say yes.

I was the guy who walked around town with my head down, trying not to be noticed.

"Where are you thinking of going?" I asked with a sinking heart.

"I don't know," Manis said as he threw an empty beer bottle overboard. "Argentina maybe." He opened the cooler and pulled out another beer. "Or Thailand. I might just walk into the airport and decide when I get to the ticket counter."

"Must be nice," I said. "To be able to live like that."

"Yeah, it is. What are you going to do? Stick to cooking and cleaning at the B and B?"

"I suppose so," I said. "I'll try to pick up more hours. Get back on a regular schedule."

Manis nodded, and in the failing light, I could feel his eyes fixing on me. Something dark was moving through his mind.

"You know, when I look at you," he began, "I see a stunted version of myself. I see what I would have been if everything in my life had gone wrong."

I didn't respond to that. I knew if I did, he would just keep going. Instead, I focused on keeping us parallel to the shore, where the lights were few and far between. As the wind picked up, I began to fear that the coming rain would obscure my view of the coast.

"We have to get back," I said. "We're still at least thirty minutes out."

"That's another thing about you," Manis said irritably. "You worry too much."

"If one of us isn't worried about getting back to the marina, we're not going to make it." The wind that had been steady out of the southeast had begun to vary, with occasional gusts from the west and north.

"No," said Manis. "I mean, in general. That's why women prefer me. You ever think about that? We look exactly alike, but they like me, not you."

"That's not true," I said. "Some of them like me." He wanted to bait me into an argument. I knew that women liked him, and I didn't care because all the women he hooked up with were boring. Good-looking, but emotionally empty. He liked shiny packages and wasn't interested in what was inside.

"Only the damaged ones like you," he said. "And you fall for them every time. You can't just have a weekend fling, can you?"

"That never was my style," I said as the wind suddenly dropped and slackened the sail for a moment. A light rain began to fall, and I scanned the shore until my eyes fixed on a string of blazing yellow lights. Probably lanterns strung along the patio of a beachside restaurant, I thought. I wanted to keep watching them, afraid to lose sight of their location, but the waves were picking up and I had to pay attention to the wheel and the sail.

"Christ, it's dark out here," Manis said. "You want one of these?"

I could hear the crinkling of a package opening, but I couldn't see what he was talking about.

"One of what?" I asked.

He shook it and it glowed bright green. "Glow stick," he said. It was the thin, flexible kind that you could chain together into bracelets and necklaces.

"I need to keep an eye on land," I said. "The glow distracts me."

I looked back toward the shore and could barely make out the line of yellow lights that had been so bright a moment earlier.

"Actually," I said, "do you mind putting that away? I can't see the—"

"Yes," Manis insisted. "Yes, I do mind. I paid for this boat, and I paid for the bungalow and the rental car and all your dinners. If I want to have a glow stick I'll have a fucking glow stick!"

As he opened a second package, his beer fell over and spilled across the deck.

"Dammit," he muttered as he made a necklace of the two glow sticks and hung it around his neck.

He stepped back toward the stern to pick up the bottle and slipped and fell on his ass, cursing again. He flung the empty bottle into the sea, then stood and tried to walk back to the cooler to get another beer.

The chop was getting rougher, and the boat rocked to port as he took a step to starboard. For a second, he just stood there on one foot, with the other suspended in midair until the boat rocked back and his bare foot came down with a thud on the deck.

"Stop drinking," I said. "And sit down."

He opened the cooler and took out another beer. "When we get back to shore—"

"*If* we get back to shore," I interrupted. "I can barely see the lights and the wind keeps shifting."

"When we get back to shore," he insisted, "you can go find a hotel."

He closed the lid of the cooler, and when it didn't go down all the way, he stepped on it.

"Don't step on that," I said, turning my eyes forward and trying desperately to see into the dark.

"Don't tell me what to do," he said.

"John, this isn't the time to fight." I turned my eyes back to the right, and panic shot through my heart. "Where's the shore? Where the hell is the shore? Do you see any lights?"

He stood on the cooler and put his hand over his brow to block out the rain.

"Get down from there," I said, because the wind had just dropped, and I had a feeling—no, a certainty—that a gust was coming from the northwest. That would push the sail back and send the boom sweeping across the deck. It would normally go over our heads, but Manis was standing up on the cooler with his head directly in its path.

I felt the boat tip, and I heard the rumpling of the sail as it slackened for a split second and then stiffened with a blast of wind from the other direction. Manis swung one arm and one foot in the air to keep his balance atop the cooler.

I should have told him we were coming about because he was too drunk to understand what was happening. The words went through my mind. "Duck! Get down!"

In the countless times I've thought about that night, I've told myself I was close enough to push him. I could have shoved him out of the way.

But I didn't push him and I didn't even warn him. The words that were on the tip of my tongue never crossed my lips. I had no conscious intention to hurt him, but some part of me wanted to hit him for being so rude and abusive, for flaunting his confidence and his easy life, for illustrating so irrefutably how far short I had fallen from what I might have been, and for rubbing it in so cruelly.

I was angry with him because he was going to abandon me. I resented him for indulging the dark side I wished he didn't have—the selfish, drinking, womanizing side. I had always hoped my better self would be above all that.

The boom whistled across the deck above my head and slammed into the back of his skull with a sickening thud. He went face-first into the sea, and from the way he toppled I knew he was unconscious before he hit the water. A person instinctively puts his hands in front of him when he falls unexpectedly, even if he's headed into the water. Manis flopped forward with one arm hanging by his side and the other trailing behind him.

My first instinct was to jump in after him, and I was about to do it. But then the boat would drift off without me. We were too far from the coast for me to swim back if I had to, and once in the water I wouldn't be able to see the lights of shore above the waves. I had to stay on board.

"John!" I called. "John!"

All I heard was the drone of rain, the slap of the waves against the boat, and the flapping of the sail in the wind. Ten feet out from the starboard side, the glowing green crescent of Manis's necklace hovered on the surface of the waves.

The boat tipped, and for a second, I lost sight of him.

"John!" I called.

I scanned the water, wondering if he'd gone under. Then I caught a glimpse of the glowing ring again, only now he was twenty feet out, drifting behind the stern.

The light disappeared behind a black swell.

"John!"

Down he went, behind a wave, and then up he came again, now thirty feet out.

I thought again about jumping in after him, but if I did, the boat would drift from me as quickly as it drifted from him, and I'd never be able to get back in. Not unless I tied myself to the stern with a rope.

Now he was forty feet out. That was the length of our longest rope. It's up at the bow, I thought, and I took my eyes off the water for a second. But if I tie myself, the boat will pull me away from him as it drifts. So what to do?

I looked back into the black chop of the sea. The glowing green ring was gone. Oh no, I thought. Oh, no! And then it rose up on a wave, so faint I could hardly see it. It might have been sixty or seventy or eighty feet away. I couldn't judge the distance anymore, I just knew it was hopelessly far.

I had to turn the boat around. I had to get back to him.

In daylight, with a calm mind and a gentle wind, I could have turned that boat around in sixty seconds. At night, in a panic, it took me... I don't know how long. Terror distorts your sense of time. Thirty seconds feels like thirty minutes. And on top of my panic about John, I still couldn't see the shore. I couldn't orient myself. I wasn't sure whether I had turned a hundred and eighty degrees or if I had turned three whole circles.

As the rain let up, I saw a familiar set of lights ahead: the marina was less than a mile away, just up to the north. That meant I had turned the boat three hundred and sixty degrees. I turned again, heading back to the south, and frantically scanned the waves for Manis.

In a few minutes, I got lucky. The glowing green necklace was just ahead. But I overshot before I could let out the sail.

"John!" I yelled as I watched the glow drift by.

I still had some hope in me that he'd woken up and was treading water, that he was just too dazed and tired to call back, that he could somehow keep himself afloat until I reached him.

I turned again and sailed north, the bow rising and plummeting on the waves. It felt like I was barely moving, but that was an illusion because the wind was at my back. The boat glided quietly over the waves, coming down the backsides with a slap or a thump.

"John!"

There was no sign of him anywhere. I found a flashlight, but searching the waves of a darkened sea is nearly impossible. For hours, I went back and forth over what seemed to be the same patch of water.

I was ready to give up when the bow thudded into something heavy. Then the green necklace, still attached to the body, drifted slowly past the starboard side.

I had earlier tied a rope around my waist, from fear I'd lose my balance and fall into the sea. Before Manis's drifting body reached the stern, I dropped the sail and the anchor, which didn't reach the bottom but did provide enough drag to slow the boat's drift.

Then I jumped in and grabbed him, which was stupid, because I didn't have a plan for getting him back on board.

I did manage to haul us both to the stern, but I didn't realize how hard it would be to push a hundred and eighty pounds of deadweight onto the boat from below.

I never was able to do it. I wound up tying the rope around his waist and dragging him back to the marina.

52

As I approached the breakwater through a steady rain and a pitch-black sea, I dropped the sails and used the electric motor to run us in. In the calm of the marina, I was able to pull him onboard.

John Manis, the confident, easygoing better version of me, lay inert on deck with a dent in the back of his head as water poured from his lifeless lungs.

I was sobbing.

You killed him, Tom. You killed him! All you had to do was warn him the boom was coming. The words were right on the tip of your tongue, but you said nothing. You killed him because you were angry and jealous. You should be the one lying there dead!

I don't remember how long I sat there, but when I finally cried myself out, I sank into numbness and stared at the body, my mind too tired and overwhelmed to think of anything at all.

Then the rain, which had been steady since I pulled in, began to let up, and I thought, If there are any people here, on any of these boats, the rain has kept them inside. Now that it's stopping, they'll come out.

That wasn't exactly true, since it was late at night. There probably wouldn't have been much activity at the marina until daylight. But I imagined people would be crawling out of their boats en masse any minute, and someone would shine a light on me sitting beside Manis's corpse.

That was all it took to set my mind racing. What if someone had seen the boat dragging the body into the marina? What if someone saw me pull him aboard? What would that look like?

229

I looked around at the other boats. No light shone from any of them. There was no noise either.

I looked toward shore, toward the end of the dock. There were no buildings there. Just a boat launch and a few empty parking spaces.

The nearest lights were almost a quarter mile away, on the patio of an outdoor restaurant. But the rain had kept people inside. Nothing moved, and there was no sound of human activity.

No one knows yet, I thought. But I need to tell someone. Who do I tell?

The police, of course. I would tell them it was an accident. They could see that. Manis was drunk. He had fallen overboard.

With a fractured skull. How would I explain that?

The police would ask for my passport, and I didn't have a passport. The state of Illinois had taken it. I was still a fugitive.

I saw myself in custody again, answering questions.

"Why didn't you warn him the boom was coming?"

"I don't know."

"It sounds like you were fighting. Were you angry with him? Did you mean to kill him?"

"I don't know."

The US consulate would send someone to get me. They'd send me back to Illinois. And when they locked me up this time, it wouldn't be in the minimum-security prison. And it wouldn't be just a couple of years. It might be for life.

Every way I looked at it, I was doomed.

Then my thoughts took a different turn.

I asked myself, Who would bother to look for John Manis? His mother is dead and his father is in a nursing home with Alzheimer's. He deliberately left his whole life behind. He erased his online profile and disappeared on purpose. He hasn't been back to the US in two years. No one's going to miss him.

You look enough like his passport photo to fool anyone. You could go back to the States. There's no other way you'll ever get back there. Not as a fugitive felon without a passport.

You could start over from scratch. How many people get that chance? You'll never have to tick that box on the job application that asks if you've been convicted of a felony, because Manis has a clean record.

You can stop being Tom Gantry. You can be a well-dressed, well-mannered, well-respected, look-you-in-the-eye kind of guy. Just play the role the same way he played it.

Now I ask you to put those options in the balance. Imprisonment and the bleak future of a convicted felon on one side. Freedom and wealth and a new life on the other.

Which would you choose?

I buried Manis in the forest, in a shallow grave where the insects could make quick work of his remains.

At sunrise, I showered. I packed up everything he had brought to the bungalow and drove south to Panama. I took his passport, his bank card, his driver's license, and his laptop. I took his mannerisms, his style, and his charm.

As I approached the port in Panama with the giant American cruise ship that would take me back to the States, I told myself it wasn't John Manis I had buried back there in Costa Rica. It was Tom Gantry. Old Tom, who never did have much will or direction, Old Tom who just couldn't seem to make anything of his life, had been laid to rest in favor of his better self.

And the first time Manis reappeared, he agreed.

"You did bury Tom back there," he said. "You buried a decent, well-meaning person. And now you've become someone else."

53

"What is it?" the doctor asked. She looked alarmed.

"What is what?" I asked. My scalp and back and armpits were soaked in sweat.

"Your face," she said. "Your whole face is contorted."

"Didn't I…" I looked at her, bewildered. My hands were shaking. "Didn't I just tell you?"

She quietly shook her head. "No, but I can see it."

"I can't," I said. "I can't go through it all again."

"That's enough for today, John."

She sent me back to my room.

The hallway was clean and well lit. Every visible line of the architecture was straight, predictable, reassuring. My bed was neatly made. The sheets were clean and crisp.

A nurse with polished nails gave me a pill and a cup of water, and when I slept, I dreamed of Marilyn, who turned into Jennifer, who held my hand while I told her everything, the words pouring out with the heat of the fierce Vegas sun, until at last I awoke from one dream into another, where Marilyn stood at the mirror in a sunlit room, brushing her long black hair.

"We should go back," she said.

"I don't want to go back," I said. "I like it here."

"So?"

"Why'd you have to spoil the mood?"

"It's just reality," she said as she laid her hairbrush on the dresser. "Everybody has to face it sometime."

"But I don't want—"

She sat on the bed beside me.

"You don't want what, Johnny?"

"I don't know. I don't know what I want."

"Johnny," she whispered. "When you were gambling, which did you like better? Winning? Or losing?"

She watched me quietly, waiting for an answer.

"Because you know there's no forgiveness for the things we can't undo."

Her hand slid from my shoulder and I awoke again.

In the hospital this time. In the quiet hospital with the spotless floors and the clockwork nurses and the paper cup on the familiar nightstand that stood unmoved by all the nightmares of all the souls that had ever passed through these doors. My guilt was mine and mine alone, and the final irreducible fact of this world that was indifferent to the suffering of its inhabitants was that it would go on spinning whether I was in it or not.

The new nurse said, "You have a meeting with the doctor this afternoon. And a policeman. The one who brought you here. We can only keep you for seventy-two hours. You know that, right? Unless the doctor decides otherwise."

54

Lou and the doctor and I sat in a meeting room with a window that looked out on a stand of tall pines. I don't remember the time because time is hard to tell when so much is happening at once. But it must have been afternoon, because that was when the nurse had said we'd meet.

"We can't keep him against his will," the doctor said. "John, you've obviously had some trauma. The anxiety medication I've prescribed will help, but I suggest you remain here for at least two weeks."

Lou watched expectantly, and for once I saw real kindness in his face, a genuine human concern that I had never guessed his stoic features could show.

"I don't know," I said. "I think Marilyn needs me."

"You need to stay away from Marilyn," Lou said.

"But she loves me."

"Marilyn doesn't love anyone and she never will. She's in trouble, John. You know that."

"No she's not. If she was in trouble, she would have brought her lawyer with her when you interviewed her at the police station."

"She *did* bring her lawyer. She's not stupid."

The doctor extended her hand toward him and said softly, "Lou." She shook her head.

Then she turned to me and said, "John, you've responded well to being here. Do you remember how you were feeling before you arrived?"

"Yeah," I said. "And I also remember what I felt like in your office yesterday."

"We may have gone too quickly to the heart of the matter. We can slow down. But it will help you to talk it out. That's why I want you to stay."

"I'm never going back there," I said. "I never want to think about that night again."

"What night?" Lou asked.

Again, the doctor raised her hand to silence him. "If you stay a couple of weeks," she said, "your body and your mind will wind down. The things that feel too raw right now will be easier to address after you've had some rest. But you need to take the time, John. There is no shortcut."

We sat in silence for a minute, and while the doctor seemed to have mostly a clinical interest in my case, Lou was on edge, fidgeting with a pen and shifting his weight from side to side in his chair. He looked at me a few times, but not with the hard stare I was used to.

I kept looking at the doctor. I wanted her to look me in the eye, to take my hand like Jennifer had and give me the look that said everything would be OK.

But she didn't. I don't think she understood.

I don't think she understood how crushing loneliness and isolation could be.

But Marilyn did. Even if she didn't know how to reassure me, even if she could never look me in the eye the way Jennifer had, Marilyn and I understood each other.

"I'm not staying," I said. "I want to see Marilyn."

Lou's head snapped up. "John, please!"

I shook my head.

"Please," he repeated.

"No, Lou. I gotta do what I gotta do."

He stood up and said, "I'm not driving you back to town. You find your own way."

<h1 style="text-align:center">55</h1>

I got a Lyft from the hospital back to town after they discharged me. It was an expensive ride, and I didn't have a lot left in the bank, but I didn't care either.

When we pulled into town around seven p.m., two police cars and a van were parked outside my apartment. Lou was on the sidewalk talking to another cop.

The Lyft driver muttered, "Looks like trouble."

"Yeah, don't go anywhere, OK?"

When I got out of the car, Lou showed me two warrants.

"This one's for the apartment," he said. "And this one's for your car."

"Try not to make a mess, Lou. I like to keep things nice and tidy."

"Stay out of the apartment and away from the car."

"OK, Lou. But you won't find anything."

"That's what I'm hoping." He gave me a look to see if I was nervous, but I wasn't. I wasn't scared of Lou Eisenfall anymore.

I had checked the news on my phone during the Lyft ride. Roland's skull and jaw still hadn't been found, so no one knew it was a murder. It didn't even seem like a murder to me anymore. It was just something I saw on TV late at night. A guy with bad manners mouthed off to the wrong person and then he was dead. Too bad.

I walked back to the Lyft and called Marilyn. It was good to hear her voice. I told her what Lou was up to.

"Great," she said. "My lawyer told me Lou has a warrant to get my call records from the phone company. Are you hungry? You want to get dinner?"

"You seem pretty relaxed about it all," I said.

"Why shouldn't I be? It's my lawyer's problem."

"I'll swing by in a few."

The Lyft driver took me up to Marilyn's.

When I rang the bell, no one answered, so I let myself in.

Marilyn was in the master bathroom, rubbing cream onto her face.

"You never asked me where I was," I said.

Her fingers stopped midswirl and without looking at me she said, "You're standing in my light."

56

"I want to go somewhere different," Marilyn said. She was in the walk-in closet, trying on a dress. This was the sixth or seventh she'd attempted in twenty minutes, and she was already on her second glass of wine.

"That one looks good," I said, a red cotton dress that hugged her hips.

"I know a place in Sonoma," she said as she pulled the dress off over her head.

"What was wrong with that one?"

She glared at me. "It's red."

"You knew that when you pulled it off the rack."

"You up for Italian?"

"Sure."

She picked a black dress and a pair of black heels. Then she poured one more glass of wine and drank it all at once.

"Sure you don't want any?" she asked.

"No thanks."

When we got outside, I told her I'd drive, but she said no, she would drive.

"All right then. I'm going to close my eyes and relax. Just don't kill us, you lush."

We arrived in Sonoma after dark. She pulled into the parking lot of an Italian place, then drove around back and parked ten feet from the dumpster between a big white SUV and a red Ford Mustang.

"Why'd you park back here?" I asked.

"Why shouldn't I?" She pulled the keys from the ignition and put them in her purse.

"There was a spot in front. And it smells like garbage back here."

"Don't pick a fight, John." She opened the door, and when we were both out of the car, she added, "We have enough pressure on us already, don't we? Do we have to turn against each other?"

I wanted to ask her why she never bothered to check in on me at the hospital, but she was already in a sour mood and I didn't want to push it.

We got a quiet table in a corner. Marilyn ordered a bottle of wine and drank two glasses before the appetizers arrived. And she kept on drinking right through the meal.

"Slow down," I said. "You're going to make yourself sick."

"You know what I want to do," she asked over pasta. Her cheeks were flushed, and her words were beginning to slur. "I want to go far away from here. Someplace tropical. I'll sit on the beach and drink piña coladas all day. Maybe I'll branch out to margaritas and daiquiris. I'll get fat and the sun will turn my skin to leather, and then I won't have to deal with men looking at me anymore."

"That doesn't sound like much of a fantasy."

"Well what do *you* know?" she asked bitterly.

"You have a lot weighing on you, Marilyn. Have you thought about talking to a counselor? Or a therapist?"

"You mean like you just did? You're all straightened out now, and you want me to join you on the sunny side of the street?"

"No, I'm just saying, you might want to get some things off your chest."

"Don't talk about my chest," she said, and she swigged down a mouthful of wine.

"Seriously," I said. "I think you're starting to crack."

"Me? *I'm* starting to crack? I'm sorry, but I'm not the one who goes around killing people. I'm not the one the cops hauled into the loony bin."

She topped off her glass, spilling a little as she poured.

"You really don't need any more wine."

"Who are you to say?"

I gave up at that point. The meal was done, and she would have another glass or two or three, and then I hoped she'd pass out on the drive home and spare me her drunken bitterness.

"You're not driving home," I said.

"Why do you think I brought you?"

I glowered at her. "You're really being a bitch, you know that?"

"I know, John." She chugged down half her glass, not even bothering to taste it. "And tomorrow I'll regret it all."

When we left, she pulled the keys from her purse and said, "Where's the car?"

"Give me the keys," I said.

"Where's the car?"

"By the dumpster, remember? Just follow the stink."

"Oh yeah."

She walked unsteadily ahead of me, rounding the corner of the building. I had to run to get in front of her.

"Give me the keys, Marilyn."

She hurried past me to the driver side of the Mercedes.

I grabbed her by the elbow and said, "Give me the keys!"

She threw them over the roof of the car, through the open window of the Mustang parked in the next spot.

"Ha!" she laughed, then put her hand to her mouth to stifle a hiccup.

"Why'd you do that?"

"Because I'm a bitch. Because I'm an awful, horrible bitch, and I'm drunk, and I wish you'd leave me."

I jerked her hard by the arm and pulled her around to the passenger side.

"Oh!" she said sarcastically. "I like a man who asserts himself."

I tried the door, but it was locked. "Wait here," I said.

"Where do you think I'd go?"

I pushed her back a couple of feet so I could look into the Mustang. It was dark inside. The seats and carpet were black, so I couldn't see a thing.

I got into the driver's seat and ran my hand along the carpet, holding the steering wheel to steady myself. I found keys poking out from beneath the passenger seat.

When I got out and shut the door, Marilyn jumped up and down and clapped. "Bravo, Johnny! You found them!"

"Shut up," I said.

I opened the Mercedes, stuffed her in, and buckled her. She fell asleep two minutes later.

Passing through town on the way to her house, I noticed my Corvette was gone.

A few minutes later, I pulled into Marilyn's drive, parked the car, and carried her up to bed.

"You're going to feel like shit in the morning," I whispered to her. "And that'll be your payback for the way you acted tonight."

Her eyes opened for a second, and she said, "Do you really love me, Johnny?"

"I do."

"I'm sorry," she said. "I told you I'm awful."

"You need help."

"Mmm. Said the pot to the kettle. I just need sleep."

She took a deep breath, her head rolled to the side, and she was out again.

I took a Lyft back to the apartment. Other than the car and my laptop being gone, the place didn't look any different than I had left it.

<h1 style="text-align:center">57</h1>

I slept hard that night. Maybe talking to that doctor had done more good than I thought. I got to relive the whole Manis incident from beginning to end, and it was painful, but it didn't kill me.

The next morning, I looked in the fridge for eggs, but Lou and his buddy must have eaten them while they were searching the apartment. The only thing in there was a bottle of beer, so I drank it.

Then I opened the leather-bound date book and checked my calendar. The whole day was empty. A few weeks ago, that would have scared me, but it didn't anymore.

I flipped back a few pages and noticed the past few days were also empty. Work had dried up.

I texted Marilyn around ten, but she didn't respond. So I called her, but she didn't answer. I figured she was sleeping off her hangover.

At ten thirty, The Lemonade Lady called about her phone, which she had accidentally put through the washing machine. Probably along with the new dress she had picked out for my next visit.

"I already have the new model," she said. "I just need help setting it up."

"What phone are you calling from?" I asked.

"My landline. Do you think you could come up for a visit today?"

"I can come up right now."

"Oh!" she said with delight. "Well, I'll need some time to prepare. How about one thirty?"

"Sure," I said. "I'll see you then."

Usually, when you buy a new phone, the people at the store activate it for you and transfer all your settings and contacts from the old phone. I knew her phone would still be in the box with the cellophane wrap, and she'd have a fresh pitcher of lemonade waiting for me on the patio.

After lunch, I got a Lyft up to her house in northern Sonoma County. The driver had such a thick Slavic accent, we gave up trying to chat after the first five minutes.

I sat back and watched the scenery roll by while Roland pestered me with questions, trying to get under my skin the way Manis used to. Lou has your car now, he said. What if he finds something in the trunk? What if there's a tiny hair, or a clothing fiber, or a microscopic drop of blood?

No, I told him. That's impossible.

I vacuumed the trunk thoroughly. I shampooed the liner, then vacuumed the bare metal underneath. Then I washed it down and vacuumed the rug again.

But wouldn't that look suspicious, Roland asked? Whose trunk is that clean? Who doesn't have a grain of sand or a little bit of grime in the nooks beneath the liner? The cops will wonder why it had been scrubbed.

Maybe he had a point. Maybe some tiny fiber had survived the cleaning. But how would they be able to match it to Roland? I had stripped his body and left it exposed to hours of rain. Then the heat and the animals had been at it. There couldn't be any clothing fibers left at the scene.

But what about hair? His hair would be at the scene. Could a stray hair have made it into my trunk? If it had, it was unlikely to have survived the vacuuming.

But what if a strand of his hair had gotten onto the seat, or the floor?

I had vacuumed those too, and had cleaned well down into the cracks and crevices to get out whatever hadn't blown away during all my hours of driving with the top down.

Would that look suspicious? That the entire car had been so thoroughly cleaned?

I leaned forward over the front seat and turned the rearview so I could look at my eyes. The driver swerved in alarm and said something I didn't understand. Maybe he thought I was lunging at him.

"If you start thinking like that again," I shouted at the mirror, "it's going to show in your eyes, and Lou will lock you up just for looking funny. So stop it!"

The driver watched me nervously from the corner of his eye.

When we pulled into The Lemonade Lady's driveway a few minutes later, I was actually looking forward to an hour of her mindless banter. It would distract me from my thoughts. But when she answered the door, the first thing she said was, "Some awful detective was up here asking about you. I didn't like his aura one bit."

She grilled me about Lou as I unpacked her new phone.

"Why would he be asking about you? He doesn't suspect you in the crash that killed the millionaire, does he? And have you seen the widow? What a stunner! She looks like the kind who'd marry an older man for money. Now she's sitting pretty on top of her very own fortune."

I wanted to strangle her.

"Is something wrong, John? You look tense."

"Tell me about your granddaughter," I said. "She's such a lovely young woman."

That got her going for forty minutes while I finished setting up her phone.

I took another Lyft home. I was going to stop by Marilyn's to see how she was holding up with her hangover, but just as I was about to call her, her car passed by, heading the other way. We were fifteen miles north of town. Where could she be going?

I dialed her number, but she didn't answer.

When we reached her house, I told the Lyft driver to pull in and wait.

Esme answered the door.

"Where is la señora?"

Esme nodded toward the north and said in Spanish, "She was angry because I couldn't find the sunscreen."

"The sunscreen?"

"Yes. But we had a happy ending. I found it in the guest bathroom. She took the sunscreen and the towels and the liquor to the lake."

"What lake?"

Esme shrugged.

I got back to my apartment at four and looked again at my date book. Every day from that day forward was empty. My heart began to sink into the dismal bottomless hole that was a thousand times worse than the mania. Worse than the agitated panic that had exploded in Vegas. Worse than the fear I'd felt after killing Roland. A pit of infinite darkness and emptiness, where you can fall forever and ever and ever, and no matter how low you go, there's still an infinity of darkness waiting beneath you.

I flipped back a few pages in the calendar, back to happier days.

Marilyn.
Marilyn.
Marilyn.
Marilyn.
Marilyn.
Marilyn.
Marilyn.

I called her, but she didn't answer.

And then the groaning fridge began to mock my solitude. It's just you and me, John, whirring and spinning forever in the emptiness.

"Shut up!" I said. I pulled the fridge away from the wall and unplugged it.

You could go to The Sage, I told myself. She was in there the first time you went, and the second. She might be there now. And if she's feeling bad about her life, you could buy her a drink.

I waited through two bourbons and four beers at The Sage, but she never showed. I texted, but she didn't answer.

So I picked up a twelve-pack of beer from the grocery and went back to my apartment.

I scrolled through the news on my phone. There were no new developments in the Roland case. They didn't call it the Roland case, because they still hadn't identified the body.

Halfway through the twelve-pack, I found an old Western on Netflix where the good guys wore white hats and the bad guys wore black. Someone had shot Roland and he was writhing in the dirt, screaming and gurgling with his hand on his jaw. The sheriff told the deputy a forensic black light test could reveal tiny bloodstains in the trunk lining of old Corvettes, and the corpse I'd planted in Costa Rica grew into a towering tree that spread its branches across the country and blotted out the sun.

Then the phone rang, and my eyes opened to a stab of angry sunlight.

"Did you hear the news?" Marilyn asked.

"What news?" My head was pounding and my mouth was dry. Twelve empty beer bottles on the coffee table. The clock said 10:17.

"Come up here. Now."

"I don't have a car." I sat up and the room began to spin. I had to lie back down.

"I know. I just ordered a delivery from the grocery store. Walk up there and find Carlos. He'll give you a ride in the van."

58

I stood up from the couch and instantly regretted it. I was so light-headed and nauseated, I had to sit back down.

What news, I asked myself. What is she talking about?

I tried to look at the news on my phone, but the tiny screen was a blur.

I got dressed and headed up to the grocery, realizing as I walked that this wasn't even the full hangover. I was still drunk, and the real pain was an hour or two away. I tried to piece together all that had happened in the past few days, but the details leaked through my aching brain like water through trembling fingers.

I was inside the grocery before I knew it. I looked around, wondering who Carlos was and how I would recognize him.

Wait, I thought. How is Marilyn going to call in an order and have them deliver it that minute? And how does she know Carlos will... Oh, yeah. Bastian was part owner of the store. Now it's hers. At least, until the banks and the IRS come to collect their debts.

A short, thickly built man with a dark mustache smiled at me. "Joan?" he said.

"Yeah, it's John. Jaaaahn."

"Come on." He waved me toward the rear of the store, and we walked through the loading dock to a white air-conditioned van that held nothing but a bag of beets and kale.

"You are friends with Miss Marilyn?" Carlos asked with a smile as we pulled onto Main Street.

"Yes," I said, turning my head to look at the two police cruisers parked in front of the station. The reflection of the sun from the car windows stabbed my brain like knives.

I turned the radio on and scanned the stations for news. I got the weather, and an update on Congress, but nothing local.

When Carlos rolled to a stop at Marilyn's house, Esme was standing at the open front door. Carlos leapt out with the bag of groceries, while I lumbered achingly from the passenger side. He handed the groceries to the housekeeper with a friendly, "Buenos días, Esmerelda." She took the bag and nodded gravely to me to go upstairs. As I ascended, I heard her and Carlos gossiping like old friends.

I found Marilyn in the bathroom wearing a black cotton dress and brushing out her long wet hair. She glanced at my reflection and said, "You look like shit, John."

"I feel like shit."

"Go to the dining room and pour yourself a drink."

"That's the last thing I want."

"It'll take the edge off your hangover. But don't drink too much, because you're driving."

"Driving where?" I asked.

She put the brush down on the counter and tugged at the ends of her hair.

"To the lake," she said. "Go get your drink."

My head was pounding so hard, I would have drunk a glass of gasoline if it promised to ease the pain.

As I turned to leave the bathroom, she said, "Wait for me in the car. I'll be right out."

On the floor beside the bedroom door sat Marilyn's black leather handbag. Beside that was a black canvas duffle bag large enough for a week-long trip. On top of the dresser, the sealed envelope had a fresh new stamp in the corner, but still no address.

59

One shot of bourbon didn't help as much as Marilyn had promised, so I had a second. That one dulled my senses just enough to make the pain bearable.

I went out to the Mercedes and sat in the driver's seat with no keys, waiting for Marilyn, who showed up five minutes later. She popped the trunk and dropped her duffle bag in, then she got in the passenger side and handed me the keys.

"Where are we going?" I asked.

"To the lake. I already told you." She pulled a compact from her handbag and checked her eye makeup.

"No," I said. "Which direction?"

"North. The way Bastian was going when he died. He was going to the lake house, remember?"

"How do you expect me to put all that together?" I asked as I started the car. "Even if I wasn't hungover."

"Just drive."

As we pulled onto the road, I told her I hadn't had time to pack a bag.

"You didn't pack one for San Francisco either, and you did just fine."

She closed the compact and slipped it back into her handbag.

"Why did you go back to San Francisco?" I asked.

"Let's not fight," she said.

"It's a simple question. Who's fighting?"

"We are," she said. "So let's change the subject. You heard the news, I take it?"

"No."

"They found Roland's car. The blue Mazda you left on the other side of the mountain."

"Shit."

"Apparently you did a number on it."

"What's that supposed to mean?"

"You left the doors and windows open through all that rain. And the fast food wrappers in the back seat attracted animals. The whole car is contaminated. They'll never get clean evidence from it."

"Well that's something," I said.

"But they know who the car belonged to because you left the license plates on. And you didn't scratch off the vehicle identification number."

"I didn't think of those things," I said. "I'm not a career criminal."

"Aren't you?" she asked coldly.

"What's that supposed to mean?"

"Nothing." I tried to read her face, but her eyes were fixed on the road ahead.

"How far is this lake?"

"About three hours."

"Three hours? How the hell did Bastian expect to drive three hours in the dark after all he had to drink?"

"He was drunk," Marilyn said. "Drunk and rational are two different things. Listen, there's a restaurant about an hour up the road, before we turn onto I-5. They have sandwiches and wraps. We can grab a couple for takeout."

We continued north on Route 29 to Clearlake, then headed east past Wilbur Springs. Marilyn seemed tense and fidgety, checking the sideview mirror every few minutes to see if anyone was following us.

"Why are you nervous?" I asked.

She was quiet for a minute. "I don't like the idea of losing you," she said softly, but something in her tone was unconvincing. "If they arrest you for that murder..." She trailed off and looked out the window so I couldn't see her face.

Over the next ten minutes, my mind worked in slow motion to piece together the situation. The cops traced the car to Roland. They'd find his physical description matched the remains less than half a mile away. Male, the right height, the right age.

With a little digging, they might be able to connect Roland to Marilyn. They'd at least know the two knew each other. They had both lived in San Francisco at the same time. They both went to the same swinger party—maybe more than one—and that's not a huge community, even in San Francisco. Someone besides Bastian must have seen them having sex by the pool.

How long would it take the cops to find all that out? A few days?

And then they'd connect the dots. Marilyn's husband dies in a suspicious accident, his corpse is robbed of over a hundred thousand dollars' worth of jewelry. Her ex-lover drove the red car that caused the crash, and then he's found murdered.

But who would want to kill the ex-lover?

Why, the new lover, of course.

That didn't look good for me, but how did it look for Marilyn? Lou Eisenfall, with his paranoid everyone-is-a-criminal mindset, would be thinking she orchestrated all of this. Get the smitten ex-lover to kill the rich husband. Then get the smitten new lover to kill the ex. That's what Lou would see.

I wouldn't be surprised if they already had warrants out for our arrest.

Marilyn kept checking the rearview, checking the speedometer, checking her watch.

"What's your plan?" I asked.

She sat up straight and stiff and pointed ahead to the right. "That's it."

"That's what? What?"

"The restaurant. Pull over and get some food."

"Jeez, you scared me." I put my hand over my heart and felt it beating hard.

"Just pull in," she said. "And relax."

As I turned into the lot I asked what kind of sandwich she wanted.

"A BLT with turkey."

"You mean a club?" I asked.

"Whatever you call it. Just get me one."

The restaurant was a one-story wood building with plate glass windows and faded yellow paint that was beginning to chip. I parked in front and Marilyn handed me a couple of twenties.

"Try the club," she said. "They're good. And get me an iced tea too."

I went inside and asked the waitress for two club sandwiches and two iced teas to go. She said I could pay at the register and she'd have them ready in a few minutes.

I glanced back at Marilyn in the car. She sat with her head down. It looked like she was writing.

"Twenty-four sixty," said the cashier. After I handed her the two twenties, I pulled my phone from my pocket and turned it off. If the cops did have a warrant for us, I didn't want them tracking my phone.

When the cashier handed me change, I turned to go outside and tell Marilyn to turn her phone off as well.

"Your sandwiches will be right up," said the cashier. "You want to grab some chips? They're free with the sandwiches."

"Huh?"

Marilyn was getting out of the car.

"Grab two bags," said the cashier, pointing at the rack of chips. "You already paid for them."

Why is she leaving the car, I wondered. Where is she going? I was about to go outside and ask when the waitress approached with two bags.

"Your sandwiches," she said, handing me the first bag. "Drinks are in here."

I took the second bag. "Thank you."

She smiled. "You have a nice day."

When I got outside, Marilyn was on the other side of the parking lot, fifty feet away, standing at a mailbox with her back to me.

"Hey!" I shouted. I ran toward her.

She didn't turn, but she pulled the door of the mailbox open.

"Hey!"

When I reached her, her hand was in the door, holding the letter, which now bore an address—the address she had just written as she sat in the car.

"Don't send that."

She looked me in the eye and dropped it into the box. The door slammed shut behind it.

I stared at her, speechless for a moment. "Why did you do that?"

"It's my life," she said.

"The only thing you had going for you was that you didn't turn in the insurance policy," I said. "Lou already suspects you. He thinks you murdered Bastian for the money. Now you just added a ten-million-dollar motive to his conspiracy theory. Why would you do that?"

She turned and walked toward the car without saying a word.

I chased her down and stopped her, pressing the two bags into her arms.

"Lou told me as soon as you turn in that policy, the insurance investigators will be all over this case."

She looked at me coolly and said, "Do you think I'm stupid, John? Do you think I don't know what I'm doing?"

The supreme confidence of her tone was a million miles from what I had expected.

"What *are* you doing?" I asked.

"I'll tell you at the lake," she said, taking the bag of sandwiches. "Just drive and try not to get pulled over."

60

When we left the lot, I told Marilyn to turn her phone off so the cops couldn't track us.

"I don't have my phone," she said as she unwrapped her sandwich.

"Why not?"

"Because I forgot it. I have a lot on my mind, OK? Give me a break." She took a bite of her sandwich.

"How can you eat at a time like this?"

"At a time like what," she asked through a mouthful of food. "No one's shooting at us."

"Yeah, but—"

"Relax, OK? This will all be settled soon."

I wanted to know what the hell she was thinking, but she didn't seem interested in talking, so I told myself I'd wait till we got to the lake. Then I'd grill her.

As we headed north up I-5, I saw John Manis lounging at ease on the deck of the boat in Costa Rica. "You need to follow her lead and relax, Tom." He smiled. "What's the point of getting worked up?"

I can't relax, I told him. This doesn't feel right.

"Just play it cool," he said as he flicked his bottle cap overboard.

I can't play it cool anymore. I'm not John Manis. I can't deal with this. I can't!

"Well then you shouldn't have gotten into it in the first place," he said. "You go around masquerading as someone else, screwing another man's wife, and then you fall apart when things get messy. If you're going to play the game, my friend, you have to play it to the end."

254

It seemed like a five-second conversation, but it must have been longer than that. Marilyn screamed, "John!" as her hand shot to the dashboard. I hit the brakes to avoid rear-ending the car in front of us.

As she picked up her sandwich from the floor, she said, "Sometimes you drift off, and I wonder where you go. You have to pay attention to what's in front of you."

From there on, I kept my eyes on the road. Marilyn tuned the radio to a classical music station and kept the volume low. That calmed me. The two of us didn't speak until we reached the lake. There, she gave directions along a narrow wooded road to an isolated lakeside cabin at the edge of the pines.

As we approached, I saw a white Ford sedan parked beside the building.

"Someone's here," I said.

"No one's here. I put that there."

I turned and looked at her.

"You don't think we're going to drive away in this thing, do you?"

61

The cabin looked bigger inside than out, but it was still cozy. The main room was a combination living room, kitchen, and eating area. To the right was a small bedroom with a closet and bath.

When I saw the liquor bottles beside the fridge, I said, "Somewhere in here are towels and sunscreen."

"How'd you know?" she asked as she dropped her duffle bag inside the front door.

"Esme told me you drove north with towels and sunscreen."

"Ah," she said with a smile. "So you were checking up on me!"

"You came all the way up here? Just to stock this place?"

She put her arms around my neck and said, "Did you think I wasn't going to take care of you?" Then she kissed me and added, "You still look like shit. How much did you drink last night?"

"Too much," I said. "I drank myself to sleep."

"Well, have another," she said as she walked toward the counter. "And then let's go for a swim. You'll be amazed at how refreshing the water is."

She opened a bottle of bourbon and three other bottles, then filled two glasses with ice as I peeked into the bedroom.

"Ever had a Sazerac?" she asked.

"No."

I went to the bathroom and looked in the mirror. Dark pouches of worry and hangover puffed out beneath my eyes. The stubble on my cheeks and chin was growing dark. The reflection of the ill-looking man was framed by the sterile background of a bare white wall. I felt like I was looking at a prisoner, and the thought of prison made my stomach churn.

"Don't act so surprised," said the voice of John Manis. "You've been a prisoner all this time. To your conscience and your guilt. To your lies and your duplicity. The only time you're ever yourself is when you're with her, and even then it depends on her mood. Nice Marilyn swells your heart, and angry Marilyn breaks it."

"Shut up," I said aloud. "What the hell do you know?"

"You're talking out loud to someone who's not even here," Manis said. "I'm dead, remember? You killed me, and no one will ever know. Will they, Tom?"

My heart began to thump. Beads of sweat appeared on my upper lip and forehead as the pulsing blood pounded through my aching head. Manis was watching me from the other side of the mirror, waiting for me to wipe the sweat away, as if that would be the sign that he had got to me. But I wasn't going to do it. I wasn't going to let him win.

The vein on the right side of my neck was throbbing as my reflection grinned back at me with malicious delight.

"You're panicking, Tom. You're losing it!" The voice was shrill, gleeful and mocking. "What are you going to do? Get drunk again? Lose yourself between Marilyn's thighs?"

"Shut up," I growled. "Shut up!"

"Why?" John asked. "Are you afraid she'll hear me?"

"You don't even exist."

"Then who are you talking to? Hmm?" He waited a second, then added, "By the way, I've been meaning to congratulate you. She's a hell of a woman, Tom. Better than anyone I could have hooked. What's your secret? What signal do you give off that a woman like her responds to?"

"Shut up!" I yelled.

"You OK in there?" Marilyn called from the other room.

"I'm fine," I said as I tore my eyes from the mirror.

"Your drink is ready," she called.

"I'll be right out."

I stood at the toilet and tried to pee, but I couldn't. My nerves were too tight. It took a full minute to loosen up and let go.

When I returned to the other room, Marilyn was on the couch—a tasteless loveseat with a faded green floral pattern and the smell of musty winter rains.

She sat smiling, one leg crossed over the other.

"John, you really do look awful. Try this."

She handed me the drink. It was strong and bitter and bracing, like a smack in the mouth.

"I like that," I said.

"I thought you would."

I sat on the couch beside her, my leg pressed against hers.

"I got us some food," she said as she sipped her drink. "There's salmon in the freezer, if you want to grill later. And crab cakes too, in case you feel like cooking inside."

"That sounds good," I said, taking two long sips of the harsh, astringent liquor.

"And a swim will do you good." She ran her hand up the inside of my thigh as she leaned in to kiss me. "It'll bring back your appetite." She kissed me and rubbed my crotch. "And your..." She looked down at her hand as it kneaded me. "You're very tense, aren't you?"

"I am," I said.

"Not ready to let go?"

"I don't think so."

"Don't worry," she said. She leaned in and whispered, "There's nothing to worry about."

She kissed me softly. "Nothing at all."

62

I awoke to see Marilyn walking into the cabin in her black bikini.

"You're back," she said with a smile. "You want to swim?"

"How long was I asleep?"

"A few hours. How's your hangover?"

"Better," I said as I sat upright on the couch.

"The sun is already behind the mountains. Let's swim before it gets dark."

"I don't have a bathing suit."

Marilyn shrugged. "Swim in the buff. I'll join you."

We undressed and two minutes later we were wading into the cold water. My shoulders were hunched up around my ears.

"God, loosen up," Marilyn said. "Of course it's going to be uncomfortable if you resist."

She ran three quick steps to where the water reached her midthigh, then dove in and went under.

She came up a few feet away with a huge smile. She pushed her hair from her face and said, "Come on!"

I waded out a little farther, then dove under the cold clear water into a world of shock.

"Whoa!" I yelled as I popped up. "Wow, that's cold!"

"But you're in," she said. "Now let's swim out to the deep water."

I followed her out about a hundred yards, to where our feet couldn't touch the bottom. The sun had dropped below the western hills, and in the fading twilight, I could see her glowing smile and the goose bumps on her arms. I pulled her toward me for a kiss. Her nipples, hard from the cold, brushed against my chest, and when my face drew back from hers, her smile was broad and radiant, like the smile she had showed me the first morning we'd spent at the pool. It was the bright, shining smile of a spirit consumed by joy, which nature lavishes so liberally upon us in childhood, before the cares of the world creep in to take it all away. Of all the moments I ever shared with her, those two moved me most.

<h1 style="text-align:center">63</h1>

An hour later, I was standing at the grill in front of the cabin, dressed in the slacks and button-down shirt I had awakened in that morning in my apartment. The coals were just hot enough to cook. Marilyn stood in the light of the doorway, wearing black underpants and a dark blue t-shirt, her right hip pressed against the frame, a drink in each hand.

"I mixed you one," she said.

"You want to bring it out here? I'm about to put the salmon on."

"The salmon can wait," she said. "Come inside."

I watched the gentle sway of her hips as she walked back toward the kitchen. I left the salmon on a plate beside the grill and followed her in.

At the counter, she handed me a Sazerac, and said, "Cheers."

"Cheers," I said. We touched glasses and our eyes locked as we each took a sip.

I turned from her, and she asked where I was going.

"To put the food on," I said.

She grabbed my hand and said, "Stop being practical for a minute. Come sit with me."

We went to the couch and sat side by side, our legs pressed together.

"What do you think of that one?" she asked. "I changed up the mix."

I took a sip of my drink. "It's more bitter than the last one."

"Is it too bitter?"

"No." I took another sip. "It tastes like medicine. Is that the absinthe?"

I pushed a strand of hair back from her face and kissed her mouth. She responded with a passionate kiss of her own. After a few seconds, I had to push her away.

"Give me a minute to breathe," I said.

I picked up my drink and took three long swigs as she watched me nervously.

"What?" I asked, wondering why she suddenly seemed so uncomfortable. "Don't take it as rejection. You know I love you."

"Goddammit, don't say that!" She was softly wringing her hands, staring at me like she was going to cry.

"What's the matter with you?" I asked. I took another sip of the drink and her eyes went wide with fear.

She pulled the drink from my lips and her voice broke as she cried, "Johnny, stop!"

The glass fell between my knees, bounced once on the shabby rug, then landed on its side, spilling ice and bitter liquor across the floor.

Marilyn leapt from the couch with a look of terror. "Don't drink any more of that. You'll die!" She pressed her hand against her heart and took a step back, her eyes fixed on me as the color drained from her face.

"What are you talking about?" I said. I felt a sudden spin, a single rotation of the room. Then the dizziness stopped.

"Johnny, can you stand?" Though she hadn't moved, Marilyn suddenly seemed a hundred feet away. "Can you stand up?" she pleaded. "Can you come to me?"

"Why do you sound so panicked?" Her fear was beginning to scare me. I lifted a leg to stand, and then heard my foot thump down onto the floor like a dead weight. The couch rocked side to side, like a boat at sea. I picked up my other leg only to hear it thud down the same way.

"Oh God," she cried with alarm. "Is it working?" She stepped toward me and stared terrified into my eyes. "Is it working? Oh, God, John, I'm so sorry. I'm so, so sorry. Please forgive me, John."

I tried to respond, but all that came out of my mouth was a slur of noise.

Marilyn turned and walked quickly to the bedroom, her hand over her mouth, choking back tears.

As the couch rolled over the waves of an invisible sea, the room began to spin and sink, like the entire world was being sucked down a drain. Then it stopped. Then it started again. Then it stopped.

I heard Marilyn's hurried steps behind the bedroom door. I must have tried to lean toward her to better hear what she was doing, because I slumped over sideways. When I tried to right myself, my muscles wouldn't move.

In a minute she came back wearing jeans and carrying the black duffle bag. She stood in front of me again for a final look and set the duffle bag at her feet.

"I told you I was horrible, Johnny. I told you to leave, but you wouldn't listen." She began to sob as she pulled the car keys from her purse. A bottle of pills fell to the floor as the keys came out, but she was too upset to notice.

Wiping the tears from her eyes, she said, "I've never felt anything more flattering than your childlike devotion. You know that? You got to me, Johnny. You got to me when I didn't think anyone still could."

She rubbed her eyes with both hands and said bitterly, "I'll never hang my fortune on the whims of another man. They're all failures in the end. They're all pathetic and weak. Fat wallets and ready cocks attached to defective brains."

She took a deep breath and zipped her purse with shaking hands. Then she said in a calm, regretful tone, "I'm sorry, Johnny. You really are a decent person. But I can't have you and you can't have me."

She picked up her duffle bag and turned to leave. As she walked through the door, she burst into tears and her final words were, "I really am sorry. I'm sorry it had to be you."

64

I woke up three times the next day. The first two times, I didn't even try to stand. My body was heavy as lead, my head was pounding, my mouth was dry, and my guts were churning.

The third time, I managed to sit up. I could tell by the light coming through the sheer curtains that the sun was high. My headache had improved to the point where I could move, but I felt like I was swimming in molasses.

After a minute or so of wondering where I was, I began to piece together fragments of the previous night. Marilyn was sobbing. Why? What had she said to me?

Then the memories flooded in.

No, I told myself. No, that was just a dream. You drank too much and passed out on the couch. Marilyn's in the bedroom. She's sleeping. Or she's out for a swim.

I saw the bottle of pills on the floor in front of the couch. I remembered her dropping them the night before. No, I thought. No. It can't be real.

I stood up slowly and was so dizzy, I almost fell backwards onto the couch. When I felt stable on my feet, I took a step forward and bent to pick up the bottle. That was too much movement at once. My brain couldn't register what my body was doing. I fell on my face and lay there for a minute as the room spun around me.

When everything stopped moving, I picked up the bottle and tried to read the label, wondering if this was what Marilyn had put in my drink. But my vision was blurred. I couldn't read. All I knew was it was some over-the-counter medicine, not a prescription. I slid the bottle into my pocket and fell back to sleep.

At twelve thirty p.m., I got up again and looked around the cabin. There was no sign of Marilyn or any of her belongings, other than the liquor bottles on the counter and a half-empty bottle of sunscreen.

Outside, the coals of the grill had burned to ash, and the uncooked salmon had been picked apart by birds. Bits of it lay in the grass, beneath swarms of flies and ants, while a few crows cawed from the trees above. The towels we had dried ourselves with after our swim hung on the backs of a pair of Adirondack chairs. The white car was gone, but Marilyn's black Mercedes remained. The keys were in the ignition.

For thirty minutes, I walked in circles around the cabin, looking for her. I scanned the lake and called her name. I walked the woods. I called her phone, but it just rang and rang.

I left a little after one and drove back to town, because I didn't know where else to go. I told myself I'd go back to the apartment and pick up the new credit card that had come in the mail. It was sitting on the kitchen counter. I hadn't even activated it yet. I told myself I'd sell the Corvette and get enough money to start over in some new town, some new life, where I could forget about Marilyn Dupree and move on.

I had that plan in my head for thirty minutes before I remembered that Lou had taken the Vette. That's how slow my mind was working under the lingering influence of whatever she had drugged me with.

I stopped twice. Once to puke, and once to eat. It was after five p.m. when I hit the stretch of road north of town. All the plans I had made on the long drive down, picking up the credit card and the car, were lies and I knew it. I wasn't going back to my place, because nothing there meant anything to me. There was only one person in the world I cared about.

I turned into Marilyn's driveway with the instinctive loyalty of an abandoned dog incapable of absorbing the betrayal of the only creature it had ever loved. I walked into the house with the impossible hope of a gambler at the roulette wheel who still believes, despite all odds, that this time his number will turn up.

I called her from the base of the stairs. "Marilyn?"

I walked into the kitchen, expecting to see her there with a glass of bourbon in her hand.

"Esme?"

No one answered.

I walked through the French doors, past the patio to the empty lounge chairs by the pool. There was no towel, no drink, no book or sunscreen or sunglasses. No indentation on the chair to indicate a human presence.

I ran back inside.

"Marilyn!"

The living room was empty. The dining room was empty.

As I ran toward the stairs, I heard cars pull into the drive outside.

"Marilyn!" I shouted as I took the stairs two at a time.

In the bedroom, the bed was neatly made and the nightstands were bare. The desk by the window was clear of papers, the dresser drawers neatly shut.

"Marilyn!"

I ran into the bathroom. Esme had wiped down all the counters, cleaned the mirrors, and swept the floor. Beside the sink was a bottle of hand soap and a hairbrush with strands of long black hair tangled in the bristles.

Someone was entering the house downstairs. My heart leapt.

"Marilyn!" I called.

Then a male voice. "He's upstairs." And the heavy footsteps of men.

I ran to the walk-in closet. Everything was in its place.

"She couldn't have gone," I thought. "She didn't pack any clothes."

The footsteps were coming up the stairs.

I opened one of the cherrywood drawers on her side. The diamonds were gone. The necklaces were gone. Everything was gone, from all her drawers.

I turned and pulled out Bastian's drawers. The watches were gone, the cuff links, everything.

Then Lou appeared with his gun drawn on me. The two cops standing behind him had their guns on me too.

"Put your hands behind your head," Lou said.

I did.

"Lock your fingers behind your neck and get down on your knees."

His gun followed me as I knelt.

One of the other cops got behind me and put on the cuffs.

"You come to clean her out?" Lou asked angrily. "Is that why you're here? To take her jewelry?"

"No, Lou. I would never do that."

"Don't give me that," he said as he shoved two of the drawers closed. "You lying bastard! You piece of shit lunatic!"

He took a step toward me, his face filled with bitter anger, and he cracked the butt of his gun down on the top of my head.

"Whoa!" One of the other cops jumped in and restrained him. "Take it easy, Lou."

"Murderer!" Lou hissed as I gritted my teeth in pain. "I can't believe you had the nerve to come back here. You fucking murderer! Why'd you kill her, John? Why?"

"I don't know what you're talking about, Lou."

65

Lou and I sat in the same small room on the second floor of the police station where he had interviewed me before, only this time I was cuffed to the chair.

"You want to talk now?" Lou asked. "Or would you like to have your attorney present?" He was pacing by the window, too wound up to sit.

"Why do I need an attorney?" I asked. "I didn't do anything wrong. And where's my car?"

Lou ignored that question. "You realize we're being recorded? You realize anything you say can and will be used against you—"

"You already told me that. After you hit me on the head with your gun, remember? I think you have an anger management problem, Lou."

"Shut up, John."

"See? Like that right there. That's no way to talk to a person."

"Where's Marilyn?" he demanded.

"Well that's the million-dollar question right there," I said.

"Where is she?" he shouted.

"How the hell should I know? She left."

"You took her up to that lake and then you killed her."

"What?" I said. "No I didn't. How'd you know we were at the lake?"

"How long have you been stealing from her?" Lou snapped.

"What the hell are you talking about? I never stole a thing from her."

Lou walked over to the door, opened it, and said in a low voice to another cop sitting in the hall, "Give me the links. That bag right there."

The cop handed him a clear plastic bag and Lou shut the door.

"Where'd these come from?" he asked as he laid the bag on the table. In it were two platinum cuff links, inlaid with sapphires.

"You got them from the guy in the hall," I said.

Lou stuck out his jaw and pursed his lips, like he was trying hard to control his temper. "They were Bastian's," he said.

"So what's that got to do with me?"

"Why were they under the sink in your bathroom?"

I shook my head. "They weren't under my sink."

"No? You deny that?"

I thought about it for a few seconds. I don't think I'd ever even opened the cabinet below the sink.

"You thinking twice?" Lou said. "If you come up with a story, lay it on me. I'm all ears."

"Lou, if you found those in my apartment, I have no idea how they got there."

A little voice inside my head said, This is when you stop the interview. This is when you ask for a lawyer. But my mind wasn't working right that day. Part of it may have been the lingering effect of the drug Marilyn had given me. Part of it was John Manis. I had played the role for so long, the guy was living inside me. And he loved to watch me squirm on the inside while I played it cool on the outside.

"Keep talking," Manis said. "Lou's got it out for you, buddy. Look how angry he is! Why don't you say something that will really piss him off?"

I said aloud, "Maybe you planted them, Lou. You seem to have it out for me."

Lou didn't take the bait. He just shook his head and said, "Try again."

Then Manis whispered, "Lou can see into you, just like Marilyn could. Tell him another lie."

I said, "Maybe Marilyn planted them."

That was at least plausible. She had been to my apartment. We had had sex, and she used the bathroom afterward. Try poking a hole in that one, Lou.

"All right, Tom," said Lou. "I have another one for you."

That sent a jolt of lightning straight down my spine. How the hell did he know to call me Tom?

Lou opened the door again and asked the guy outside for something.

Then he shut the door and laid Bastian's watch on the table. It wasn't the watch Bastian was wearing when he died. I had thrown that one off the Golden Gate Bridge. It was the one I had hocked in San Francisco with Marilyn.

"You know where I got that?" he asked.

I swallowed hard, wondering what this meant. Was he going to say I stole it from Marilyn and then charge me with theft? He couldn't, unless Marilyn decided to press charges, and Marilyn was gone. Besides, Marilyn had been with me when I hocked it.

"The guy in the pawnshop described you perfectly," Lou said.

I was about to tell Lou the guy could have described Marilyn too, because she was with me. Then I remembered Marilyn didn't go into the pawnshop that day. She stayed in the car.

"You want to explain that?" Lou asked.

"I don't know, Lou. That's a long story." I thought back to that day when the appraisers had been in her house, to the fight between Marilyn and me, her rage and fear and her irrational, panicky obsession with money. I was just trying to soothe her when we sold that watch. I had a feeling Lou would choose not to understand. He would twist the whole story into something that made me look guilty.

"All right," Lou said, "I'm not even that concerned about the watch. The piece that really concerns me is the other one you hocked there. The bracelet Bastian was wearing the night he died."

That really shook me, and Lou could see it. While Tom Gantry writhed in fear, John Manis could barely contain his delight. Part of my mind kept asking, What do I say? What do I say? Meanwhile, Manis, easy and cool and almost laughing, said, "It doesn't matter what you say now. Just keep talking!"

"I saw it on Bastian's wrist," Lou said. "The night he died. You remember? I was called to the restaurant and I drove Marilyn home. Bastian was wearing the bracelet that night. So how did it come to be in your possession?"

Lou stood there glowering at me, but I couldn't think of anything to say. Part of me thought, OK, he's bluffing. If he had the bracelet, he would have shown it to me, like he showed me the watch. He doesn't have it, so he can't prove anything. All he can say is that the pawnbroker told him I sold a bracelet that resembled Bastian's, and that's a far cry from solid, tangible evidence. I mean, how many platinum bracelets are there in this world?

Finally, Lou got tired of looking angry and took a break to stare out the window.

But wait, I thought. The bracelet had Bastian's initials on it. BAC. How many platinum bracelets are there in the world with those letters spelled out in diamonds? My heart sank, and Manis said, "Keep your chin up, boy! He's trying to bury you alive. All you have to do is keep breathing."

After half a minute, Lou spoke again in a calmer voice.

"That bracelet meant a lot to Marilyn," he said, still gazing through the window, still with his back to me. "She went all the way to San Francisco to get it out of hock."

"Wait, what?" This was a whole new shock. "What?"

"The pawnbroker described her too. Matter of fact, he has it all on video. You sold him the bracelet. Then you came back and sold him the watch. Then Marilyn came in and bought the bracelet back at a pretty steep price."

Oh my God! I tried to leap up from my chair, but the handcuffs yanked me back down. It all came to me in one blinding flash.

"What is it?" Lou asked. "You have something to say?"

The bracelet! Was that what Roland was after when he robbed Bastian of his jewelry the night of the crash? Was that what he was supposed to give her the day she went to the overlook and he didn't show up?

And then, a few days later, when I asked Marilyn at the poolside about the inscription, she looked at me in shock and I saw murder in her eyes. "How did you know it had an inscription?" she asked.

And then the fight in her bedroom a few days later, her insistence on selling Bastian's watch! It was all a ruse! "Where would you sell a watch like this?" she asked. She fought and cried. She knew how to get to me. And she was so persistent! She made me drive her there. Right to the pawnshop where I had sold the bracelet. And when I handed her the cash, all the weight lifted from her, her mood lightened, and she was like a carefree girl. Not because of the money, but because I had led her to what she'd been looking for.

After we'd returned from San Francisco, she went back. Esme told me she had gone to the city, and I couldn't understand why, because we had just come from there.

And I knew now why she wanted that bracelet.

"Lou," I swallowed hard. "You know Bastian put ten million dollars into a cryptocurrency account."

Lou perked up and took a step closer to me. "Yeah?" He had an eager look on his face.

"Were you watching the account?" I asked.

His eyes narrowed with suspicion. "What are you getting at?"

"Was that account emptied out, by any chance? Recently?"

Lou nodded, not in agreement, but the way a person nods when you confirm what they've been thinking. "Funny you know that," he said. "Because that's not the sort of thing an innocent person would know."

It all clicked. Marilyn must have known about the Ethereum account for some time. She had ready access to Bastian's backup disk and could have seen all the documents and messages I had seen. When I told her about the Ethereum account in the car on the way to San Francisco, she reacted indifferently, like it was old news. At the time, I assumed that was because her lawyer had told her about it a few days before, but how long had she really known?

And the bracelet, the inscription on the back of the bracelet, that nonsense word that didn't mean anything in any language—that was the password to the account.

"Lou," I blurted. "I had a bottle of pills in my pocket when you arrested me. What was it?"

He looked at me kind of funny, like he couldn't make out what I was after.

"What kind of pills were they?"

"Dramamine," he said. "Why? Don't you remember?"

"Oh my God!" I tried to put my hand up to my face, but it was cuffed to the chair.

"What is it?" Lou asked, looking confused.

I thought back to the day I had walked into the deli to find Bastian and Marilyn arguing about whether it was possible to travel outside the US without a passport. Was Marilyn planning to run away even then? Is that why the question was on her mind?

And then—oh, how it stung! I had laid out the whole plan for her. Go down to South Texas, I said. Hire a private boat and pay the captain to drop you off on an empty beach in Mexico.

"Does it have to be Texas?" she asked.

"No. It could be Southern California."

Or Northern California. Just be sure to bring your Dramamine, so you don't get seasick.

I started to shake as the questions raced through my mind. Why would she need to travel without a passport? Was it because she was planning on running off with Bastian's money, and she didn't want to be traced? Or was it because she was planning something worse—like this, like Lou thinking she was murdered—and she knew she couldn't travel under her own name when she was supposed to be dead?

A shudder ran through me and I let out a groan.

Lou reacted immediately, as if he were pouncing on an involuntary admission of guilt. "Where is she, Tom? Where'd you put the body?"

"There is no body," I said. "I didn't kill her."

"Bullshit," Lou said. "Where is she?"

"She's probably on her way to Mexico," I sighed.

Lou stepped up and smacked me on the side of the head. "Where is she?" he shouted.

"I don't know, Lou. I really don't know. Why do you think I killed her? I would never kill Marilyn. Never in a million years. I'd sooner kill myself."

"Don't bother killing yourself," Lou said. "The state will take care of that. Premeditated murder for financial gain is a capital offense in California. Which brings me to something else."

He paused and watched the fear of those words sink in. A capital offense? I couldn't absorb any more, but he was still piling it on.

"Tell me about John Manis," he said. "How did you come to have his passport and license?"

I shook my head in woe. "That's a long story."

"Didn't take you long to empty out his bank account. To sell off all his stocks. How the hell did you blow through all that money in nine months?"

"I'm cursed, Lou. I'm cursed."

"No," he said as he walked back to the window. "You're just stupid, like a lot of other criminals. But let's forget about Manis for now. That one's outside my jurisdiction, so I'll let the FBI handle it. Let's talk about something a little closer to home. Let's talk about Roland Marchand."

"Oh, God," I groaned. "Oh, God."

"That's not the reaction I'd expect from an innocent man," Lou said. He wasn't even looking at me. He was enjoying the view of the mountain outside. "I know Roland and Marilyn had a relationship. I assume you know it too?"

He turned and looked at me now. "I talked to a couple of Bastian's friends from San Francisco. They told me Bastian didn't like Roland. Seems you didn't like him either. So you shot him, didn't you?"

"What? No."

"Well someone did. Shot him right in the jaw. We found the bone the other day, two hundred yards below the overlook. It was shattered, with traces of copper and gunpowder. We didn't tell the news media because I was afraid you might take off."

My heart began to slow and fill with dread. My hands and feet grew cold, and an icy sweat broke out on my scalp and forehead.

I started to say, "I want... I want..." But I couldn't get the last words out.

"What?" asked Manis, laughing. "A lawyer? Is that what you want?"

Yes, I thought.

"Well then say it," Manis gloated. "All you have to do is say the words. *I want a lawyer. Watch out for the boom.* You know the words. Speak them. Speak!"

But I couldn't. The room was spinning, and I couldn't say a thing.

"Don't go to sleep on me," Lou said. "We're not done." He went to the door and had a word with the man outside.

When he returned a few seconds later, he was holding something behind his back.

"Let's get back to Marilyn," he said. "You going to stick to your story, Tom? You going to tell me you didn't kill her?"

I shook my head. "I didn't kill her, Lou. And why do you keep calling me Tom?"

I knew he knew who I was. I just wanted to know how he found out.

"That's your name, isn't it? Thomas Alfred Gantry. Born in Momence, Illinois and spent two years in a minimum-security prison for theft and wire fraud. Well let me tell you something. The place you're going to is nothing like minimum security. It's a whole different world."

Lou's threats and his arrogant self-assurance stirred my anger, and I used the energy to build a case inside my mind that would give me reassurance.

He had no solid evidence to convict me of the most serious crimes. Marilyn wasn't dead, so there was no crime there. No one would ever find Manis's body, so no one could ever know for sure how he died. And no one could place me at the scene of Roland's death. If there had been a witness, he would have come forward already. If the cops had recovered fingerprints or other evidence from Roland's car or from mine, Lou would have mentioned it by now. He would have proudly asked me to explain it so he could watch me squirm.

The smaller crimes were another matter. Maybe they could convict me of those, but it wouldn't be the end of the world. It wouldn't be a death sentence, or even a life sentence, and minor crimes don't warrant a maximum-security prison.

Having the cuff links might amount to petty theft. Hocking the watch might be something a prosecutor could twist into a crime, even though I'd done it at Marilyn's request. The bracelet, though, was trickier. I could tell the truth about how I'd found it. Lou knew I was on that stretch of road the night of the crash. He even had video of us talking about it in this very room.

But I had told him in that interview I hadn't seen the crash. I had told him I'd passed that point of the highway before the crash happened, and I hadn't seen a thing.

It would look bad if now I had to say I'd been lying, if now I had to change my story and place myself at the scene before the medics arrived.

Before Lou revealed what he was holding behind his back, I started calculating how much time I might have to serve. One count of theft for the bracelet. One count for the watch. One count for the cuff links, which I didn't even steal. One count of obstruction of justice for lying to Lou about not being at the scene the night of the crash. Maybe one count of leaving the scene of a fatal accident.

That already added up to a lot, but I still had hope. A decent lawyer could get half the charges thrown out, and plant enough doubt in the jurors' minds to get me off one or two others. I might be facing a couple of years, and I already knew I could handle that.

Then Lou showed me his trump card, and of all the things that shocked me that day, this one stung the most. This was a knife right through my heart.

"How do you explain this?" he asked as he revealed what he'd been holding behind his back.

It was the letter from Marilyn. The one she had kissed and sealed the first day I visited her. The "insurance policy" that had sat for weeks on her dresser, unstamped and unaddressed, until, on our last day together, she dropped it into a mailbox right before my eyes.

There on the front of the envelope, in her generous, looping hand, was the name Detective Lou Eisenfall, and the address of the building we were sitting in.

"This arrived this afternoon," Lou said. "At twelve forty-five."

As he unfolded the letter, I saw the imprint of the lips I had once loved to kiss. Lou turned the pages around and showed me the mug shot of Tom Gantry from his arrest in Illinois. Below it was a handwritten note. I remembered watching her write it that very first day as I sat on the bed and she stood at the dresser.

"You want me to read it to you?" Lou asked.

I shook my head in woe as my spirit drained away and a crushing pain throbbed through my heart.

"It says..." And then Lou read aloud: "He's not who he says he is. He's been stealing from me since we met. When I confronted him, he threatened to kill me. He's taken my phone, and he's taking me to Shasta Lake to murder me. Please help."

Lou looked at me and said, "Talk your way out of that one, Tom."

If I had had my wits about me, I would have said, "Think about it, Lou. How would she have time to look up my record on the internet and print it out and write all that if I was going to kill her? Did she just whip it off the printer while I was warming up the car?" I would have pointed out the graceful handwriting. I would have asked, "Is that the hand of a woman who's about to be murdered?"

But I was already guilty in Lou's mind, and my heart was so broken, I couldn't say a word. She had betrayed me from the beginning. I was her ticket out, her insurance policy to guarantee a clean getaway. No one would bother tracking her down if they thought she was dead.

She knew who I was the night we first spoke, the night at the bar, when my mug shot appeared on Bastian's phone.

"We're not always born who we want to be," she had told me at her house. "Sometimes we have to make it happen."

"I understand that," I said.

And what had she replied?

"I thought you would."

On the drive up to the lake, she had asked why I didn't scratch out the vehicle identification number of Roland's car.

"I'm not a career criminal," I said.

"Aren't you?"

Why had I been so blind? Why could I not see through her? Even when she warned me, I refused to see it, because I so badly wanted her to be who I thought she was.

"You're awfully quiet," Lou said. "And a lot less cocky than when you came in here."

"Lou," I moaned as I slumped in my chair. "I feel sick." Sick as much at my own blindness and stupidity as at her betrayal. I sat doubled over with my head hanging above my knees. Only the handcuffs kept me from falling off the chair.

Lou stood over me, gloating. "Doesn't feel so good now, does it, Tom? And I have one more for you too. We got an anonymous tip last night about a red Mustang parked behind an Italian restaurant in Sonoma. It's got a white scrape on the front right quarter panel."

That was the side of the car I couldn't see. We had parked beside the driver's door of the Mustang that night. Marilyn threw the keys in and made me get them. I thought she was just being drunk and difficult. She had played it all in character. So perfectly in character.

She had even jumped up and down and clapped. "Bravo, Johnny! You found them!"

"The paint on the Mustang looks like a match for Bastian's Mercedes," Lou said. "We're testing it now. You want to tell me how Tom Gantry's fingerprints got on the steering wheel and door of the car that ran Bastian into the back of that steamroller?"

I shook my head in defeat.

"Come on, Tom. I'm giving you a chance here. All you have to do is explain away the evidence and you can walk free."

What could I say? What could I possibly say?

Marilyn's words as she mailed her betrayal letter rang bitterly in my mind. "Do you think I'm stupid, John? Do you think I don't know what I'm doing?"

No, Marilyn. You're a genius. You're an absolute fucking genius. You've even outsmarted Lou.

Lou let out a long breath and said calmly, "We know which cabin you were in. The crew's been searching for hours now. The woods. The lake. You want to start to make things right, you can tell us where the body is."

"There is no body," I whispered.

"Come on, Tom. You drove back in her car. Alone. Where'd you put her?"

I shook my head and muttered something even I didn't understand.

"What's that?" Lou asked. There was a note of triumph in his voice. "Speak up, Tom, I can't hear you."

"Please," I whispered. "Please just kill me. Put a bullet through my heart."

And at last John Manis broke down. At last his mighty confidence failed him, and with eyes cast down, in a humble, shaking voice he said, "Do you get it now, Tom? Do you understand how much it hurts to be betrayed?"

66

The most fundamental elements of our character—our desires and our fears—were written into us as speechless children by a world we could not comprehend. We discover how they rule us only when life gives us the chance to act out what's inside. And we must act it out, or else we know we have not lived.

All I needed was to stumble across the people I was hoping to find—Manis, who I wanted to be; Marilyn, who I wanted to love; and Lou, because there had to be someone I couldn't lie to, someone to see me for who I was.

In the feverish years of my panic-stricken freedom, I was looking for something to impose upon the chaos of my life an order I couldn't violate. Stepping into Manis's life wasn't going to cut it. Obsessive love for Marilyn wouldn't do it either. I needed someone to bring the hammer down on me.

But I couldn't have articulated that at the time, however deeply I might have felt it, because the driving force of my life was a compulsion to be lived, not a word to be named or a feeling to be described.

At night I dream of John and Marilyn beneath the full white sail of the boat, gliding silently on an aqua-green sea of boundless promise.

Manis is confident and sure in the warmth of that abundant sun. He knows he doesn't need to run anymore. He has found in her what he was looking for.

Marilyn smiles as she looks at him—the broad white smile of joy that lit the two shining moments of my life and told me at long last that what I had always wanted really did exist.

Then I awake to scratchy prison sheets and the clang of steel bars.

Within these narrow confines is the certainty, the order I always craved. I can measure in inches the grey horizons of my cell and touch every boundary that contains me.

I am infinitely less terrified in this world I cannot ruin, in this world where nothing will change today, or tomorrow, or the day after that. The numbers on fortune's wheel have all gone blank, and I have no chips left to play.

I am safe here in a world I cannot escape, in a world I will not leave alive. There will be no new surprises, no further disappointments in this life I once hoped would be beautiful and good.

ACKNOWLEDGMENTS

I would like to thank my editor, Jacque Ben-Zekry, whose invaluable input vastly improved this book. I'm grateful to Dorian Box (author of *Psycho Tropics*) and Sophia Morris (an all-around lovely person) for their feedback on the initial draft of *Johnny Manic*. Thank you, Lindsay Heider Diamond, for your insightful editorial comments and excellent cover design. And thank you, Meredith Tennant, for another superb proofreading job.

ABOUT THE AUTHOR

Andrew Diamond writes mystery, crime, and noir. His books feature cinematic prose, strong characterization, twisting plots, and dark humor. *Impala*, in which a hacker accidentally inherits a stolen fortune, was named a best of the month mystery by Amazon.com and a best of 2016 book by IndieReader. It won the Readers' Favorite Gold Medal for mystery and the 24th Annual Writer's Digest award for genre fiction.

In *Gate 76*, a tough detective must track down the last surviving witness to a crime that has captivated the nation—a troubled woman who doesn't want to be found. BestThrillers.com called *Gate 76* one of the best thrillers of the year, and the book was named to Kirkus Reviews' Best Indie Books of 2018.

You can follow Andrew online at https://adiamond.me, on Goodreads, or at https://facebook.com/adiamond.me.

Impala

After four years on the straight and narrow, Russell Fitzpatrick has a boring job, the wrong woman, and an itch for something more.

When he receives a cryptic email from a legendary and slightly deranged fellow hacker—his old friend, Charlie, whom he knows to be dead—he tries to tell himself it's none of his concern. But the guy who stalks him across town at night, the two thugs waiting in the alley, and a ruthless FBI agent let him know his days are numbered if he doesn't turn over the money Charlie stole.

The problem is, Russ doesn't have it. As his enemies close in from all sides, Russ slowly unwinds the mystery of his old friend's paranoid mind and finds that Charlie left behind something worth much more than the money. And no one but him is onto it...

Impala was named a best mystery of the month by Amazon.com editors upon its release in 2016, and went on to win the Writer's Digest award for genre fiction, the Readers' Favorite Gold Medal for mystery and a best of the year nod from IndieReader.

[Diamond] gets all the little things right, as well as the big ones, in this riveting novel...A convincing, complex cyberthriller. — *Kirkus Reviews*

A smart, wholly engrossing cyber crime novel... full of hard-hitting insights that ring true. A must-read for any thriller fan. — *BestThrillers.com*

A compelling, unexpected mystery that's hard to put down and satisfyingly complex to the end. — *D. Donovan, Senior Reviewer, Midwest Book Review*